THE ICARUS AFFAIR

By the same author:

Ages 9-12:

Celia and Granny Meg go to Paris

Celia and Granny Meg Return to Paris

Young Adult:

Chief Inspector Maigret Visits London

Max Survives Paris

Night Train to Berlin

THE
ICARUS
AFFAIR

MARGARET DE ROHAN

Matador
9 Priory Business Park,
Wistow Road, Kibworth Beauchamp,
Leicestershire. LE8 0RX
Tel: (+44) 116 279 2299
Fax: (+44) 116 279 2277
Email: books@troubador.co.uk
Web: www.troubador.co.uk/matador

ISBN 978 1800463 875

British Library Cataloguing in Publication Data.
A catalogue record for this book is available from the British Library.

Printed and bound by CPI Group (UK) Ltd, Croydon, CR0 4YY
Typeset in 11pt Aldine by Troubador Publishing Ltd, Leicester, UK

Matador is an imprint of Troubador Publishing Ltd

FSC
www.fsc.org
MIX
Paper from
responsible sources
FSC® C013056

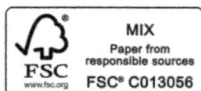

This book is dedicated to the people who died, or were injured in Paris on the night of Friday 13th November 2015.

But it is a work of fiction: I have no knowledge of the terrible events that occurred that night other than what I, and millions of others, watched on television or read in the newspapers.

However, I have used the real name of a restaurant which was attacked; 'La Belle Equipe' because it seemed appropriate to do so. I mean no disrespect to those who died there; may they rest in Peace and may Light eternal shine upon them. And for their relatives and the survivors who continue to suffer long after the flowers have wilted and the candles burn out: love, healing, and the peace that passes all understanding.

"Vengeance is mine; I will repay, saith the Lord."
Deuteronomy 32:35 KJV
Romans 12:19

Margaret de Rohan
Adelaide, December 2020

ONE

David Quinn and his enigmatic friends melted quietly away from Berlin before they could be asked any awkward questions. He never did resume his position with GCHQ, the British Government's listening post in Cheltenham. Rumour has it that he's either writing a book, or planning to stand for parliament – or both.

Patrick Evremond flew back to London the next day, also without answering any difficult questions, although he went with Philippe Maigret's blessing. But Nat, fresh from hospital and fully recovered, stayed on in Berlin with his family for a few more days.

Early on the Saturday morning the three detectives also left Berlin travelling once again in the British Embassy's Jaguar with Georges Martin, in his element, driving all the way to Paris.

On his first night home Philippe Maigret collected the feisty furry one from his mother's apartment on the Avenue Foch, and then walked her in the neighbourhood park. She seemed happy to see him; she

1

purred occasionally and only scratched him once. When they returned to their Rive Gauche apartment Philippe was scarcely inside the door before the phone rang. It was Megan.

'I'll be home soon, darling,' she said. 'Tom's consultant believes a medivac flight to Paris around the middle of next week should be possible, and his children have asked me to accompany them.'

'And what then for us, my love?'

'What do you mean?'

'You *know* what I mean, Megan.'

'Not now, Philippe. We'll talk about *everything* when I'm home.'

'Our life together. Can it ever be the same as it was before Berlin?'

There was a significant pause on the other end of the line.

'Maybe not *quite* the same,' she said carefully.

★

Police Nationale HQ, Paris
Early November 2015

As he was pouring himself a second cup of coffee, Philippe Maigret's phone rang. It was Chief Inspector Clive Scott of the Met police in London.

'I believe congratulations are in order, *mon ami*,' he roared down the line.

'Oh?'

'Don't play the novice with me, mate; my spies are everywhere and I know everything, as you should realise by now.'

Maigret groaned.

'Who's been talking? If it's one of my men he'll...'

'Not one of your squad, someone far higher up the totem pole than that! The source was impeccably Gallic.'

'Christophe Saint-Valéry, I suppose. Or someone who works in his department,' he said with one of his famous sighs. 'It's not enough that he's forced a promotion on me with the collusion of my wife, but to leap two ranks in one move is unacceptable. And to think he's one of my closest friends. I should have retired rather than take the upgrade.'

'Need I remind you that Monsieur Christophe is your Minister of Police? He can do as he sees fit, *Chief Superintendent* Maigret. Besides, what did you expect after you prevented a terrorist attack in Berlin that could have killed hundreds of people and wiped out a third of the German Cabinet including the Chancellor herself?'

'I was just doing my job, Clive, and I had a great deal of help; you played a significant role yourself.'

'Yes, but you *recognised* the importance of David Quinn's approach to your wife – *"Are you going to Scarborough Fair?"* – at *Les Invalides* and that started the whole shebang.'

'But was I acting as one of *Police Nationale's* chief inspectors at the time or an anxious husband? It's quite possible I'm a fraud motivated by self-interest,' he said, sighing again.

'You think too much, my friend. What difference would your intentions have made to the outcome? But since you've opened that particular door how are things between you and the missus these days?'

'In most ways our life is the same as it was before... before the events in Berlin. Except that now she spends an hour two or three times a week at the American Hospital playing Florence Nightingale to the man who was her first love. And you can imagine how that makes me feel.'

'How's Tom Aitkens doing? Any progress on his spinal injury?' Clive said hoping to prod Maigret into a change of direction.

'He can't walk yet, but he's faithfully following his therapy schedule so I believe he'll definitely walk again, contrary to the medical diagnosis when he was shot.'

'Then he'll return to New York, won't he? So just be patient. After all, he *did* put himself between you and a bullet from a rifle – two bullets actually – and you'd be dead now if it wasn't for him.'

'That's what I keep hearing from my wife.'

'Because it's the truth. And nothing you can say will change that fact.'

'So out of eternal gratitude, I'm supposed to gift him my wife – is that it?'

'Don't be ridiculous. That woman knows her own mind; if she's living with you and er... keeping your bed warm it's because that's where she wants to be. I presume everything is er... still *acceptable* in the... er garden of good and evil...'

'Everything is fine. Never better, which may seem *perverse* but that's the way it is.'

'Then thank your luck and move on. Let your missus do what she needs to do until Aitkens is back on his feet or back in the US.'

'Not going to happen.'

'But you said…'

'Back on his feet – maybe. But he's not returning to the States. He's bought a magnificent apartment on the Avenue Foch not far from where my mother lives, and plans to move in when he leaves hospital. He's going to live in Paris; he's already running his company from here.'

'How do you know all this?'

'Certainly not from my wife. If she knows about it she hasn't mentioned anything to me.'

'Oh. Well, how about a change of scene? An escape from Paris for a week or so…'

'I've tried that already but it didn't work. I suggested a week in Provence but she said not now, maybe later. So that's it.'

There was silence on the other end of the line for a few moments before Clive spoke again.

'How much do you know about the 6th Earl of Leicester, Philippe?'

'Is this a joke?'

'No.'

'I have no idea who the 6th Earl of Leicester is.'

'Well that's obvious otherwise you'd have used past tense. The 6th Earl, Simon de Montfort, died on 4th August 1265…'

'Wait – I know about this; not long ago his body was found buried under a supermarket carpark…'

'No,' Clive said patiently, '*that* was Richard the Third, King of England. In 1264, Simon de Montfort, the 6ᵗʰ Earl of Leicester, won the battle of Lewes, usurped Henry the third, and became the *de facto* King of England. Of course he was French-born, ergo trouble-maker! He married the king's sister, Eleanor of Leicester, a powerful woman in her own right, and she supported him against her brother.'

'At this point I'm tempted to say "so what", Clive – even though that would be rude…'

'So this – Simon de Montfort played a significant role in English history: he set up the first English parliaments.'

'Good for him! Is this one of your shaggy dog stories? Because if it is I really don't have…'

'No unkempt canines involved, but very pertinent to a case I'm working on. A murder case. The wife of a retired judge died two or three months ago and last week Thames Valley police found their daughter dead in her car down an embankment on the M40, which is the main highway from London to Oxford.'

'Cause of death?'

'That's the great unknown. When the judge's wife died the Thames Valley force treated it as an accidental death…'

'Accidental?'

'She fell down the stairs in the middle of the night and broke her neck.'

'Oh.'

'However, it seems that his Honour never agreed with that conclusion because his wife was fit and walked regularly, so no frailty. And now I quote from the transcript of his first interview with the Thames Valley detectives: "Elisabeth was not some decrepit old dame who took sleeping pills and roamed around during the night in a semi-somnolent state not knowing her aristocratic arse from her egalitarian elbow." But after their daughter's body was found we've had to consider other options for his wife's death too.'

'The daughter's death was not an accident?'

'No, although it was *designed* to look like one, but her body was obviously found earlier than the killer had anticipated. And because of that the post-mortem found a high level of drugs in her body which would have rendered her incapable of driving a car *then*, much less many hours before. They also found a small mark behind her ear presumed to be from an injection of some kind.'

'A tragedy for the judge to lose his wife and daughter in a short space of time. But we have murders to deal with too. Far too many for comfort and we're coping with an elevated terrorist threat too. I can't see how I can help...'

'Okay. Then will you do something for me?'
'What?'

'Ask your missus if she remembers a girl named Fleur who lived near them in Hampstead years ago.'
'Why?'

'Because earlier today a young woman came to the Met and *begged,* in a deluge of tears, for help to find a Mrs Megan Lisle who she said was her mother's best friend. Of course I immediately recognised that was your wife's former name…'

'A coincidence, it has to be. It's some other woman with a similar name.'

'But you don't believe in coincidences do you, *Chief Superintendent* Maigret?'

'No.'

'Then humour me. Ask your wife if she remembers Fleur and her mother Angela.'

'Okay, I will.'

'Ask her now if you can because the matter is rather urgent.'

'A missing person enquiry – urgent? I thought you had a suspicious death and the murder of a relative of a retired judge…'

'Fleur is the granddaughter of Ambrose Carpenter, the judge in question. And it's her mother Angela and her grandmother Elisabeth, who have died within months of each other. You don't have to be a genius to figure out who might be the next victim in the killer's sights.'

'*Merde.* Now I understand; I'll ask Meg and get back to you as soon as I can. But what does all this have to do with the 6th Earl of Leicester?'

'Ask your wife first. The Earl can wait; he's not going anywhere these days.'

'What's the girl's surname?'

'I was trying to avoid telling you that at this point. It's de Montfort, although she prefers to be known simply as Fleur Montfort now.'

'Ah, so that's the connection with the 6th Earl,' Maigret said, as he mentally assembled the pieces to form an intriguing pattern.

'That's not the half of it. I haven't mentioned Fleur's uncle yet, and what a hellish moment that will be when I do. Or rather, *if* I do, because that all depends on whether your wife remember Fleur.'

'For the love of my sanity mention the uncle now!'

Clive Scott swore softly.

'Okay, if you insist. Fleur's uncle, and Angela's brother-in-law is a constant pain in my *derriere*.'

'How?'

'He's a very clever, very successful criminal barrister. We lock 'em up and he gets them off! Time and time again. He's the scourge of the English criminal justice system and that's putting it mildly.'

'And his name is…'

'Giles de Montfort, QC. Or, as he is known within the confines of the Met, the Spawn of Satan.'

Maigret laughed.

'You really do have your hands full, don't you? And he's another Earl of Leicester?'

'No, Simon de Montfort flew too close to the sun when he opposed the king so he crashed and burned. Consequently the title was forfeit for hundreds of years.'

'What happened to the de Montfort titles…?'

'Search me, mate, I'm not the BBC. I only report the news, I don't create it. The Spawn is a mere pleb like the rest of us, but it is only because of Giles bloody de Montfort and the song and dance routine he's been performing, that the Met's become involved. The case rightfully belongs to Thames Valley as Elisabeth and Ambrose Carpenter's home is within their jurisdiction and Angela's body was found well inside the Oxfordshire border too. But de Montfort, egged on by the judge has considerable influence, so the orders have come down from on high that the Met has to deal with it and pretty damn sharpish too. Which translated means find the killer and wrap up the case to the satisfaction of both the judge and the Spawn without any careers being damaged in the process.'

After his conversation with Clive, Philippe thought for a few moments before phoning his wife. She took longer than usual to answer and seemed breathless when she did.

'Just back from walking kitty in the park love,' she explained. 'We stayed there for almost an hour because it's such a beautiful day.'

I can't do this to her by phone, he thought.

'Yes, it is a beautiful day, Madame. How would you like to have lunch with me at our favourite restaurant by the river? I could send Jacques with the car to drive you there.'

'I'd *love* it. But this is unexpected. Are we celebrating your double promotion at long last?'

'Nothing to celebrate there.'

'But there is, so don't be grumpy. It was well-deserved and appropriate.'

'Hmm.'

'What time for lunch?'

'Would 1 pm suit you? And Jacques about fifteen minutes earlier?'

'Fine by me, *Chief Superintendent,*' she replied mischievously, then pressed the end key before he could respond.

Over lunch Maigret quizzed her gently. Gently, and subtly. Or so he thought. He mentioned earlier times in her life when her children were young; he already knew that she and Michael Lisle had lived in Hampstead. She went along with this interrogation but she was not fooled. Not for a second. She relished the challenge of answering his questions honestly while not *volunteering* any new information. And all the while she was trying to figure out what he might be up to: after three years of marriage to this complex Frenchman she was aware that he had little interest in her former life or her first marriage. Yet here he was, harking back to that time and asking questions. Why? *But at least he's giving my relationship with Tom Aitkens in New York a rest,* she thought, *and that's something for which to be thankful.*

'What's all this about, love?' She asked when her patience was finally exhausted. 'What do you really want to know? Just ask me!'

He laughed, embarrassed to have been caught out.

'You can blame Clive Scott for the questions, it's to do with a case he has in London.'

'Well, why didn't you just say that at the beginning, you idiot. What does he want to know, and how can I help?'

'Do you remember a young woman whose name was Fleur Montfort?'

She gasped.

'Goodness, that's a memory from the past. Yes I do, or I did, know a girl named Fleur, but her surname was actually de Montfort; her mother was a close friend of mine at one time.'

'Angela de Montfort?'

'Yes. How did you know her name?' He didn't answer, so after a moment she continued. 'Yes, Angie and I were good friends, but we… er lost touch over the years.'

'How? Why?'

She hesitated.

'Because of our husbands. Michael and Robert were two motivated men who always competed with each other. You name it, they competed: careers, investments, sport. It was always the same. Then Michael said he wanted to move to Kensington – to get away from Robert probably – and Angie and I gradually drifted apart. But I want you to know that I'd never make a choice like that again.'

'I'd never ask you to.'

Oh no, she thought. *So what about Tom Aitkens and my obligation to him, and yours too?*

'You'd like Angela. I'm sure you would. And Fleur too, who always insisted on being called Flo, which infuriated her father; she was quite bolshie. Although she might be different now. I haven't seen the de Montfort family for a long time.'

'Bolshie?'

'An archaic reference; difficult to manage, politically radical and or left wing. Slang for Bolshevik.'

'Fleur de Montfort was a communist?' He said incredulously. 'But her uncle's a Queen's Counsel.'

'Is he? I didn't know. Nor do I believe Flo was ever a communist. It was teenage rebellion and she was none the worse for that; I've always been very fond of her.'

He left his seat to stand behind her. He put his arms around her, kissed her cheek and whispered softly in her ear. 'Darling, Fleur would very much like to see you again. And… and there's something else. Angela's body was found recently. It seems she was murdered.'

He felt the long slow tremor run through her as his words made their impact. Then, despite his arms she began to slide slowly off her chair. He caught her just before she reached the cold tiled floor.

It was the first time in her entire life that she had fainted.

TWO

After that, restrained panic. Waiters scrambled to supply smelling salts and brandy while Maigret, still fussing over his wife, was aware that his phone was buzzing. He ignored it twice, but finally answered. It was Clive Scott, as he knew it would be.

'I thought you said you'd get back to me ASAP, so why...?'

'I'm dealing with a domestic situation *mon ami*. But the answer is a definite yes.'

'You're not damaged are you; I know your missus sometimes has a short-ish fuse.'

'I'm fine. But the shock of hearing the news...'

'A fainter, is she? I'd never have thought it.'

Maigret chuckled.

'No, she's not. This was a one-off, I hope.'

'What do you want me to tell the daughter? Okay to give her your personal contact details?'

'Not yet. I'll get back to you later about that. But if you have any information regarding er... any arrangements perhaps you'd text me those details.'

'The funeral?'

'Exactly.'

'Will do. The pathologist's not willing to release the body yet; he's still trying to discover what was injected into the victim's neck. We might be looking at another few days before he's satisfied. Do you think your missus will want to come?'

'Definitely.'

'You too?'

'Yes.'

'I look forward to seeing you, mate. Want me to arrange accommodation for you? Maybe a nice Met safe house somewhere south of the river.'

'Thanks for the offer, but I think we'd prefer something a little more salubrious.'

'Your embassy?'

'No, it will be a private visit if I have any say in the matter.'

'Right-Oh. Over and out.'

As they left the restaurant Philippe glanced at his watch hoping that Meg wouldn't notice. She didn't. It was 2.30 – about the time she would usually take a taxi to the American Hospital to play cheerleader while Tom Aitkens went through his physiotherapy program. *Will she still want to go today?* He asked his subconscious? He received his reply from an unexpected source.

'I don't think I'll go to the hospital today.'

'Is he expecting you?'

'Yes. I'll send him a text.'

She did, and received an immediate reply, followed by two more texts which registered with him although he said nothing. *Trying to change her mind by laying on the guilt, he thought.*

'Could we walk for a while or do you need to go straight back to HQ?'

'I'm at your disposal darling, especially if you want to tell me about Angela. Do you?'

'No. Not yet.'

'Then when you're ready, I'll be here.'

'I know. Thank you, love. Did Clive say when Angela's…?'

'No. There are… er certain formalities to be completed.'

'The post-mortem.'

'Yes.'

He took hold of her hand, kissed it then tucked it under his arm. She looked up at him and smiled.

It really was a glorious day, unusually warm for November; the sky a cloudless blue, and by the Seine the winds were light. They sauntered arm-in-arm along the riverside promenade not speaking; there was no need. But although he appeared relaxed he was really working – observing; seeking; recording and feeling. Paris was his city. He loved it, but something was amiss. There was a new mood; one that unsettled and challenged him, but he wasn't yet able to discern what that vibe might be.

It had been the same in the days leading up to the 7th January: something not quite right. Something in the wind and in the air. Then the terrible events in the 11th. The savagery, the casual carnage, the total contempt for human life. And the blood. So much blood – running like sluices through the city of light and love.

What use frail flesh when pitted against assault rifles, grenades and the like, he thought. The attack on the Charlie Hebdo offices. Twelve dead, murdered in cold blood and eleven wounded. Then the assault on the Jewish supermarket with the hostage-taking and the senseless slaughter of a young woman police officer. *The obscenity of it: and the demand for revenge taking root inside of him.*

Jacques Laurent, his loyal sergeant for eight years had been wounded twice that day, barely escaping death. His right lung, pierced by a shard of metal compressed inside a weapon – as yet unidentified – meant he was painfully breathless at times; yet he would not accept medical retirement while, as he said, "there remains a job to be done." But he was unaware that Maigret had vowed never to risk him in the field again no matter what the provocation.

And time and time again the question in his mind: *what do these bâtards* want? The answer was sickeningly simple: complete world domination. The whole of humanity forced to submit to their brutal interpretation of Islam. So away with you Beethoven, and your 'Ode to Joy', and you too, Mozart and Liszt and Chopin and Grieg, and all the rest of you whom the enlightened world hails as geniuses. No music, no joy, no beauty, no carefree children playing their innocent games or the glory of the Creator revealed in the loveliness of unshackled women. Only the drab, colourless world of ignorant misfits and petty criminals who presumed to know better than the rest of civilisation.

Some say we are living in the last days. Are we? He asked himself. *Not for us to know* came the swift reply. And if we did know, what would we, what *could* we do differently?

When they approached *Pont Neuf* he saw what he was looking for, or rather, *who* he was looking for; a small cluster of 'our other friends,' as he referred to them, bunched together sharing a bottle of red wine. Four men of indeterminate age and one elderly woman dressed entirely in black apart from an absurdly flamboyant red hat which covered her unruly hair.

'Wait here a moment,' he whispered, 'I need to speak with these people.'

'Can't I come with you? Do they bite?'

'No, they don't bite. But neither do they speak English.'

'Well, that will help my French.'

They really were gentle people, she thought, as Philippe introduced her. Rheumatic limbs struggled to stand on weary feet while tired old backs bent themselves into courtly bows. She could feel tears pricking at her eyes, but she controlled herself. However, when the frighteningly thin woman almost fell struggling to make a curtsey in her honour, she stepped forward to save her.

'Well done, my love. I'll de-louse you when we get home.' She thought he was joking but she couldn't be sure. She certainly *hoped* he was.

But after that impulsive gesture they all became friends. One of the men rummaged around in the shadows of the bridge where their precious belongings were hidden until he found an ancient, rickety chair. With a theatrical flourish he invited her to sit on it, dusting it energetically with a tattered handkerchief before she did.

She sat quietly and observed while he questioned them. He did so gently, and without the slightest indication of the difference in their status. Quite the opposite in fact; at times he seemed deferential, especially to Madeleine, the woman. If she had been a duchess he could hardly have displayed more gallantry.

I have never loved you more than I do at this very moment Philippe Maigret, she told him silently. *And perhaps I never will.*

He looked over at her as though he had read her mind and smiled his wonderful smile. Then she nodded and he winked – again there was no need for words.

At one stage he drew Madeleine off to the side and spoke intensely with her. Meg tried to follow the conversation but couldn't. Except for one word that he kept repeating urgently *"quand?"* he asked. *"Quand? Quand? Quand?"* It was the French word for when. At first Madeleine either shook her head or shrugged. Then finally she uttered just one word – *"bientôt"* – soon. She saw the shadow pass over his face: it was the word he had not wanted to hear.

As the general questioning resumed, with many a shrug or a vehement denial, she realised that Madeleine had been slowly moving closer until finally she was standing almost on top of her. *I think she wants to feel my clothes,* she thought. *Or maybe it's my silk scarf.* She removed the scarf and offered it to the old lady who immediately draped it carefully across her shoulders before preening and strutting around looking very pleased with herself.

'How do I say it matches your lovely hat,' she called softly to him.

'*Elle correspond* à votre belle chapeau.'

'*Merci,* Monsieur. I suppose I should have remembered that.'

'*Oui,* Madame,' he said, winking again.

'Please tell her it's hers.'

'No – have a stab at it yourself.'

'Okay, but you'd better cover your ears if you don't want to hear your native language being tortured.'

'Do your worst my shoulders are broad.'

She took a deep breath.

'*Madame, il est un cadeau pour vous.*'

'*Pour moi, Madame?*'

'*Oui.*'

'Well,' she said, looking at him. 'How'd I do?'

'Not bad– except that it should have been 'elle' instead of 'il' because the scarf's feminine.'

'Why is a scarf feminine?'

He shrugged.

'Why not? It's just the way things are with the French language.'

She murmured something almost under her breath.

'*Comment?*'

'Nothing.'

'I have excellent hearing, my love.'

'If you already knew why did you ask?'

'Because I wanted to tell you that "an impossible language" is *exactly* what I said about English when I was having lessons. And look at me now.'

'Yes, look at you now – I've created a monster.'

'What?'

'When we first met you were polite, reserved; quite reticent in fact, but now…'

He laughed.

'That was because I was terrified of putting a foot wrong and ending our relationship before it actually began.'

'Really?'

'Yes, really.'

'But your fate was sealed the moment I laid eyes on you that day at the Hotel Celeste. Didn't you realise that?'

'You mean…?'

'I mean there was no escape for you, Monsieur; not after our paths crossed.'

'You might have said something; it would have spared me a great deal of anguish.'

'I thought I did. Not in words, of course but…'

'You wouldn't let me look at your room!'

'Well, no; I had standards to maintain. I *had* been at Greenham Common towards the end of the women's peace camp there…'

'Before or after New York?' He asked quickly.

'Just after, but before Michael and I were married. He had to bail me out…'

'You were *arrested?*'

'Yes twice, actually. But it was a mistake both times. Well at least the first time was a mistake because although the police found me holding the bolt-cutters I didn't cut the fence...'

'You were arrested?' he repeated. 'What fence?'

'The perimeter fence around the RAF base at Greenham Common where the American cruise missiles were being kept.'

'So that's criminal damage...'

'No – I said I *didn't* cut the fence, I was just unfortunately holding the bolt-cutters when the police arrived and they jumped to the wrong conclusion...'

By now he was laughing.

'I fail to see the humour in the situation I'm describing,' she said haughtily, about to walk off. Her words triggered increased laughter.

'Wait!' He said when he could finally speak. 'If you didn't cut the fence why were you holding the bolt-cutters?'

'Because Tiggy asked me to.'

'Tiggy?'

'Her real name was Miranda, but everyone called her Tiggy. She and I were two of the youngest women at the camp then so we became friends. She was a very posh girl; her father was a duke or an earl... something like that, but she was as game as Ned Kelly, was young Tigs.'

'What? Who?'

'Ned Kelly, Australian bushranger and folk hero, hanged in Melbourne jail sometime in the 19th century.'

'And she asked you to hold the bolt-cutters?'

'Yes. She said "hang on to these for a mo"…'

'Why?'

'Isn't it obvious,' she sighed. 'Because she didn't want to take them inside the fence with her in case she was caught by the guards. Besides, they were too heavy for her to carry very far; she was quite petite.'

'So you were arrested and charged with criminal damage and…'

'Going equipped. But the police *knew* I hadn't cut the fence because they had seen the back of Tiggy as she climbed through, but they were too far away to identify her.'

'Then why were you arrested?'

'It was pure spite because I wouldn't tell them who she was. And that made them very angry – so they said my fingerprints would be on the bolt-cutters and threw me and some of the other women in the back of a Black Maria and…'

'What?'

'A police van with darkened windows; they treated us very roughly, and that's why I wasn't prepared to submit to French brutality that day at the Hotel Celeste.'

'Brutality? All I wanted was to confirm that your room was secure.'

'So you say.'

He smiled, and caught hold of her hand.

'What a very dull life I must have led before I met you, my love. Let's go home before you confess to murdering Marat in his bath.'

'Don't be ridiculous, Charlotte Corday confessed

to his murder and you guillotined her for her courage. How can you say your life was dull when you'd been a police officer for twenty-something years and were shot four times in the performance of your duty?'

'All as nothing compared with what's happened to me since I met you, Madame! Now let's go home. I have some thinking to do about what the people we just met told me, and some de-lousing too, remember?'

'You were closer to them than I was…'

'*Précisément.* So you'll check me and I'll check you; forensically, if necessary.'

'I'm hoping de-lousing is a euphemism for something far more pleasurable.'

'You know me too well.'

As they entered their apartment on the Rive Gauche Philippe's phone rang. It was Clive Scott again.

'The funeral's at noon on Friday,' he said without preamble.

'But you said the pathologist…'

'He's thrown in the towel, at least for now. His best guess is that it's a kind of spider venom, or a derivative thereof. He's kept some tissue samples for further analysis and released the body for burial. Want me to text you the details?'

'Yes. What about the victim's husband, Fleur's father? It occurs to me that there's been no mention of him so far.'

'Sad case, Philippe; he's been in a nursing home for the past few months or so. Early onset dementia. Robert de Montfort scarcely recognises his nearest and dearest from one day to the next. He hasn't been told that his wife and mother-in-law are dead.'

'Oh, the poor girl – so tragic for her.'

'Yes. And bad news for us because the Spawn QC is now both family protector and inquisitor-in-chief. It's a damn nightmare, I can tell you!'

'Can you send me Fleur's contact details? I'm sure Meg will want to be in touch with her.'

'Will do.'

'Want me to meet you at St Pancras?'

'You're going to the funeral, Clive?'

'Of course, wouldn't you? And we'll have some plain clothes lads taking discreet photos of everyone there too.'

'The killer stalking his next victim?'

'Got it in one, mate.'

As the call ended, she said.

'I think I've sussed what that conversation was about; when's Angie's funeral?'

'Noon on Friday.'

'You'll come with me?'

'Of course.'

'Good. Now tell me about Madeleine, please.'

'Not now,' he said, enfolding her in his arms, 'later. I have other plans for you right now, Madame Maigret.'

THREE

Madeleine's story

'Let me say at the beginning that no one on earth knows Madeleine's complete story, not even Madeleine herself,' Philippe said. 'She did know it *all* at one time of course, but I've realised over the years that, by the Grace of God, she has forgotten a large part of it: the mind protecting itself from what would otherwise be intolerable torment.

She was born in a small rural backwater of France that time seems to have chosen to bypass, if not utterly disown. From what I can gather a feudal system still operated there although that was abolished at the time of the Revolution. Madeleine can't remember where that village was, and I can't decode her accent. It's definitely regional, but it has so many overlays from all the places she's lived during her life that her original accent has been lost.

We don't even know her real name; that's another thing she either can't remember, or more likely, has chosen to forget: the mind protecting itself again. We named her Madeleine because when she first arrived in

Paris many years ago she set up camp near the entrance to the basement foyer of La Madeleine Church on the flower market side. This was a wise decision; as you know there's a restaurant in the basement, run by volunteers I believe, where a good meal can be enjoyed for a modest amount. Not that Madeleine had much money, but the volunteers were kind and often brought her food that would have otherwise gone to waste. And so, as time passed, her own little court formed around her. There is a kind of fellowship hierarchy on the streets and it seems to have been recognised early on that she had received a decent education, which most of them had not. But how would a poor country girl be educated in those days? Certainly not in the few years she spent in the village school.

Little by little, Madeleine began to confide in me. On the edge of the village was a large handsome house. In it lived a retired gentleman and his placid wife, who were upright God-fearing people. Unfortunately they had not been blessed with children, so when the gentleman's wife and their elderly house-keeper died within months of each other, he cast his eye around the village to find someone to take care of both himself and his comfortable home. And that was how, at the age of about fourteen, Madeleine became a live-in servant to the gentleman, who she always refers to as 'his lordship' – although he was probably not of the aristocracy, nor did she know how his money had been made. However, he paid her a small salary on top of all her living expenses being met which many similar employers did not. All of that money Madeleine gave to her widowed mother when she visited her on her day off, which was Sunday.

In time the employer and the servant grew very fond of each other. He treated her as though she were the granddaughter he never would have, and set about educating her. He introduced her to music and art, and the classics, which he insisted she read to him even though at first she stumbled over many unfamiliar words. He pretended that his sight was failing and so she persisted with her reading lessons which at the beginning were a chore but later became the source of much joy. And so the two of them – elderly gentleman and young village girl – lived together happily for a number of years. A long time ago she described that time to me as the happiest of her life; her very own *"belle époque"*.

Then disaster arrived at their door. Her beloved gentleman died and his late wife's brutish cousin and his equally unpleasant wife inherited the fine house and everything in it. And that, he assumed, included the pretty young Madeleine. Within days, and with the full compliance of his wife, he raped Madeline without mercy. Over and over for many weeks until, predictably, he impregnated her. When the pregnancy became obvious to his wife she beat Madeleine so savagely that she lost the baby she was carrying. This pattern was repeated twice more, but she told no one. Not her ailing mother who depended on the income she provided, nor her brother, nor her friends, and especially not the young man with whom she was in love.

However, with the third pregnancy, despite the beatings, she did not miscarry as early as the other times. She carried the unfortunate child long enough to feel its movement within her. Consequently, when the inevitable happened, she almost died and the doctor had to be called. He immediately realised what had been happening and informed the local authorities who shrugged their shoulders and decided it was none of their business if thuggish rich men despoiled young country virgins.'

Philippe paused for a moment.

'Shall I go on my love, or have you heard enough misery for now?'

'Go on, please. It's almost more than I can bear but I need to hear all of it, terrible though it is.'

'Very well. And we're almost at the end of Madeleine's story anyway, although now we have two versions of how the story ends.'

'Two?'

'Yes and the Lord alone knows which one – if indeed either – is the truth, or close to the truth, because Madeleine has told me both stories with what I judged to be complete sincerity, at various times over the years.'

He took a deep breath and continued.

'Version one: the doctor who saved her life at the time of the third miscarriage had daughters of his own. And he knew, despite all the years he had devoted to tending the sick and injured, that if one of his precious lambs had suffered even a hundredth of what Madeleine had endured he would have killed the man responsible with his bare hands.

Except that, being a medical man, he didn't need to resort to bare hands because he had more sophisticated ways to put down a rabid dog. He carefully perused his medical kit until he found what he was looking for: a small brown bottle of something similar to insulin which he knew would not only simulate a heart attack but would quickly be eliminated from the body afterwards.

So that is what he did. By some ruse he persuaded the rabid dog that it would be to his benefit to swallow the potion, so he did. The doctor's only regret was that it would probably kill him too quickly. However he consoled himself with the knowledge that what pain there was would be extreme *intense* pain at the very least, and that was a small price to pay for his act to remain undetected. Not that he considered what he did was a crime: it was a mercy killing.

As soon as she had recovered her strength Madeline gave what money she had to her mother and brother. Then she left the village forever.

Now the second version. In some way Madeleine's lover – although there had apparently been no consummation of their love – became aware of what she had suffered at the hands of the rabid dog. He ranted, he raved, and then he broke into that house of unspeakable horror with murder in his heart. Murder and revenge. But by that time the brute was already dead. Already cold to the touch, already prostrate before his Maker, already facing eternal condemnation. His depraved widow was wailing, tearing at her clothes, and cursing anyone in sight, especially the innocent girl. This so enraged young

Pierre, who was by now aware of her sadistic compliance, that in the coldest of cold blood, he slashed her throat.

Of course, when the authorities discovered the two murders they assumed that Pierre was responsible for both, and in a very short space of time he was tried, found guilty, and summarily executed. And that was when Madeleine's heart finally broke.

As soon as she was fit enough to travel, she vowed to leave that village forever. But then a change of fortune. Her beloved 'lordship' had remembered her in his Will. To him it was a modest amount; to her it was a fortune. Most of her inheritance she gave to her mother. The small amount she kept for herself allowed her to travel far, far away from that unhappy place. And from that time onwards she has never wanted to live within four walls again. Bad things happened to her in a house – a fine, architecturally-designed house – and the only place she feels safe now is on the streets.'

Before Philippe had finished speaking, she was in tears.

'Oh, we must help her,' she cried. 'What can we do, Philippe?'

'Don't you think that's what I've been trying to do for a long time? Year after year, on whatever pretext I can invent, she's admitted to hospital as winter approaches. She's given a bath regularly, her hair deloused, washed and cut and given the vitamins and medicines she needs, new clothes and good food. But after a week or two she discharges herself and she's off to the streets again.'

'How old is she?'

'If she can't remember her name or the place where she was born, how can she remember her age?' He sighed. 'At a rough guess I'd say she won't see seventy again. But there's no doubt life on the streets ages people prematurely, so who really knows? Not me, for sure.'

'That's the classic way to do it, of course.'

'Do what?'

'Destroy someone. Abuse the body; demean the spirit; the heart breaks; the mind has gone.'

A violent tremor ran through him.

'I think someone's just walked over my grave,' he said.

FOUR

London, early November 2015

Chief Inspector Scott was waiting on the platform when their EuroStar rolled into St Pancras on the day of Angela de Montfort's funeral.

'Where are you staying?' He asked as he greeted them. 'The fancy-mancy on Mount Street?'

'No, The Stafford in St James's Place,' Philippe replied.

'I thought the Connaught was your favourite.'

'Once maybe, but Madame insisted on a change.'

'Do you want to check-in now? Do you need to freshen up?'

'No and no. But a cup of coffee would be very welcome if we have the time.'

'We do, and I know just the place – it's on the way.'

The day was blue-skied and sunny. *There is no justice in the world,* Meg thought as she walked, black-clothed and heavy-hearted, through the garden towards the parish church of St John in Hampstead. *On this day there should at least be a partial eclipse of the sun. Or wild winds with torrential rain. Or knee-deep snow. Anything – anything at all. But not the*

obscenity of sunshine and calm air. And the birds! If I could get my
hands around their throats the dawn chorus would be decimated.

John Constable, the illustrious English landscape artist
was buried in the graveyard which had long since been
closed to further tenants. But Angela had been a regular
communicant and her fellow parishioners knew her
worth. Therefore a special dispensation had been made to
allow her earthly remains to repose forever in this tranquil
corner of London. Her quiet good deeds were numerous.
No gentleman of the road had ever been turned away
from her door. A generous sandwich and a good strong
cup of tea or coffee was the usual fare. This was often
served in her own kitchen and on her best china. Nor
were those rovers sent on their way without the jangle of
a few pound coins in their well-worn pockets, courtesy of
'The Missus' as she was known to that particular band of
friends. And her husband's clothing trudged many a long
mile on a humbler, less upright back, often before he even
knew he no longer needed it.

A dangerous practice, some might believe in these
troubled days, but none of Angela's 'gents' (as she
called them) had ever caused her a moment's concern.
They were there now, hanging back on the fringe of
events, paying their respects to her, battered old hats
gripped tightly in their hands, like so many advocates of
Chaucer's courtly love, venerating their Lady from afar.

As they walked towards the graveyard after the church
service, Meg caught sight of a familiar figure. He was

standing back in the shadows of a small copse, looking like he wanted to remain incognito. Philippe and Clive had paused a few feet behind her and were deep in conversation; oblivious to anything other than their own concerns. She hesitated, unsure whether to acknowledge him or not. Then he beckoned her, and she shook her head. He beckoned again, and this time someone else noticed. It was Fleur, holding on to her grandfather's arm, while at the same time hurrying him along in an attempt to catch up with her.

'How do you know David Quinn?' She asked, while Ambrose Carpenter struggled to breathe normally.

'How do you, Flo?' She countered.

'That's simple; he and I were engaged to be married.'

'Past tense?'

'Yes, very much so.'

'And yet, here he is.'

By now Ambrose had recovered his breath and was desperate to join the conversation.

'Megan, my dear, it's really good to see you after all this time, even if the circumstances…'

'I know, Ambrose…if only the circumstances were different.'

'Exactly. If only.' He made a valiant attempt to lighten the conversation. 'What have you been doing with yourself? I heard you married some French ponce and…'

'Grandad!'

'French, yes sir, but ponce most definitely and

happily not.' It was Philippe arriving within earshot at exactly the wrong moment.

'Oh dear. Have I put my big foot in it again?'

'Yes, Gramps you have!'

'Oh dear. Er… er je suis… très er désolâtes Monsieur, je… et per favore excuse.'

'It is of no consequence, sir. Philippe Maigret at your service,' he said, as they shook hands.

'*Chief Superintendent Maigret, actually,*' Flo hissed behind her hand, 'and he speaks excellent English so mind your manners.'

Her perfect little oval face, capped by a long fringe and a dark bob of hair, was devoid of the arty makeup Megan remembered from times past. Her eyes were heavy with unshed tears and she was very pale. The black designer-tat garb of her early teenage years had been discarded in favour of a charcoal houndstooth fine-woollen suit, with a high collar, edged with black velvet, and a fashionably short skirt offset by black opaque tights. Out were the Doc Marten's: in were demurely classic black pumps of Italian origin. Megan was amazed to see the transformation. Yet despite the sophisticated clothes, Fleur still looked younger than her years.

'I repeat: how do you know David Quinn,' she said.

'He kidnapped me and my grandson from the night train from Paris to Berlin.'

'What?'

'Well, actually, in the end, he didn't really kidnap us because we went with him willingly.'

'What?'

'It's a long story, Flo, and this is the wrong time for me to tell it; sufficient to say that his actions, although unorthodox, were justified.'

At that moment, Meg noticed that one of Angela's gents was being reluctantly pushed forward towards Flo. Without knowing why, she intercepted him.

'Can I help you, sir?'

'Er…er… you a rozzer?'

'No, I'm a friend of the late Mrs de Montfort.'

She looked over her shoulder and saw that Fleur was now engaged in earnest conversation with Philippe and Clive. 'Do you have something to say?'

'Perhaps.'

'Well – do you, or don't you?'

'She were a good woman, weren't she, our Missus. A very good woman.' He said, twisting his cap nervously.

'Yes she was. One of the very best.'

'Why would someone want to do her in?'

'That's what the police are trying to discover.'

'We reckons there's two reasons why someone would do for a woman like our Missus was.'

'Oh? And what would they be?'

'Money or revenge. We reckons it was an inside job, we does,' he whispered, 'tell the rozzers that but remember – you didn't hear it from me.'

He turned, about to walk away.

'Wait! Do you mean someone in the family?'

He shook his head.

'Not that close. But close enough. And that's all I know.'

'How do you come by that information, sir?'

He tapped the side of his nose and adopted a conspiratorial air.

'We knows what we knows. We hear things on the streets. Sees 'em too. It's about the moolah, innit? The old judge geezer's loaded, ain't he?'

And with that comment he walked off to re-join his companions. She watched his departing figure while re-running their conversation in her mind.

'What did he want?' Flo called, as she hurried towards her, 'the two of you looked quite engrossed in your tête-à-tête.'

'Did we?'

'So?'

'Not now. I need time to absorb what he said.'

'Okay. Come and say hello to Uncle Giles then.'

'Uncle Giles, QC?'

'The very same.'

'You'll have to introduce us. We've never met.'

'Are you sure?'

'Absolutely.'

By this time, the Queen's Counsel and the Chief Superintendent were chatting cordially while Clive Scott had decided to make a tactical exit to speak with his plainclothes men. The women joined them just in time to hear the end of Giles de Montfort's lengthy exposition.

'So, in your experience what's the most common motive – revenge, greed, or love?'

Meg gasped and suddenly all eyes were fixed on her.

'My goodness, that's almost exactly what I was thinking.'

Giles de Montfort raised an elegant eyebrow and looked at her as though she was some bizarre specimen on a dissecting table. 'And what conclusion did you reach, Madame Maigret?'

'I'd have to say love, since I'm living in Paris and married to a Frenchman!'

They laughed and she breathed a silent sigh and relaxed.

'I can see there's no need for me to introduce you two; I knew you must have met before,' Fleur said.

'No, we haven't.'

'But we have.'

'When and where?'

'At one of Angie's summer soirees yonks ago,' he replied.

'I'm sorry, I really don't remember.'

'Of course you had a different name and husband then…'

'You make it sound like I change my husbands as often as I change my handbags,' she said quickly, feathers ruffled. 'Michael Lisle died six years ago.'

'I'm sorry… I didn't mean to cause offence.'

Philippe took a mental step backwards, the better to fathom the nuances of the scene playing out in front of him. He ran the conversation through his mind, and then ran it again. *What just happened,* he thought. *Why is Meg upset?* Don't ask us, Phil, his subconscious replied, she's your wife. *Unhelpful,* he protested. *If I live to be a hundred I'll never understand how the female mind works. Might as well give up the struggle right now.* Bravo, his subconscious replied, that's the spirit!

'I think the burial service is about to begin,' Fleur said, linking her arm through Meg's, 'perhaps it's time to move to the graveyard.'

'He did that deliberately, didn't he?' She asked as soon as they were out of earshot.

'Oh, yes. Uncle Giles rarely does anything by accident.'

'But why?'

'My guess is that he was testing your mettle.'

'Why should my mettle need testing? I'm nothing to him.'

'He likes to figure out people – see what they're made of; it seems to intrigue him. I think he separates them into the sheep and the goats. Or, in his case, the worthy and the un.'

'Did I pass the test?'

'Definitely I'd say, by the look on his face. He'll know better than to bait you again.'

'So am I in the worthy or un camp?'

'Only he would know. His rules, his judgement.'

'Then rhubarb to him and his stupid mind games.'

'Indeed – rhubarb, rhubarb.'

After Angela's coffin had been laid in her grave they each threw a handful of earth on top of it, followed by myriads of rose petals. Then they walked towards the waiting cars.

'Darling, would you hate me for ever if I missed the er… Reception or whatever you call it?' Philippe whispered.

'You *know* I could *never* hate you, love. And we call it a Wake.'

'*Merci.*'

'However,' she paused for effect, 'however… you *might* be cast into outer darkness…'

'Forever?'

'Quite likely.'

He stopped walking and looked at her steadily with his grey-blue eyes.

'How long do I need to stay at the… Wake to avoid this hideous fate?'

She laughed.

'Forty-five minutes; then make a discreet exit. Where are you going, by the way – as if I didn't know?'

'Clive and I have watch lists to exchange…'

'I thought MI6 dealt with those kinds of issues. Or your DGSE or DGSI.'

'How do you know…?'

'You sometimes talk in your sleep,' she said quickly.

'Hmm. Well if I do, which I strongly deny, I doubt I speak in English. Have you been snooping in the vicinity of my desk again?'

'I occasionally attempt to tidy your desk; and I dislike your use of the word snooping.'

'Then stay away from my papers. God help us, you might be the biggest security threat we're currently facing! What am I supposed to do at this er Wake?'

'Mingle.'

'Sorry?'

'You mingle… from the verb to ming.'

'Are you two arguing?' Flo asked as she joined them.

'No, I'm just explaining that what one does at a Wake is er… *circulate*.'

'You *said* mingle…'

'It's the same thing, Philippe. Just spread your Gallic charm around the room and you'll set every female heart aflutter.'

'Why do I have the feeling that I'm being setup by the two of you?'

'Because you're a detective?' She managed to say before she began laughing.

Philippe did his duty then took his leave of Ambrose Carpenter, Fleur, and Giles de Montfort.

'Shall I arrange for Clive to send a car or are you happy to take a taxi to the hotel?' He asked before leaving.

'No, I'll make my own arrangements. Fleur has asked me to go with her to visit Robert in his nursing home in Highgate and I'm not sure how long we'll stay. It depends on whether he's having a good day or not.'

'This er Highgate – it's a long way?'

'No, quite close; something like fifteen minutes by car.'

'The unfortunate Robert suffers from dementia – yes?'

'Yes. And that's a tragedy for Flo who has now lost both her mother and her grandmother. It's such a pity; Robert was a lovely man with a fine mind. Goodness knows how much of the man he was remains.'

'What work did he do?'

'He had a senior position in a bank in the City – NatWest, I think. But his real love was devising crosswords for various newspapers; I believe he did very well out of that financially.'

'It takes a particular mind-set to be able to finish a crossword, much less actually devise one.'

'It certainly does. And Robert created cryptic crosswords as well as the more basic ones. In fact I'd say they were his forte.'

'Sounds like he'd have made a good spy,' Philippe said thoughtfully. Then he kissed her and murmured 'à bientôt'.

'Yes, see you soon.'

But he had already gone.

FIVE

Another pair of eyes watched Maigret leave. They were David Quinn's; he had been attempting to speak with Meg but each time he tried someone else claimed her attention first.

'Why have you been deliberately avoiding me?' He asked as he finally pounced.

'Why should I avoid you, David?'

'Hah! The lawyers' trick; crude but surprisingly effective.'

'What do you actually *want?*'

'I want to discover what you know about Icarus.'

'His father made him a pair of wings so he could fly but it didn't end well.'

'Very droll, but not *that* Icarus…'

'There's another one?'

He swore softly.

'Surely you haven't forgotten Jamal Ahmadi and what he did for us in Berlin?'

'Of course not. But why mention him now…?'

'You know that after Berlin he was offered a job with the British security service don't you?'

She nodded.

'That's the code name MI6 gave him – Icarus.'

'I'm supposed to know that how…?'

She did know. Philippe had mentioned Icarus during pillow talk one night. But she was not prepared to share that intimate detail with Quinn or anyone else.

'What about *him*?'

'Assuming you're referring to Philippe…'

'You know I am.'

'I have no idea what he knows about Jamal Ahmadi post-Berlin. How would he know *anything* at all? What's this about anyway?'

'Jamal Ahmadi has disappeared and MI6 has no idea where he is, or even if he's still alive.'

'Or whether he's gone back to his old ways and dangerous associates?'

'Exactly. If he's dead, well that's bad luck, but they'll move on and probably put up a discreet plaque somewhere in his honour. But if he's gone rogue then…'

'You're a ruthless damn bunch aren't you?' She said angrily. 'Yet you're supposed to be the good guys. I'm sorry you're apparently working for them again.'

'Defence of the Realm, Sunshine. And this is a once only assignment because of my previous connection with the missing person.'

'What connection? It was Philippe and Clive Scott – Tom Aitkens too, who actually knew him not you; I'd know as much about him as you do. They're using you, aren't they? If you find yourself in trouble they'll deny all knowledge. And if you should turn up dead somewhere then maybe M16 will put up a discreet plaque in *your* memory too – you idiot!'

'Ah, but you see I have *knowledge* of him, and the fewer people who do, the better our secretive friends believe. So for the sake of auld lang syne I advise you to keep quiet about knowing about him if you don't want to get the same virtual knock on your door as I did.'

'Come on Meg!' It was Fleur calling from the doorway. 'We need to go. Dad will be expecting me; that's if he remembers.'

'Ask Maigret if he's heard anything recently about Icarus…'

'I certainly will not! Do you really think I'd involve him in something as dangerous as this game of yours?'

And with that comment she hurried off to join Fleur.

'You're very quiet,' Flo said as they passed the familiar Horses' Pond in Hampstead on their way to Highgate. 'Did Quinn say something to upset you?'

'No. I was just thinking of the times we spent walking on Hampstead Heath all those years ago. And the lovely summer picnics we had too.'

'Long ago – if not far away.'

'Yes,' she replied, opening her window. 'Listen – can you hear the spirit voices whispering through the trees?'

'It's just the wind, nothing more ghostly than that.' Her voice was strong, but she shivered as she spoke.

They drove on in silence again, each looking back, remembering different events. Finally, Fleur spoke.

'What were you and Quinn talking about anyway? You both looked serious.'

'It was nothing very important. How will Ambrose get back to Oxfordshire tonight?'

'He's not going home he's staying at his Club for the next week or so. I'm having dinner with him tonight. Have to keep an eye on the dear old boy.'

'He seemed quite sprightly to me.'

'And so he is. He's okay during the day but he gets lonely in that big house at night, although he won't admit that to me or anyone else.'

They drove on again in silence for a few more minutes.

'What went wrong between you and David Quinn?'

'Oh, lots of things. He's a short-back-and-sides kind of person and I'm not. By the way I like the length of Philippe's hair – very sexy for a cop. But then he is a total studmuffin, isn't he?'

'Flo! Quinn's a decent man; I know that from experience.'

'Yes he is, in his own way. We're just wired differently; although the sex was good. Very good, in fact…'

'Whoa, that's too much information and especially on this of all days.'

'Mum wouldn't mind. She was very fond of Quinn; she treated him like the son she never had. But when did you become such a prude? There was a time when I could tell you almost anything and you'd be completely unshockable.'

'Yes, but that was when I realised you were inventing your scandalous stories. But now, well, it's different when it's real life…'

'Do you know where he worked? And for *whom* he worked?'

'I know where he *formerly* worked.'

'So bloody GCHQ! How could a poacher like me marry a game-keeper like him?'

'Have you never heard of opposites attracting?'

'Yeah, I have. But not *that* opposite. And not Quinn and me.'

'Then I think it's your loss, my dear. I really do.'

'If I tell you something, do you promise not to laugh at me?'

'Of course.'

'Promise anyway.'

She did.

'Mum spoke to me this morning. Not aloud of course, but… well, it was like er… mind to mind. I was in the shower, feeling very sad about… *everything*… I heard – no, I *felt* her say, 'don't be sad, my darling…' Her voice broke as she said the last two words. 'Do you believe that's possible?'

'Not only possible, dearest Flo, but very, very likely. Do you know that the Greek Orthodox people believe that the souls of the departed stay close to their loved ones for six weeks after they've died?'

'Do *you* believe that?'

'Yes I do. How could the love between you and your Mum disappear in a matter of days? Or weeks? Or even years? That love will last forever – have no doubt about that. And she will always be near you, especially during your times of need. As for David Quinn, well I do believe…'

'We're here,' Flo said brightly, pulling up in front of Willows Glen, a pleasant three-storied, cream brick building in a tree-lined street. *And not a minute too soon,* her subconscious remarked. *She's on to you, my girl; she knows you're still in love with David Quinn.*

Weeks later, when lost in her personal hell, Meg would remember that visit with Robert de Montfort in his sheltered environment. But at the time it seemed mostly unremarkable: just an old friend visiting someone down on their luck, making polite conversation.

But that was when she was deep in love, and knew that she was loved in exactly the same way. That was when her world had been perfect.

Robert appeared to be having a good day; he recognised his daughter immediately and gave her an enthusiastic hug and a noisy kiss. He *seemed* to remember Meg too, although he couldn't quite recall her name until Flo reminded him. However he had obviously connected her with his wife because he asked her why Angie hadn't come too. Aware that Robert had not been told of Angela's death she had mumbled something that even as she said the words made no sense to her, but it seemed to satisfy him: he immediately asked Fleur if she could arrange some afternoon tea.

How much he was aware of his diminished mental capacity or why he was no longer living at home, she couldn't fathom. He was less robust than she remembered, while his hair was changing from speckled grey to white, but he looked remarkably well: she was grateful that whatever had ravaged his fine mind had, at least for the time-being, largely left his body alone.

As soon as Flo went to see about the tea, Robert rummaged around in the drawer of the small cabinet next to his armchair and produced a notebook. It was well dog-eared but quite ordinary. However what was significant was the collection of different coloured pills half-wrapped in a tissue that the book had been covering. Robert quickly closed the drawer.

'See this?' He asked, turning immediately to the last page. 'This is my Bastille prison log.' On the paper were many little strokes, like the number 1. 'Count them,' he said, 'they're the number of days since my Angie has been to see me.'

She automatically registered that there were fourteen marks. *That's probably about right*, she thought, but she said nothing.

'The fox is in the hen house,' he whispered. 'And the home is lost. *Sturm and drang – sturm and drang*. There's a canker at the heart of our culture.'

For the next few moments he repeated these phrases over and over like a religious litany.

'Rob… I don't think…'

'*They…* the God-denying pontificators who say everything and believe nothing… say the canker is *poverty*.

But I know it's not. It's *hypocrisy*... utter, unadulterated, top-down *hypocrisy!*'

He almost spat out the last word then slumped back exhausted in his chair and began to quietly weep. She stood up quickly to put her arms around him.

'There, there, Rob. There's no need to worry – *all shall be well, and all shall be well, and all manner of thing shall be well.*'

He turned slightly to look up at her and smiled.

'Good old Thomas Stearns,' he said, mopping his eyes with a fresh handkerchief from his pocket, 'always ready with the poetry of reassurance and resurrection.'

'True; but not forgetting Mother Julian of Norwich who wrote the words centuries before Eliot did.'

Robert nodded.

'Indeed. God bless them both.'

Just then they heard footsteps coming down the hallway then a fumbling on the handle before the door opened.

'Anyone for tea?' Flo said cheerily, somewhat unsteady under the weight of the tea tray. 'Shall I be... shall I pour?' She peered intently at her father, 'Daddy, have you been crying? Has something upset you?'

'No, no, darling girl. Not at all. I'm just a silly sentimental old fool these days.'

'You are are not!'

And all the while Meg was thinking about Robert. And about the origin of the pills he'd obviously not taken, and the strange chanting recitation – angry, accusatory yet at the same time despondent.

There had been no repetition of that sequence after Flo's return. Had she provoked this outburst from him, or had something stirred in his mind? He knew she had seen the pills, yet said nothing. Did he know she wouldn't mention them to Flo?

As they were leaving Willows Glen, Meg said, as casually as she could manage, 'Do you think your father's had any other visitors recently?'

'Why?'

'Oh, just wondering…'

'I repeat – why?'

'He just seemed a little… *disturbed* about something at times. I wondered if someone might have upset him…'

'We can soon find out,' she said pragmatically, 'let's ask Matron.'

But Matron was not there so they asked Muriel, her deputy instead, who immediately retrieved the visitors' book from a shelf under the Reception counter.

'Well now, let's see. Mr Giles came on Wednesday as he always does. But that's about it – oh, wait, yes there it is, and I'd completely forgotten. Your dear father had another visitor the Friday before. We hadn't been expecting him, he said he was just passing and thought he'd pop in to say a quick hello.'

'Who was he? Had he been before? What did he look like?' Flo rattled off in ten seconds.

'He was a Mr Livingstone. Mr Henry Livingstone. A posh gent, very well-spoken. Oh yes – he was wearing one of those Club ties, the MCC, perhaps. No, I think it was a Regimental tie of some kind.'

'Age?'

'Err… not really old – late forties or thereabouts, I'd say.'

Civil servant, Flo whispered to Meg, as they took their leave of Muriel. She nodded and mouthed *defo* in response.

'Do you think Livingstone was his real name?' She asked when they were back in the car.

'Not a cat's chance in hell.'

'Think he'll come back?'

'Probably not, but Muriel will message me if he does.'

Will I go in feet first, or should I be more subtle? She asked her subconscious as they drove off. You might as well go for the direct approach; she's probably going to react whatever you say.

'Flo, how certain are you that Rob's suffering from dementia? He seemed quite lucid to me for most of the time.'

'That's the nature of the illness, unfortunately. Good days clear days – bad days, confused days. And some days are a mixture of both when he'd struggle to tell you what he had for breakfast, much less his own name. He's been evaluated by four doctors, all well-respected in their field. We tried Mum and me, to keep him at home and all was fine for a while. Then earlier this year; around the beginning of March, he disappeared for three days and we almost went crazy with worry. The police finally found him; or rather a member of the public did. He was wandering around south London asking people how he could get to Canary Wharf of all places, and she phoned the police. After that episode his health really took a massive nose-dive.'

'Oh, poor dear man…'

'The thing that struck us as odd at the time was that there was hardly a mark on him. He was clean, tidy – with only a little stubble – and yet he must have been sleeping rough.'

'Or else the woman who found him took him in…'

'For *three days*, when she'd know someone would be looking for him? No, she told the police that she'd come across him while walking her dog that very morning.'

'Maybe he'd been in a homeless shelter somewhere…'

'Not as far as we could discover.'

'So where had he been for those three days?'

'You tell me. Dad certainly couldn't remember anything; the police said it would be a waste of their resources to attempt to find out. He was back with his family again, so no harm done. End of case as far as they were concerned.'

Meg took a deep breath.

'Do the words 'stem and drank', mean anything to you, Flo?'

'What!' She pulled off to the side of the road and hit the brakes. 'What?' She repeated.

'That's what Rob said – something like stem and drank.'

'Or might it have been *sturm and drang?*'

'Yes! That's what he said.'

Flo laughed.

'Oh boy, your visit must have rattled him big time to dig up a memory like that! The German words – *sturm and drang* – were the answer to one of his most famous cryptic crosswords years ago. Some of his readers had nightmares trying to decipher the clue.'

'What was it?'

'I just knew you were going to ask me that. It was too long ago, I can't remember. You know how these cryptics work, of course. *Like Penny's back with a vengeance.* To which the answer would be…'

'Portcullis – because that was the image on the back of a British penny. And that's the extent of my knowledge of cryptic crosswords.'

'Bravo. Yes, Penny's back is an old favourite of crossword creators, but it's not one of Dad's. His clue was more obscure, as was his way. Something like *the fight has not entirely left the emotional old Huns…*'

'And the answer to that was… er sturm and drang? I don't get it.'

'Few did, hence all the angst, because the answer had to be a seven letter *word* and clearly sturm and drang wouldn't fit. It was a clue within a clue. Sturm and drang was a late 18th century German literary movement known for stirring action and high drama which often dealt with a personal revolt against society.'

'For pity's sake, what was the answer?'

'The modern day equivalent of sturm and drang – *turmoil.*'

SIX

While all this drama was happening in Highgate, clear
across London on the leafy Victoria Embankment,
Philippe Maigret was being entertained by Chief
Inspector Scott of the Metropolitan Police. Perhaps
'entertained' is not the right word for what was actually
happening. Clive Scott was a talker: Philippe Maigret
was not, although he was by no means reticent. He
simply preferred to speak when he felt he had something
useful to say. So he sat quietly while Clive rumbled
on about everything that irritated, vexed, or generally
frustrated him, while he skirted around the subject that
would be the main topic. And that was the disappearance
of Jamal Ahmadi and Clive's reluctant secondment
to the British security service, MI6. True, it was for a
single-assignment and a limited time, but it did not
sit well with the Presbyterian who, although born in
Berlin during his father's service with the British Army
of the Rhine in post-war Berlin, had spent his teenage
and early adult years in Edinburgh. That changed when

he met a sweet-faced English girl, Katie Stirling, at the Festival Fringe one year. Within five months they were married, and a few months after that he transferred from the Police Service of Scotland to New Scotland Yard and the Met in London. Once there he had kept his head down, worked diligently and promotions followed on a satisfyingly steady basis.

As his monologue, delivered in a soothing Scots burr continued, Philippe experienced the full hypnotic effect. It had been an early departure from Paris that morning, while the funeral, although he had not known Angela, had proved surprisingly emotional. Nor had the two glasses of wine at the Wake helped his energy levels. He stretched his impressively lean frame to its full six foot plus extent, rested his head against the soft leather wingback chair, closed his eyes and relaxed.

Clive was alarmed by this languid behaviour. *He's gone to sleep,* he thought. *What do I do now? He's a guest of the Met, and he out-ranks me, even if he serves in a foreign force. Moreover he's my friend.* He cleared his throat noisily, without result. He cleared it again, even more loudly, which also failed to produce any change in Philippe's behaviour. Finally, after the third attempt, the Frenchman spoke.

'Do you need a glass of water Clive, or did you just want to discover if I was still awake? As you can see, I am and have been for the entire time that you've been beating around that damn mulberry bush: I only respond now in hope of something being left for you to prune next year. Out with it man – what is it that you're trying to tell me?'

Clive went red, squirmed in his seat, and then laughed.

'Were you going to wait until I'd completely tied myself up in knots, or were you hoping I'd hang myself, my *former* friend?'

'Get on with it,' was the laconic reply and so he did.

Jamal Ahmadi had, in a relatively short time, proved to be a significant asset for MI6, and a useful amount of information had been gained through his infiltration of various fledgling terrorist groups, particularly in Europe; the new centre of Islamic radicalisation. In fact his most recent foray into this dangerous arena had been a few months earlier. He had received an email from an unknown source which read *Icarus will crash and burn in Brussels before the next full moon*. He had reported that to his superiors at the time, and that had been virtually the last trace MI6 had of him.

Maigret snapped to an upright position, frowned, and said something in French under his breath.

'Sorry?' Clive said, 'my second language is German not French, remember?'

'When was that full moon? And when is the next, and who speaks in those terms?'

'What? Greek mythology?'

'No, the phases of the moon. She said bientôt…' 'You're havering man; talk sense. Start with who said what.'

'I have to get back to Paris. The duchess said *bientôt* – soon, and she would know…'

Just then his phone rang; it was Meg.

'Are you still with Clive Scott?' She asked anxiously.

'*Oui.*'

'Good. Then please ask him what he knows about *sturm and drang.*'

'What?'

But Clive had heard her.

'Good God,' he muttered. 'Who's she been talking to now?'

'You know?'

He nodded.

'So what's this... whatever my wife mentioned...?'

'Hello, hello – I'm still here, you know...' She protested from the other end of the line.

'Sorry, my love. I'm just about to leave. I'll see you at the hotel soon.'

'Promise?'

'*Oui bien sûr.*'

'Now where were we?' Clive asked.

'You were explaining what... what my wife said.'

'Oh yes. Well sturm and drang,' he sighed, before continuing. 'It's about our stock in trade; the things that keep us awake at night and on our toes during the day. It's *turmoil*. And on a grand sodding scale.'

'What?'

'Put it this way: it means the world's going to hell in a handcart...'

'We already *knew* that! What's different now?'

'To reiterate, the difference is apparently in the *scale* of whatever it is we're facing. '*Something evil this way comes*' and we might not know how to confront it.'

'So who pricked their thumbs this time?' Maigret said, picking up the Scottish play reference.

'That's what we need to find out – and fast.'

Maigret stood up and in one seemingly fluid, graceful movement batted a foppish lock of hair out of his eye, smoothed his somewhat crumpled clothes and offered his hand to Clive to shake. *How the hell did he manage to do all that without falling over?* An impressed Clive thought.

'*Mon ami*, I know nothing of this matter. But if and when I do, I promise I'll share any information I have with you no matter how many red lines I have to cross to do it.'

And with those words he quickly shook Clive's hand again, patted him on the shoulder, opened the heavy door and left.

When he returned to their hotel in St James's he was not happy to be informed that Madame was waiting for him in the American Bar with a gentleman who had recently arrived to see her. He had been looking forward to an early dinner *a deux,* with a good bottle of red, and the uninterrupted pleasure of his wife's company. He was even less pleased to discover that the visitor was David Quinn.

'What's *he* doing here?' He whispered, as he bent to kiss her. Some might have thought that he hissed, rather than whispered; she certainly did.

'Good evening, sir,' Quinn said, standing as Maigret made his entrance.

They shook hands in a perfunctory way. Quinn felt certain his hands were already clammy and that this would have been obvious to the detective. He could feel himself unravelling mentally after barely a minute in his presence.

'Please sit down, enjoy a glass of this excellent wine David has ordered and try not to be grumpy.'

'I'm sorry, Madame – it has been a difficult day.'

'All the more reason to relax now. And, in answer to your question, David's here because I invited him. Something happened at the nursing home this afternoon and I need you to both hear about it at the same time because I don't want to tell it again.'

Both men immediately took a large slurp of their wine. *Good,* she thought, *it looks like I have the upper-hand in this battle of the sexes, even if only temporarily.*

'If you're comfortable, I'll begin.' Both men nodded and took another generous swig of their wine.

'This afternoon Fleur and I visited her father at the Willows Glenn nursing home. He seemed calm and *reasonably* focussed, though at first he didn't know who I was. However, we realised that at some point that he'd associated me with Angie, because he asked why she didn't come with me. I knew he hadn't been told about… about… what had happened to her so I fudged my reply, which I regret now because I remember that there was something in his eyes – an almost begging look – when he asked the question. I think he knows more than we give him credit for, but I only realised that afterwards.'

At that point her emotions took over and she began to cry. The men looked at each other in consternation. *Do something,* Quinn telegraphed, *she's your wife!* But the police officer, despite having dealt with considerable human anguish during his career, had not yet found a way to cope with his wife's tears.

He was spared further indecision by the prompt arrival of the man in charge of the bar; Charles, a Frenchman as were all the waiters in the American Bar.

'Come, come, Madame, surely the wine is not as bad as all that. Please allow me to fetch you a glass of excellent champagne.'

These words were delivered with eyes twinkling, in a Gallic accent overlaid with authentic Cockney; Charles had come to London when he was nineteen and learnt his English in the East End over the following three or more decades.

'Do you think champagne solves most of Life's problems?'

'Yes. But if now you should tell me that it does not, Madame, then I would be… distraught.'

'Then I will certainly not say that, Monsieur. But nor do I need a glass of champagne; this is a very good wine although I thank you for the kind thought.'

Charles smiled and bustled off to rescue the next mature damsel in distress.

'That's a great marketing strategy he has,' Maigret observed, 'but he lingered too long over the hand-kissing routine.'

'Well, I liked it! But I digress, and apologies for the tears…'

'A little while after we arrived, Rob asked Flo if she could organise some afternoon tea; I believe that was a deliberate ploy. As soon as she left the room he opened the drawer of the little cabinet next to him and produced a piece of paper on which there were numerous small pencil strokes. There were about fourteen in all. He said they were his 'Bastille diary record'– he'd been counting the number of days since Angie had visited. That was when I first began to doubt the dementia diagnosis.

When he opened the drawer I noticed a collection of pills which he quickly covered when he realised I'd seen them. There might have been twenty or more. Some were white and there were yellow ones too, but most were blue…'

'Diazepam – Valium, in differing strengths.' Quinn said. 'Blue's the strongest – 10 mg per pill, while white's the weakest at 2 mg. And yellow's 5 mg.'

'How come you know so much about this, David?'

'Elementary; veritable tools of the trade. Then there are the antipsychotics which are the real heavy-duty stuff: if he's only getting Valium he's probably one of the lucky ones.'

'Is it… er… would it be *ethical* to give them to a dementia patient?'

'Ethical? When did you last hear anyone mention ethics! Long since killed off along with morality and personal responsibility. Now it's all *nuanced conversations* – how I loathe the duplicity of that expression – and shades of grey, or rather all colours of the rainbow. But I suppose that if the mind confusion became extreme enough to cause problems or if the patient was agitated or aggressive, mind-altering drugs might be used. Lesser of two evils; means justifying the end, and so forth.'

'Mmm... I see,' she said, thinking of Robert's strange repetitive chanting. *Strange definitely, but no sign of aggression. The anger had come later.*

'Did you challenge him on the subject...?'

'No, I didn't say anything, wimp that I am. I was afraid what his reaction might be.'

She hesitated for a moment, took several sips of her wine, before resuming her account.

'Then his behaviour changed and he did become agitated. He started a kind of rant. Or was it more like sacred chanting? I can't be sure. He kept up a recitation about the fox in the hen-house, and the home being lost. Then he began saying *sturm and drang, sturm and drang,* over and over. He said there was a canker at the heart of British society, and that canker was hypocrisy. He repeated these phrases like a litany for the next few minutes.'

'*Mon Dieu,* what has been done to this poor man's mind?'

'Have you heard those German words before, David?'

'No. What do they mean?'

She sighed.

'Apparently they refer to some old German literary movement, late 19th Century I believe Fleur said, and they were part of the answer to one of Rob's cryptic crosswords.'

'Weird: thirteen letters to fit into the crossword squares.'

'No, no. I said they were only *part* of the clue. When they were distilled to meet cryptic criteria the answer was *turmoil*. And, with the benefit of hindsight, I now realise that was the theme of Rob's rant or recitation.'

'Hmm. And the thing that keeps us awake at night and terrified during the day,' Maigret said thoughtfully.

'What?'

'I mentioned those words, on my wife's insistence, at my meeting earlier this afternoon, and that was the reply I received from a fluent German speaker.'

'Clive Scott,' his wife said, 'but wait, there's more, much more. And worse to come.'

'Then I think I'd better order another bottle of wine and something on which to graze.'

'No, it's my turn,' Maigret said, signalling to Charles, and speaking rapidly in French.

Meg continued.

'Rob said that *they*... the almighty pontificating *they* who say everything yet believe nothing – as he described them – would allege that the canker is *poverty*. But he knew that it was *hypocrisy*... utter, top-down *hypocrisy*. He practically spat out that word then fell back in his chair and wept. It was a pitiful sight; I can't get the image out of my mind. I tried to comfort him, and then my subconscious must have taken over because I found myself reciting Eliot . He smiled, "Good old Thomas

Stearns, always ready with the poetry of redemption and resurrection," he said.'

The refreshments arrived and they were magnificent. Not a trace of olives, nuts or crisps, but *proper* food, as Maigret described it. Delicate little savoury quiches, and smoked salmon crepes. A gently spicy terrine and blinis too, with chopped onion, crème fraiche and other subtle accoutrement. It was a feast for both eyes and taste-buds.

'This is more like it,' said Quinn, chomping contentedly on yet another sautéed mushroom.

'Indeed,' replied Maigret, who had his eyes fixed on a tempting plate of whitebait. 'And I'm so content that Charles suggested we switch to this excellent Sancerre.'

'Shall I continue?' Meg asked, when she saw that both men were almost replete. They both nodded.

'It was just after the Eliot lines that we heard Fleur coming down the hallway. As soon as she opened the door she could tell that Rob had been crying, and she looked at me in a rather accusatory way.'

'That's my girl,' Quinn said wryly, 'or rather, that *was* my girl until recently…'

'*Comment?*'

'David and Fleur were engaged to be married,' she whispered.

'There's no need to spare my feelings, my heart's ventricles have almost healed now…'

'*Comment?*' Maigret repeated, feeling he must have drifted off at some point.

'Ssh… I'll explain later. Rob assured Flo that he was just a little emotional and shortly afterwards we left. But I kept thinking about what had prompted his unusual behaviour. If it wasn't me, had there been any other visitors for him recently? It turns out that there had been an unexpected visitor the previous week. He said that he had been in Highgate and had made an impulsive decision to visit Rob who he described as an old friend. He said his name was Henry Livingstone, but Flo was adamant that her father had no friend by that name. We both thought his name seemed unlikely anyway.

According to the matron's deputy, he was a posh gent of medium height, possibly with a moustache, wearing something similar to a Regimental tie, although she couldn't recall the actual colours. She thought he might have been in his late forties or so.'

'Civil servant,' Quinn said. 'Low level pen-pusher in the Department of Defence or one of its auxiliaries. But what the hell did he want with poor old Rob?'

'That was the question Flo and I discussed as we left the nursing home. I had another question too; how reliable was the diagnosis of dementia? He had seemed pretty lucid to me – at least for most of the time. She said that was the nature of dementia; good days, bad days, and some days were a combination of both. Four experienced doctors had agreed on the diagnosis. They tried to keep him at home as long as possible and all went well for a while. But then came Flo's bombshell: without warning Rob disappeared for three days.'

'What? When? How?' It was Quinn speaking; his face suddenly flushed. 'This is complete news to me.'

'Sometime earlier this year, and after that he ended up in Willows Glen.'

'It must have been about the time that Fleur and I were having er… shall we say… difficulties. But where did they find him?'

'They didn't, nor did the police. A woman in South London found him wandering in the street and thought he looked confused. She contacted the local police, they checked their missing persons' file, and brought him home. But the strangest part of the episode was that when he was found there was no sign of any injury and he was clean, tidy and almost whisker-free and yet he'd presumably been sleeping rough for three days. Now what do you think of all that?'

'The woman had looked after him…'

'For *three days*? No, she told the police that she'd found him while walking her dog that morning.'

'He must have been in a homeless shelter…'

'Not as far as anyone could discover, David.'

'Then where had he been during that time? Surely the police must have had some idea. Or Rob himself.'

'Rob couldn't remember anything, except for talking with the woman with the dog. And it appears that the police had no interest in taking the matter further – waste of resources they said. The lost sheep had been returned to the family fold, so all was well as far as they were concerned.'

'All very strange, *non?*

'Strange doesn't even *begin* to describe it. So tell me clever gentlemen, who could do that?'

'Do what?' Maigret and Quinn said at the same time.

'Make someone disappear for three days then wipe his memory and return him to the streets again, apparently unscathed?'

SEVEN

'Apparently unscathed?' Quinn queried, shifting uneasily in his chair exactly mirroring Maigret's movements at the same time.

'Yes, *apparently;* definitely not actually. After that episode his mental health plummeted according to Fleur. And that's why he finally had to be admitted to the nursing home.'

'Well now… let me think…'

'Surely there's no need for anyone to think! Only… *instruments* of the State – in some form – would be able to execute something like that without any consequences…'

'Lower your voice Meg,' Quinn said, looking around anxiously.

'And the worst part is that they know exactly where to find him. Hence the unscheduled visit of the mysterious Henry Livingstone.'

'But why?'

'Why what?'

'Why should these… er *instruments* be interested in an ordinary man living a quiet life in Hampstead?'

'That's for you to find out, David. You have the contacts and after all Rob *was* almost your father-in-law.'

'Why would Livingstone choose to visit him now when he's been in that place for months?'

That question hung in the air for a few minutes without anyone answering. Then Maigret spoke. His voice was slow and deliberate, with an edge to it.

'To discover whether there had been any *change* in his condition since the last time they had met.'

'You're probably right, sir. Why else would he suddenly appear like that?'

'If he had *improved* – what then?' She asked.

'There would probably have been some… concerns,' Quinn replied.

'He might not be out of danger yet?'

'Exactly. Was there any CCTV at the nursing home?'

'I didn't notice any but I wasn't really looking; I admit I was nervous about seeing Robert again, although I'm not sure why. But that's certainly a good place for you to start. I suggest you ask Fleur to go with you.'

'Why?'

'Because I don't think she's an entirely lost cause as far as you're concerned.'

'Feminine intuition?'

'Yes. And that's all I'll say.'

Just then Maigret's phone rang. He glanced at the screen, said *'merde'* softly, excused himself then walked quickly out to the cobble-stoned courtyard.

She watched him through the large window directly opposite her. He was pacing restlessly; sometimes to and fro, other times in circles, his shoulders slightly hunched, his brow creased, speaking rapidly in his native language.

She observed him with a heavy heart. Two things she knew for certain; it was bad news, and he was speaking with Inspector Georges Martin, his right-hand man at *Police Nationale*.

He was gone for a long time. When he finally returned his shoulders were now sagging – either from tiredness or despair – and he looked lost. He sank down in his chair and took a draught of wine emptying the glass.

'What's happened, darling?' she whispered. He ran his fingers through his hair in a potent gesture of distress but said nothing.

'Please speak to me, Philippe.' But he remained silent and so did she and Quinn.

They stayed like that for almost ten minutes while worried waiters came and went, topping up their wine and removing empty plates. When Maigret finally spoke his voice was hoarse and hesitant.

'*Nos autres Amis,*' He said. 'Nos autres Amis…'

'Yes, yes – our other friends. What about them?'

'*Mort.*' He fell back in his chair again. Both Quinn and Meg thought the same thing; he was utterly devastated.

After a few minutes, Quinn shifted slightly, hoping that the movement would draw Meg's attention away from her husband. It did. *What is he talking about?* He signalled. *What friends – where? The street people who live near the Seine I think,* she mouthed. *He introduced me to them a few days ago.*

Without warning Maigret launched into a fast-flowing stream of words, thoughts, feelings and names in no cohesive pattern, as far as she could tell. The words Gervais, the Duchess or Madeleine, did register with her at various times, and were regularly repeated, but that was about all she could follow; her French was too basic for this torrent. And still words continued spilling from his mouth as though a dam-burst had occurred in his brain. Or his heart.

'English please,' she murmured.

But by then David Quinn, fluent in both French and Hebrew, had begun an impromptu translation.

'He says that the body of a man has been found in the Seine, he was one of his other friends, and his name was Gervais. He… this doesn't make sense – something about dusting off an old chair…'

She nodded.

'I know what that means – go on.'

'He was a quiet old man who never wronged anyone in his entire life – gentle… gentlemanly. Had he ever reviled anyone for practising their religion even though… No, never. Yet for his gentility and er… *forbearance,* for his patient… tolerance… beaten then his throat cut… May they burn in the hottest flames of Hell! Next the coldness of the river for his grave. Poor, dear, troubled man. Oh… God in Heaven why this for him? Oh, gentle Jesus. Madeleine… likely dead… somewhere. Georges… why can't you find her… You ask too much of me, Lord. Why do you… it's far too long… But still I try… I go on… when will it ever be over? How long, Lord… how much longer… When comes the longed for day of peace? Hail, Mary, full of Grace…'

At that point David stopped translating, although Philippe's out-pouring continued: a constant flow of verbal anguish.

She looked enquiringly at him.

'It's more of the same,' he whispered. 'It's all gut-wrenching stuff; painful to hear and even worse to translate. The man's soul is in turmoil – he's twisting on the bloody rack – and that's no exaggeration.'

She stood to put her arms around Philippe. He stopped speaking and looked up at her with his eyes full of unshed tears: a sight she had not witnessed before.

'Come on darling, it's time for us to go upstairs now,' she said, darting a quick glance at Quinn, who rose to the moment.

'Yes, yes, I must be going too. I'll settle up here. And let's keep in touch, if I don't manage to see you before your return to Paris.'

'I don't think you will; we have a family lunch planned for tomorrow, and we're on an early EuroStar the next morning. But you will follow-up on er the matters concerning Robert, won't you? And you'll take Fleur with you, if she agrees?'

'Of course. Leave everything to me, and I'll keep you informed.'

They were still waiting for the lift in the Lobby when Quinn joined them again. Philippe smiled, and shook his hand.

'*Merci, mon ami,*' he said. 'I appreciate your courtesy

and discretion. I will give you whatever assistance I, and my officers, might be able to provide.'

'Thank you, sir. Does this mean I'm finally off the hook for abducting Meg and Nat from the night train to Berlin?' He replied cheekily.

'Yes. I know better than anyone that it is almost impossible to persuade Madame to do anything she's not inclined to do! And, for the record, my name's Philippe.'

When the lift arrived at their floor they stepped out quickly and went straight to their room. Philippe sighed as he closed the door on the outside world, then sank down in the nearest chair, loosened his tie and removed his shoes.

'Oh, no you don't, *Monsieur le grand fromage,*' she said lightly, desperate to avoid a return to his dark mood.

'What kind of big cheese am I supposed to be?'

'You can be any kind of cheese you like, as long as you're my cheese.'

'Well then, I think I'll be …'

'How is anyone supposed to govern a country that has two hundred and forty-six different kinds of cheese? As Napoleon once said.'

'No darling, it was General de Gaulle.'

'Was it? Well… well… maybe he was quoting Napoleon at the time.'

Philippe laughed.

'Yes, maybe he was.'

'And anyway you haven't answered my question. What kind of cheese would you choose to be?'

'Brie.'

'Why?'

'Because I know it's your favourite.' He was rewarded with a kiss.

'Let's get ready for bed. It's been quite a day, one way or another.'

'It's too early to sleep,' he said, glancing at his watch.

'Who said anything about *sleeping*? We could read, or watch television, or…'

'I like the sound of the second or…'

'So do I, as long as Georges is not phoning or texting you for half the night.'

'He won't. I told him we'll speak again first thing in the morning. See – I'm switching my off my phone right now. But I do need return to Paris as soon as possible. You stay on longer if you wish, but…'

'Not without you. Why don't you phone Georges and ask him to change our Eurostar tickets from Sunday morning to tomorrow night?'

'Are you sure?'

'Yes.'

'What time would suit you?'

'Seven or eight? Something like that. The grandkids will want you to stay as long as possible and maybe have a game of cricket too. The old leather on willow…'

'So they can laugh when I get out first ball as usual and tell me that the French can't play cricket…?'

'They adore you, as you are very well aware.'

'Hmm. What is this leather on willow?'

'The outside of a cricket ball's made of leather and

the bat is made from the wood of the willow tree. It's the sound of summer when those two are pitted against each other.'

'But it is November: the summer has long gone.'

'That's a metaphor for Life in a way, isn't it?' She regretted the words as soon as they left her mouth, fearing that they might trigger another deluge of pain from him. He looked at her and smiled.

'Don't worry, I'm okay now.'

'Been doing a spot of mind-reading again, Monsieur?'

'Something like that. Have to keep my hand in.'

As he spoke her phone rang; it was Flo.

'What have you been telling Quinn?' She demanded.

'About what?'

'You tell me! He rolled in here by taxi twenty minutes ago, reeking of alcohol and clutching a bunch of droopy red roses, gibbering about hidden pills… and… *Agents of the State* and CCTV cameras. Then, worst of all, he went all mushy. He actually tried to get down on one knee to propose again saying that he couldn't live without me. But he lost his balance fell sideways and I had to help him up.'

'*In vino veritas,* Flo.'

'What?'

'People tend to tell the truth when they're…'

'He's not *drunk*; just very, very… relaxed. It's all very well for you to laugh but I need to leave soon to have dinner with Granddad and the old boy's a stickler for punctuality.'

'Then go.'

'And leave Quinn here by himself…?'

'Why not? He's not likely to throw a wild party or burn the house down, is he?'

'I should just let him stay…?'

'I would.'

'Oh Lord – now he's lolling about in Dad's favourite armchair, reciting some maudlin poetry.'

'A tenner says it's Keats; *La belle dame sans merci*.'

'I think you're right. He just mumbled something about a spotty knight on a windy hill whining on about some fairy who done him seriously wrong. How did you know?'

'It figured. Abandonment, death and a beautiful heartless female creature. It's the depressives Charter, isn't it? Therefore it's Keats.'

EIGHT

They had their family lunch the next day, followed by the obligatory game of cricket in which Philippe, much to everyone's surprise not least his own, scored an impressive twenty-four runs before being caught by Tim.

He also showed some promise as a wicket keeper, although it took considerable discussion to brief him on the requirements of this important role.

'But why should it be necessary to watch the man who is batting?'

'So you can be ready to stump him.' Tim explained.

'Or run him out when the possibility arises,' Max added. 'It's probably just like catching criminals. You keep watching until they slip-up and then – Gotcha! Voila! – you're nicked, mister.'

Late that night: Gare du Nord, Paris

Their EuroStar rumbled into Gare du Nord on schedule and Georges Martin met them on the platform and carried their bags as he always did, although his chief complained that this assistance made him feel decrepit.

'What have you done with the car, Georges?' He asked.

'It's right out front, Chief and Jacques is with it.'

Maigret tutted.

'You shouldn't have let him come at this time of night; he's not a well man.'

'I did attempt to dissuade him, but you know Jacques; when he's determined to do something there's no stopping him.'

Maigret sighed.

'You're right, of course. He's a terrier at times.'

When they reached the car they found Jacques standing by, doors and boot open, with a beaming smile on his face. Maigret noted that he looked more robust and his breathing was less laboured.

'Madame, do you wish to go via the Avenue Foch to collect the little furry one from Madame Maigret senior?'

'No, let's not disturb them this late Jacques; I'm sure they will all be in their beds by now. Did you know that Ms Moggs sleeps with Brodie in his basket when she has these little holidays at her Granny's house? Although she probably thinks it's *her* basket really and she's doing *him* the favour.'

'What happened to them fighting like cats and dogs?' Georges asked.

'They never did. They immediately accepted each other as part of the family and that was that.'

As they drove through the dark near-deserted streets, Jacques carefully avoiding the night club areas, she snuggled into Philippe and yawned.

'Feel free to use French all of you; I'm planning to have a little nap next to this charming man I met on the EuroStar tonight.'

They all laughed.

'Are you planning to *keep* him, Madame?' Jacques asked.

'I thought I *might*. He definitely shows promise; we'll just have to see how well house-trained he is.'

She wasn't really planning to nap: it was her way of overcoming their scruples about using a language, in which she was far from fluent, in front of her. *Gentlemen to a fault,* she always thought, *and thank heaven for that indulgence.*

But nor could she avoid hearing the conversation, and parts of it she could piece together. Madeleine had still not been found, nor had any member of her select coterie. That was the bad news. The good news was that no more bodies had turned up in the Seine. Maigret muttered a few words of thanks heavenwards when he was given that information.

Their pleasant return to Paris seemed to set the tone for the next few days and their life settled into a familiar routine. Meg had morning coffee with the still beautiful Louise Maigret the next morning and brought Kitty home afterwards. Philippe joined the continuing search for Madeleine, or anyone who might have known her, and re-checked the hospitals. All futile, he realised, since it had already been done thrice over by his squad, every one of whom knew something of the abuse Madeleine had suffered when young, and their chief's devotion to her as a consequence.

In fact, as she looked back on that time, she was amazed at how very *ordinary* life had been. Of course she was sorry that Madeleine had not been found but even more concerned about Robert, in his nursing home in Highgate, and the cache of pills he had not taken. The Thursday morning after their return Fleur phoned with an update, but each new piece of information only deepened her anxiety rather than relieved it.

She and Quinn had visited Willows Glen the previous day and found there was CCTV in operation. After some trawling backwards and forwards through the film they found a grainy image of the mysterious Henry Livingstone: they suspected that his glasses and moustache were probably part of a disguise. Quinn subsequently checked the photograph on the data bases to which he, after some pleading and calling in of past favours, had access, but there was no trace of him. MI5 declared they had no knowledge of him and so did MI6.

'I asked Dad about Livingstone,' Flo said, 'but he became quite vague at that point. Said he *thought* he might know him, but couldn't be sure. Then he clammed up for a while, so I asked him about the pills…'

'Oh Flo! Was that wise…?'

'Who knows? I thought it was worth a try. Do you know what he said? He said they were sleeping pills…

sleeping pills, can you imagine that, because that's what someone had told him.'

'Why didn't he take them?'

'He felt he didn't need anything to help him sleep. Said he slept too much as it was, and he didn't want his mind to be foggy all the time.'

'Good for him: that degree of self-awareness is impressive for someone in his situation.'

'That's what we thought. But after that Quinn, for reasons known only to him, asked Dad if he knew the strengths of the different colours. And that was a real surprise. Dad very confidently went through the colours: the blue, were the weakest...'

'What?'

'Bear with me, Meg. So – the blue were the weakest, the yellow were a little stronger, while the white were the strongest of all.'

'He was deliberately given the wrong information, but who would...'

'There's worse. David signalled that I should divert Dad's attention; I'd brought an old photograph album with me for that purpose, while he searched the pill drawer. And what do you think he found...?'

'So it is *David* now – is it?'

'Sush... we're er... *might* be trying to work things out...'

'Hallelujah!'

'Right at the back of the drawer he found four more pills. Two were a dark yellow, and two were an evil-looking red-brown colour. He didn't like the look of them so he wrapped them in a tissue and put them in his pocket.'

'And?'

'He had a chemist friend run them through his lab and they turned out to be antipsychotic drugs: Risperdal or Risperidone, something like that. The yellow were 0.25 mg strength and the evil-coloured ones were 0.5 mg. And both were for the treatment of moderate to severe bi-polar illness.'

Meg gasped.

'And to think that in my innocence I questioned the ethics of giving a dementia patient mere Valium! What's going on at that place? Who's running it – Josef Mengele and his concentration camp doctors?'

'Strange that you should mention those vile times and experiments because David said almost the same thing. We think it might be something like illegal drug trials, but we can't fathom why when there are already so many drugs on the market and approved for use.'

'Indeed. Almost overkill, one might say.'

'Then, just as we were getting ready to leave, I asked Dad again about Livingstone. This time he didn't dither around as he'd done before. This time he was quite clear. Livingstone had said they'd met at The Horseshoe pub in Hampstead, but I reminded Dad that he usually went to The Flask in winter and the Spaniard's Inn in the summer because he enjoyed walking across the Heath. But he just shrugged and said that *usually* was not a synonym for *always*.'

'Well he would certainly know; clever old crossword

creator that he was. But it's still very strange and getting weirder by the minute, in my opinion.'

'Mine too. But at least we solved the pill mystery, and I confiscated the Valium David had left behind. We'll see if any more turn up in that drawer.'

'How did he manage not to swallow them? Isn't a member of staff supposed to watch while the patient takes their medication?'

'Yes. But my cunning old lad had perfected a trick of somehow slipping the pill into a gap between two of his back teeth while he swallowed the water. I tried it with an aspirin at home and I really couldn't do it, but he could, God love him.'

Friday 13th November 2015
Avant le déluge (Before the flood)

The next afternoon, as she was deciding on what to wear for her regular dinner *a deux* with Philippe, a custom they had observed almost every Friday night since their marriage, her phone rang. It was him, and immediately she knew by his voice that something was amiss.

'What's wrong, love?'

'Nothing.' Then silence, while she waited for him to continue. Eventually he said, 'Everything. Everything, and yet nothing. Nothing that can be explained. Paris is off her axis; she's moved both latitude and longitude and the music is all discord. It's jarring, jangling; strident. I can't fathom it. *For now we see through a glass darkly…*'

'*Madeleine?* Has she been found?'

'Not yet.'

'Then what? Try French, love... I might have a better chance of understanding.'

Another long silence, broken by an even deeper sigh.

'Why don't we leave the discussion until you're home? Come home early so we can have a drink and talk before we go to dinner.'

'That's just it. I... er wondered if we might not go out tonight.'

'Don't you feel well...?

'No, no – I'm fine. It's just that...'

'What?'

'There's something wrong. Not with me: everything! Something harsh and shrill. The squad feels it too. Even the birds know something's in the wind. I took a long walk at lunchtime and no birds were singing. None! Don't the birds fall silent long before the tsunami hits the shore? That's it! A tsunami's coming and the birds sense it.'

'A tsunami in Paris?'

'Yes. Not actually of course, but...'

'Then trust your judgement. I'll make us something simple and we'll have a quiet night in.'

'I'd like that.'

'Then it's done. Stay safe...'

'Why did you say that?'

'It's what I always say, isn't it?'

'Hmm. Maybe.'

'You're frightening me now,' she said, but he had already ended the call.

He *did* come home early, and as he walked through their door he felt the apartment wrap its arms around him, whispering *you are safe now, relax and lay down your burdens.*

Delicious smells wafted from the kitchen while only the table lamps were lit creating a warm glow; there were fresh flowers on the hall and sitting room tables.

Next came the patter of soft paws and Kitty arrived. She looked up at him and meowed.

'Come on then, Ms Moggs,' he said, opening his arms into which she leapt with unerring precision.

'Hey, Monsieur! Don't I get a kiss before the cat?'

'Certainly, Madame. But should I kiss you below the ear as I do with the furry one, or should I follow my natural inclination?'

They dispensed with their usual pre-dinner drinks in favour of eating early. She had made a zesty smoked salmon roulade, served with a crisp lettuce, tomato and avocado salad. This was one of his favourite meals.

'What's this?' He asked suspiciously, as he raised his wine glass. 'It looks like one of our fine wines but it doesn't smell like it. Oh – nor does it taste like one.'

'It's an electrolyte drink mixed with coconut juice.'

'Are you trying to poison me, Madame?'

'Drink it, it's good for you. Your mother told me that she'd read all about it in…'

He groaned.

'Not another of *maman's* new age concoctions? Saints preserve us.'

'You may scoff but your mother looks fantastic for her age. For any age actually; she has to practically fight off would-be suitors with a stick.'

He held his nose and drained the glass.

'Yuk. Now may I have some wine?'

'Yes, but not yet; best to let the electrolytes do their work first.'

'How long?'

'Twenty minutes should do it. Have some more roulade and salad while you wait.'

He did. Afterwards she cleared the table while he stacked the dishwasher; he could always load more even after she felt it was full. Then she fed the cat while he read the paper in his favourite chair in the sitting room.

The first phone call came at 9.55 pm. And after that no one rested easy that night: Paris was a city in *turmoil*.

NINE

The phone call was from Philippe's university friend, now the Minister of Police, Christophe Saint-Valéry.

'Our world's in turmoil, Philippe. Paris is under attack! I'm receiving multiple reports of mass shootings; both the 10th and 11th are being simultaneously hit.'

'What do you want me to do, Christophe?'

'I want you to make a wide slow sweep of the 10th and the 11th to discover the extent of the chaos so we can determine our best response. Be my eyes and ears on the ground: observe, assess and report back at brief regular intervals. Keep me informed but be discreet. No frontline heroics. Just painstaking police work. Is that understood?'

'And where exactly is the frontline?'

'God knows. Use your best judgement. Hold on, my other phone's ringing.' He heard the Minister's exclamations very clearly. 'Mère de Dieu! Another attack. Catastrophic? Where? Outside the Stade de France? Mon

Dieu, the President's there; we're playing Germany. He is? Thank the Lord. Philippe – are you still there?'

'I'm here, Minister.'

'Did you get any of that?'

'Yes, but I only heard clearly what you said…'

'Well, let me fill you in. There's been an explosion in Avenue Jules Rimet, outside the stadium. Now two more bombs have exploded; the second in the same avenue as the first, the third nearby in Rue de Cokerie. Four dead. Three suicide bombers and an innocent man who was in the wrong place at the wrong time. The President's safe and on his way to the Elysee.'

'What's our next move?'

'Hold on – my other phone's ringing again. I'll get back to you ASAP.'

When he did, his voice was sombre.

'Now it seems I can tell you where the front line is. Three attackers armed with assault weapons have entered the Bataclan and opened fire during a gig by some American band. It seems they're shooting people indiscriminately as they try to escape. Many dead, many injured. Get there as fast as you can. Make a sweep of the area but stay safe.'

As soon as the Minister finished speaking Maigret began rushing around the apartment. First he went to the safe in the study and removed the revolver he wore above his right ankle in times of danger. He checked that it was fully loaded then quickly wrapped the holder around his ankle, secured it, and pushed the revolver into the tight pouch. Next he removed his Sig Sauer, the weapon of choice for the French police and confirmed that it too was loaded. Then he switched off his official phone, placed it in the safe and removed what he referred to as 'the vanilla version': nothing on it would yield any useful information to either terrorist or criminal. He quickly retrieved his padded jacket from the hall closet and thrust the Sig into the inside pocket. Meg, who had been silently following him from room to room, her anxiety rising with every step, finally spoke.

'Why the weapons, Philippe?'

He smiled, hoping to reassure her.

'It's for *insurance*, my love, just like carrying an umbrella to keep the rain away.'

As he spoke the apartment's intercom buzzed. It was Miguel the night concierge at the ground floor Reception desk.

'Madame Maigret, Inspector Martin has arrived with the Chief Superintendent's car.'

Philippe, who had been expecting the call, signalled 'three minutes', to her. She nodded and relayed the message.

Now came the moment they dreaded.

'Why is it *always* you at times like this?'

'It's not always me…'

'You're really too old to be…'

'Too old, am I? That's not what you said last night. I'm sure I heard you murmur words of appreciation to someone described as a *love god*.'

'In your dreams, Monsieur,' she said, laughing despite her fear.

'So you question my memory, do you? Then for the sake of my honour I must insist on a reprise at the earliest opportunity.'

'Agreed, my darling,' she said, walking to the door with him. 'Now button up your jacket and stay warm and…' Her words ended with a sob.

'Don't, please don't. How can I leave when you're…?'

'I'm okay now,' she said, keeping her voice steady despite being aware that every corpuscle in her body was screaming *don't let him go*!

As he walked through their door, he turned.

'Close the curtains and stay away from the windows, my love. Don't open the door to anyone; not even someone you know. I'll call you as soon as I can. If *maman* should phone tell her er tell her I'm in a meeting with Christophe and can't be disturbed but that I'll call her in the morning. Oh – and don't watch the news channels!'

Then he was gone.

'Too late,' she whispered after him, 'much too late. I already know that all hell's broken loose out there and you will be in the thick of it.'

'Where too, Chief?' Georges Martin asked as Maigret walked out of the lift.

'Wait. Miguel, lock and bar the front door as soon as we've left and don't open it again unless you are very sure about the person on the other side.'

'Understood, sir. Everything will be done as you have instructed.'

'Good man.'

'Where to, Chief?' Georges repeated as they reached the car.

'We're to reconnoitre the area around the Bataclan concert hall on the Boulevard Voltaire. Do you know it?'

'Yes sir, I've been to a few concerts there but not recently.'

'Get there as fast as you can but try not to injure any pedestrians we encounter on the way.'

'Gotcha, sir. Watching out for pedestrians.'

However, they had not driven for more than ten minutes before Maigret's phone rang.

'Hello?' He said, cautiously.

'It's Central, sir. I have new orders for you.'

'How did you know to use this number? And be very careful how you reply: no names or ranks.'

'Understood, sir. I tried er the *alternative* first. This is listed as an... acceptable option.'

'Very well. Continue.'

'New orders: abort previous orders...'

'Is that situation now secure?'

'Negative, sir. But specialist units in operation or en route which it's thought will deliver force majeure.'

'I hope to Heaven that whoever made that judgement is correct.'

'Indeed, sir.'

'Where now?'

'92 Rue de Charonne… sitrep only, no intervention. I repeat – sitrep only, no intervention.'

'But that's…'

'Correct. Not far out of your way, sir. Over and out.'

'So no Bataclan for us, boss?' Georges asked when the conversation ended.

'Apparently not. From what our cautious control officer said, I imagine that the specialist units are the GIGN corps of the *Gendarmerie*. They'll position crack snipers on the adjacent roofs to eliminate as many of the enemy as they can.'

'The enemy?'

'Of course, they're the enemy! They can call themselves ISIS or Islamic State, or Jihadis, Islamists – whatever the hell they like – but we are at war now, and make no mistake about that. If we don't protect our way of life these barbarians will wipe us out, one by one, if necessary. Make a U-turn, we need to change direction.'

'Where?'

'Not far from where we were headed, still in the 11th but off the other end of the Boulevard Voltaire.'

'What kind of establishment?'

'Don't know, but following the pattern already established I'd say it was either a restaurant or a bar.'

Maigret was right. The 'La Belle Equipe' was a bustling restaurant that night.

Georges made a screeching U-turn with lights flashing and siren shrieking.

'Let's go silent now, no need to advertise who we are and what we're about.'

'Yes, sir. Silent approach now.'

The terrorists must have known some French history, or done their homework, because the Boulevard Voltaire is a significant boulevard in the 11th arrondissement of Paris. It was created by Baron Georges-Eugène Haussmann during the reign of Emperor Napoleon III. Originally named Boulevard du Prince-Eugène, it was renamed Boulevard Voltaire on the 25th October 1870 in honour of the French Enlightenment writer, historian, and philosopher Voltaire: *"those who can make you believe absurdities, can make you commit atrocities"*.

The boulevard is a great axis joining two historical squares associated with the French revolution: the Place de la République and the Place de la Nation, and is a main hub for left-wing demonstrations with the Republic and Nation squares as the focal point.

So: hit us where it will hurt most, Maigret thought – *in the very heart and soul of our democracy. You've made your point, you death-loving hell-hounds, and now we will make ours.*

They drove silently down the boulevard, lined with platanus trees. When they turned on to Rue de Charonne it was the pungent smell of Nitro-glycerine from recently-discharged weapons that assaulted their senses first, together with the muted sound of explosions and more gunfire in the distance. Then further down the rue the smell of free-flowing blood, running over the footpaths and down into the gutters.

'Slow right down and turn off the lights, Georges, we're almost there.'

As he spoke they saw the full horror that awaited them. A small group of people standing quietly, a respectful distance from the sprawled, bleeding bodies on the pavement. They had been dining in the 'Septime' restaurant next door to the ill-fated 'La Belle Equipe'.

The first-fruits of those swept away by the tsunami of evil, Maigret thought as he regarded the victims. *But how many more will there be tonight.*

'Oh God! Stop the car; I'll go on foot now. Leave it somewhere down the first side street you come to then double back and wait on the other side of the restaurant.'

'Sir – those are not our orders!'

'Stop, I said! To hell with our orders. Where is the rest of our squad?'

Georges reluctantly stopped the car and Maigret prepared to get out.

'They have different orders from Control HQ. They're deployed here, there and everywhere as far as I can tell.'

'And what are your orders, Inspector Martin? And from whence did they come?'

'Chief, I can't say. You know that.'

'Never mind, it was a rhetorical question. I already know. And, to be perfectly clear, I'm now countermanding those orders and I take full responsibility for doing so. Now do as I say and drive on!'

Maigret walked quickly towards 'La Belle Equipe'.

'They're all dead, sir,' a man in the pavement cluster said. 'But I don't know about those inside.'

'Police officer,' he said briskly, producing his official ID for them to see. 'I suggest you go back inside the restaurant, bolt the door, and wait. Police cars are on the way and the officers will want to interview you as soon as we're satisfied that 'La Belle Equipe' is secure.'

They filed silently away to the sanctuary of the 'Septime'.

When they had gone he initiated his own form of triage. He checked breathing, felt for the throat and wrist pulse, and observed. At first he believed that they were indeed all dead. Then he saw a slight hand movement further down the pavement. It was from a young woman; her dead lover and two of their friends lying face down on either side of her. He could see her wound; a gaping hole, pouring blood, close to her liver. He snatched the cloth off the table, bent over her, and applied pressure to the injury. She cried out, her lovely face masked with pain.

'Forgive me, dear mademoiselle – I did not mean to hurt you but I must stop the bleeding. I'm a police officer and I'm here to help you.'

'Monsieur,' she whispered, 'they... they are still inside.'

'Yes, I know. Don't be afraid, I will stay with you and keep you safe.' He made a pillow with some of the other tablecloths bundled together and lifted her head gently on to it. He noticed that she had closed her eyes.

'Open your eyes please m'dear. What is your name?'

She made a valiant effort to open her eyes, but failed. 'Marianne,' she murmured. Then the gentle soft sigh as her soul fled from agony to the haven of her Maker.

He stared at her in awe for some time: before his very eyes her face, so recently contorted with pain, was subtly being restored to its former loveliness.

He fell to his knees.

'Father in Heaven! Do you see this poor child? How could you let this happen? What was her sin that her young life should end in this brutal manner?' He railed on and on at the sky. Then he bowed his head and wept.

And still the assault weapons rang out.

How long he remained like that, or how long he wept, he had no idea. Time and space meant nothing to him. All that mattered in the entire Universe was that this beautiful lost life should be respectfully mourned. *If not me, who will mourn her at this moment? Bells will come for her later and many, many tears. But for now there's just me, and I pray she knows the depth of my anguish for her.*

He leant across to kiss her cheek, as he covered her with a table-cloth shroud. As he did his Sig fell from the inside pocket of his coat. This was something that, in all his years as a police officer, had never happened before. He stared at the weapon in disbelief then instinctively pushed it and his ID carefully under Marianne's body, out of sight. As he stood, rubbing his knees, he heard the sound of the restaurant door handle turning. He reached for his revolver but fumbled its removal. *Damn, what's wrong with my hands? Why won't they work properly? Perhaps Meg's right – I am too old.*

'Sir!' It was Georges, further off crossing the boulevard and running towards him.

The door opened and two men looked at each other from a distance of mere metres. The one with the assault weapon smiled in an unpleasant sign of recognition and prepared to fire. But Georges Martin fired first: the bullet grazed the gunman's ear as it whizzed past him and he fired as he fell. Maigret was hit and sank slowly to the ground.

Georges saw him fall just before he was dealt a blow to the side of his head delivered with extreme malice. As he began to lose consciousness he witnessed another gunman drag his bloodied chief inside the restaurant.

His last conscious act was to press the 'officer needs assistance' key on his phone.

TEN

Après le déluge (After the flood)
Paris. Saturday 14 November 2015.
before dawn

> *I am poured out like water,*
> *and all my bones are out of joint*
> *My heart has turned to wax;*
> *it has melted within me.*

She watched the news channels: flicking constantly between them in the hope of catching a glimpse of Philippe until she could bear it no longer. She didn't see him, nor did she know that his orders had been changed and he was not at the siege of the Bataclan. Time passed inexorably without any word from him. Minute by minute her fears increased. Nor did the strange behaviour of their rescue cat help; for some time she had been roaming around the apartment meowing loudly as she went.

'Kitty – stop!' She cried, nerves jangling, 'come to the kitchen and I'll give you a treat.'

The cat stood her ground and continued with her

yowling. The standoff continued for a few minutes, each of them staring at the other.

'Okay, you win Moggs, but please shut-up,' she said, sitting down again. 'He's not here. You must know that since you've been in every room at least ten times already. I don't know where he is, or even *how* he is.'

As she spoke the feline ran over to her, stood on her hind legs holding on to her skirt for support, and looked directly into her eyes.

'Meow, meow, meow,' she cried. This Meg translated as 'do something – and right now!'

She lifted Kitty into her arms and tried to soothe her but was scratched twice before the cat leapt out of her grasp to begin her roaming pattern again.

Who could I call at this time of night? It is long past midnight. Yes, but who will be asleep tonight – no one! Not Paris, her subconscious advised, phone Clive Scott, he'll have heard the news, he will still be awake. And he was.

'Where is he?' The chief inspector said, as he answered. 'And what took you so damn long to call me?'

After she had spoken to Clive she walked purposefully into their bathroom and retrieved Philippe's nightclothes – boxer shorts and a white t-shirt – from a hook there. She held his clothes close to her heart and inhaled his familiar smell. For a few moments she was overcome with such longing that she couldn't move. After a while she realised that Kitty was standing in the doorway, watching her. She went into their bedroom and shaped his clothes into a little nest on his side of the bed close to his pillows. She had scarcely finished before the cat jumped on the bed and into the nest, sniffing, pawing, and then rolling back and forth across his clothes in ecstasy. Finally she settled down inside the nest and began purring.

Peace at last, she thought, *it's a pity it is not that simple for me.* She remembered Clive's final words to her.

'Get some sleep if you can, and I'll phone you in the morning. Things will look better then.'

She laid, fully clothed except for her shoes, on top of the duvet and tried to relax. Kitty's purring was soothing. Reassuring too. Eventually she fell asleep.

Paris, Saturday 14th November 2015

At six o'clock that morning, her phone buzzed but she was already awake. It was Philippe's mother.

'Is he home? Is he safe?' She asked urgently.

She hesitated to steady herself, aware that her mother-in-law was no longer young.

'He's not home yet.'

'But is he safe?'

'I don't know, Louise, his phone's switched off. But Georges Martin was with him, so I'm sure they'll be…'

'Has Christophe Saint-Valéry been in touch with you?'

'No, not yet.'

'Or Georges Martin?'

'He's not answering his phone either; nor is anyone else I can think to call. I'm sure they're all exhausted after the hellfire they went through last night. As soon as I hear anything from anyone I promise I'll call you.'

'Thank you, my dear. I know you must be as worried as I am yet you sound so calm, and that helps me a great deal.'

Not calm, she thought as they ended the call, *just exhausted. But I pray I'll be given the strength to do what I need to do today.*

At 7 am Christophe Saint-Valéry phoned on the landline. Her heart missed several beats when she recognised his voice. It was very like Philippe's but perhaps half a tone deeper; just as clear and strong. A man quite confident in giving orders. An honest, *good* man.

'Please be assured that I phone to allay your fears, not as the bearer of bad news, my dear.' She tried to speak but found she couldn't. 'I apologise for asking you to do this, I'd have much preferred to come to your apartment, but that would be unwise, given the... er *current* circumstances. If I send a car for you in an hour would you come to my... er would you meet with me in an informal setting?'

She found her voice.

'If you have any news to give me, Christophe then please just do it now.'

There was a sigh from the other end.

'I would prefer to speak with you in person...'

'Philippe hasn't come home and I haven't heard from him, so I ask you directly – is he...?'

'We have... evidence that he is alive. We also have... evidence that he may have been wounded...'

'Then where is he?'

'I will answer all your questions when we meet. Is a car to your apartment in an hour agreeable to you, Madame?'

'Yes. You can make it half an hour if you wish. Oh, and I'd like Louise Maigret to come with me. Would that be acceptable?'

Her question was not immediately answered.

'Not a good idea,' he said eventually. 'We have decided to speak with next-of-kin only at this stage.'

'For the love of Heaven, Christophe! She's his mother.'

'Even so, our decision stands. And bearing in mind her age, I believe it is for the best.'

'She's a feisty, wonderful woman…'

'That she is. But this is one of those occasions when… when certain *filters* might need to be applied.'

'I'll tell her everything you tell me anyway,' she said defiantly.

'And that will be *your* decision, as it should be. The car will be with you within the hour. It will not be an official vehicle; that might attract too much interest, but the driver, a woman, is a valued member of my department. She will be driving her own car, a white Renault, and we shall call her… er Carole. That is not her real name, but it would be better if you and she appeared to be two old friends meeting to do some shopping together…'

'Shopping – after a night of carnage in Paris?'

'Well – having coffee together, then.'

'Why the cloak-and-dagger stuff?'

'There's a great deal of speculation wafting around Paris today, most of it from an overwrought media. Supposition, outright deception, deliberate misinformation and cruel lies. And that's just from those who are supposed to be on our side! I'd be very surprised if there wasn't a reporter or two slithering in the undergrowth near your apartment. Photographers too, with long lenses.'

'They know where we live?'

'I'm afraid they do, many of them anyway. But they keep the information to themselves; otherwise they know they'd never get another briefing from us.'

'Will they know he hasn't come home?'

'They will before long, but don't worry, we're working on a cover story. *A bientôt*, m'dear.'

'Wait, please. Georges Martin, where is he, and why isn't he answering his phone?'

A heavy sigh from the other end.

'Inspector Martin is in hospital under police guard because he's a witness.'

'He's been shot?'

'No. He suffered a vicious blow to the side of his head from the butt of a rifle.'

'Oh, dear Lord. Will he be alright?'

'Time will tell. He could have a subdural hematoma; that's a collection of blood outside the brain. The doctors tell me that bleeding with increased pressure on the brain is potentially life-threatening. They might decide to place him in an induced coma to relieve the pressure. *A bientôt*,' he repeated.

'Yes, soon.'

As he ended the call her mobile rang. It was Clive Scott.

'Good morning. Any news – preferably good?'

'Are you clairvoyant, Clive?'

'Why?'

'I've just had an official phone call from…'

'He's not – tell me he's not…'

'I'll tell you everything, and then I want you to give me your take on it. But we need to be quick, there's a car coming for me in an hour.'

After she had related her conversation with the Minister he didn't speak for a few moments.

'So, to be clear, he used the word 'evidence' twice. Is that correct?'

'Yes. I wondered about that. Is evidence the same as proof?'

'No, and that's one of the first things we coppers are taught: evidence is suggestive, it can point us in the right direction, but it's not conclusive. Proof, on the other-hand, is absolute. Monsieur Christophe was choosing his words carefully by the sound of things.'

'So?'

'So, proof takes time and it's very early days. Confusion reigns, I'd say. It's the same at this end; everyone's worried that London might be next. But rumour has it that some of the attackers helpfully left fingerprints and their identities are already known.'

'The usual suspects?'

'Oh yes. And probably long since scarpered back from whence they came. Although I've heard that squads of French police have crossed into Belgium and they're currently turning Brussels upside-down in a very er *determined* fashion. There is another rumour going the rounds too. But I'm not sure I should say anything further until I've checked it out properly. On second thoughts maybe it's something you could quiz Monsieur Christophe about when you see him; his reaction might be very revealing.'

'Tell me.'

'Okay. Remember it's only an unverified rumour, but it does come via our people in Paris. It seems that a senior police official has not yet been accounted for following last night's bastardry.'

There was a sharp intake of breath from her.

'Official or officer, Clive?'

'That's the unknown, I'm afraid. I'll contact David Quinn shortly to see if he's heard anything from his old mates at GCHQ. Will you be in touch after your meeting, or should I phone you later this afternoon?'

'Let me contact you, Clive. I'll ask the driver to take me directly to Philippe's mother's apartment after Christophe and I have had our meeting.'

'Right-Oh. Mind how you go. Mrs S sends her heartfelt best wishes to you.'

Before she went downstairs to wait for Carole, she phoned Louise Maigret to tell her about her conversation with Christophe. She had already decided that she would commit the sin of omission during that call; she would not mention that Philippe's blood had been found at the scene of one of the attacks, but would tell her that the police had evidence that he was alive. This approach left the older woman confused.

'But if they know he's alive, how can they not know where he is?' She queried. It was a question for which Meg was prepared.

'Er, I think they might have a witness, Louise. And that could very well be Georges Martin. But as I've already said, he's in no state to be interviewed.'

'Oh, yes, I see. A witness.'

'I promise I will ask Christophe that question during our meeting. Afterwards I'll come to see you, to tell you everything I've managed to discover.'

'The Lord be with you, my dear.'

'And also with you, Louise.'

The white Renault, with a jaunty curly-haired Carole at the wheel and a cheery toot from its horn, arrived on schedule and they greeted each other like friends. As Carole brushed the side of her face with a pretend kiss she whispered, 'they're here.'

'The media?'

'*Oui*, a reporter's close: the photographer's on the other side of the street.'

As they walked briskly towards the car the reporter shouted a question in French.

'Where's your husband, Madame Maigret? And how's he doing this morning? Going to the hospital are you?'

She said nothing, but Carole replied angrily in French.

'I didn't understand everything you said, Carole,' she remarked as they secured their seatbelts before speeding off.

'Probably just as well. None of it was complimentary to the Fourth Estate, and most of it would be frowned on by my parish priest.'

'That's what I thought. I understood the word parasite because it's the same in English; it was the adjectives either side of the noun that I struggled with.'

They drove in silence for about ten minutes by a circuitous route that baffled her.

'Lost yet?' Carole asked.

'You lost me a long time ago.'

'Just making sure we're not being followed.'

'Are we?'

'I can't tell. I might just be paranoid; it's an occupational hazard at times like this. If we are, I'll attempt to lose them at the next roundabout.' She did.

Eventually they stopped halfway down a narrow, somewhat shabby rue, little more than an alley really, which as far as she could tell was somewhere in the vicinity of the Place Vendôme, the popular square to the north of the Tuileries Gardens and east of the Madeleine Church. She might not have been wrong.

'Where are we?'

'Back entrance. Quickly, go inside the first door – it will be open and there will be someone to look after you. I'll be here when the meeting with… when your meeting is finished.'

'How will you know when that happens?'

Carole smiled, brushing an unruly lock of hair out of her eyes as she did.

'Ways and means, Madame. Now – *vite, vite!*'

She left the car walking quickly towards the door and pushed it open, surprised by how heavy it was. Then she found herself in a dark, poky little space with another door directly in front of her. She blinked several times, willing her eyes to adjust to the inferior quality of light. As she did the door ahead of her swung open to reveal a tall gangly bespectacled young man. He was dressed with the casual elegance that only the French can achieve. Impeccably-cut black trousers, a crisply-ironed white shirt – sleeves rolled up twice from the cuffs and open at the neck – topped by a fine pin-striped waistcoat which was nonchalantly unbuttoned. This vision was so far from what she had been expecting that she had an almost overwhelming urge to giggle.

'My good God,' she gasped.

'No, Madame Maigret, just his feeble servant. *Bonjour*, my name is Bernard and I'm the Minister's office factotum. I regret to inform you that the Minister is slightly behind schedule but will be with you shortly.'

His English was as close to an Oxbridge accent as any Frenchman could hope to aspire.

'*Bonjour,* Bernard. And I regret to inform *you* that… that you have a cornflake stuck to your right cheek!'

And with that comment she completely lost her composure and was reduced to inappropriate laughter.

ELEVEN

'Oh, my dear. Please tell me that you didn't *actually* mention the naughty cornflake to the unfortunate young man.'

'I'm afraid I did, Louise. I thought it was kinder for me to do it rather than Christophe his boss. Think of the embarrassment he would have suffered if that had happened, especially as he was such a *vision* of perfection otherwise.'

'Hmm. I suppose, when you put it that way, you did the... *humane* thing.'

'I hope so, and he did take it in good part; we laughed about it together. "The perils of being a batchelor," he said. "No wife to cast a discerning eye over me before I'm permitted to leave the house!"'

This conversation took place within the subtle elegance of Louise Maigret's drawing room in the Avenue Foch apartment.

The Avenue, a wide residential boulevard in the 16th arrondissement, connects the Arc de Triomphe with Porte Dauphine. It was named in honour of General Ferdinand Foch who served as the Supreme Allied Commander during the First World War, accepted the German surrender in 1918, and was present at the Armistice on the eleventh of November 1918.

How ironic then, but surely not accidental, that 84 Avenue Foch should have been chosen as the Parisian HQ of the counter-intelligence branch of the SS during the German occupation of Northern France in World War two. The buildings either side of 84 were also commandeered by the Germans. But 84 was used for the interrogation of allied Special Operations Executive (SOE) agents captured in France. Prisoners were regularly brought to the building from Fresnes prison on the outskirts of Paris.

Folklore testifies that after the Liberation of Paris in August 1944, all three premises were thoroughly exorcised by means of a series of solemn Requiem Masses for the repose of the souls of those tortured and murdered therein. Copious amounts of Holy Water were also required before anyone would put so much as a foot inside any of those notorious buildings much less consider living there.

But those were old, unhappy times from long ago, and hardly anyone chose to mention them these days. Fortunately Louise's apartment was not situated at any of those addresses, and it was very beautiful. So was the owner, or rather she had been. Now, in her eighties she was merely *unforgettably* lovely. And kind, hospitable, and usually full of fun. However she had something of a past. In her youth, when she was one of the most celebrated beauties in the whole of Paris, Louise Villiers had been a bohemian and quite wild. She had posed, in very little

112

clothing (if indeed she wore any clothing at all) for many of the rakish artists who lived up at Montmartre, and she frequently drank more champagne that was good for her.

But all that changed when Fate intervened one night and she met Daniel Maigret. It was love at first sight for both of them, *a coupe de foudre,* a thunderbolt of emotion that left neither of them in any doubt that they had found 'the one'.

He was a young engineering student at an unfashionable university with not a cent – or sou as it was in those far off days – to his name, while she was from a wealthy family with aristocratic connections. Her family was appalled and threatened to disinherit her.

But in the end, they married and lived happily ever after. Their happiness increased when not only did Louise's family *not* disinherit her but the unassuming Daniel did something quite unexpected and amazing: he invented a small aeronautical component which saved the French aircraft industry millions and millions of *francs.* So that was how the Avenue Foch apartment came to be bought. And it is also but a mere fragment of the extraordinary story of Daniel and Louise Maigret's life together.

'Now then,' Louise said as Rosa, her young Colombian housekeeper entered the room carrying a tray replete with coffee and dainty home-made croissants. 'Tell me everything Christophe said. Every word; please don't leave anything out. And Rosa please, I'd like you to stay. If that's acceptable to you,' she said, with a nod to her daughter-in-law.

'Of course it is. Rosa's been part of the family longer than I have. But I'm not hungry and I don't need any more coffee. I feel I've overdosed already this morning.'

'How about a small sherry then?'

'It's a little early for me; it's not even noon yet.'

'Nonsense – it will do you much good.'

And, strangely enough it did. It seemed to calm her inner turmoil, but paradoxically, after a couple of sips from what was actually a generous measure, she felt her mind becoming more focussed; she could recall everything Christophe had said with great clarity. *How can this be,* she thought, *surely it's counter-intuitive for alcohol to sharpen the mind?* Don't question the gift; cometh the emergency, cometh the grace, her subconscious replied.

She took a breath and began her report.

'Firstly, I must stress that what Christophe told me was in strict confidence, so not one word must leave this apartment. If the enemies of France, both foreign and domestic, should discover what we know, Philippe's life might be in great danger.'

By now Rosa's eyes were heading towards saucer-size and her face was pale. She had long considered Philippe Maigret to be the most elegant, sophisticated, and *desirable* man in the whole of Paris, even though she accepted that he was almost old enough to have been her father. She would have suffered the same fate as Jeanne d'Arc rather than reveal anything that might endanger him.

'Last night – the last, terrible night – Philippe and Georges Martin were instructed to attend the atrocity at the Bataclan theatre. Or rather, they were told to drive slowly around the area, assessing the developing situation, while making their recommendations at frequent intervals as to how the security forces should best be deployed. They were expressly told not to take part in the actual police response.

However, while they were en route, reports were received of another terrorist outrage at 'La Belle Equipe' a restaurant in Rue de Charonne in the 11th, and HQ diverted them there. Once again it was to be observation and analysis only; no direct physical involvement. Next door to 'La Belle Equipe' there's another restaurant, 'Septime' which, for whatever reason, was not attacked. They heard the gunfire and the screams, but did not venture outside until everything went quiet; eerily quiet, was how some witnesses described it. When they did eventually go out they were confronted by the bodies of those who had been dining at tables outside; they were sprawled over the pavement while their blood ran down to the gutters. They tried to help but believed they were all dead.

Then they noticed a dark car – which some of them identified as an unmarked police car – driving slowly down the rue. The two men inside appeared to be having a heated discussion. The car stopped near the scene of the attack and a tall man, with greying hair got out while the car drove on. The witnesses told him that all the victims were dead, at which point he identified himself as a police officer. He told them to go back inside the 'Septime' and lock the doors; other officers would be with them very soon.

While they watched through 'Septime's front windows, the police officer – who we now know was Philippe – examined each person to discover if anyone was still alive. Apparently, there was one young woman who was; but only just. It appears he spoke to her and he certainly attempted to staunch the blood from her injury. But sadly she died.'

She took another few sips of sherry; she had not noticed that her glass had been re-filled by Rosa while she was delivering her account. She felt suddenly tired, and desperate to return to the sanctuary of their apartment. She glanced at Louise, who was holding herself quite still: *she looks like a lovely porcelain figurine,* she thought. Rosa had been quietly weeping for some time.

Shall I go on? She asked her subconscious, *or should I apply Christophe's filter now?* Tell them, came the swift response, but go easy on the ruddy gore.

'Philippe's ID, and his Sig Sauer, were both found underneath the body of that young woman when it was removed. Some of the witnesses inside 'Septime' heard more gun shots very close to them at some stage. Some say they heard two, others three or more. It's known that Georges Martin fired his Sig and some witnesses believe Philippe attempted to fire the revolver he wears above his ankle. But that was not found at the scene.'

'But where is he now?' Louise asked in a voice barely above a whisper. 'What has happened to my lovely boy?'

This is the hard part, Meg thought. *We're down to the nitty-gritty moment.*

'That's the great unknown, as Christophe said. The police assume that he was dragged inside 'La Belle Equipe' by one of the terrorists, but that has not yet been confirmed. Those still alive inside the restaurant were all, quite obviously, in shock when they were finally rescued. None of them has been interviewed yet, and it might be several days before they are well enough for that to be done.'

'Was he wounded?'

'He may have been, Louise. Some of his blood *was* found at the scene, but only a little. There was nothing to suggest a serious wound.'

'And the bad men?' Rosa asked, finding her voice at last.

'Gone. Long gone. But the hunt for them is on, all over Europe. They won't escape. The Minister swore to me that they will be hunted down like the vermin they are until every last one of them faces justice.'

"Dead, or alive – we don't much care – one way or another they will pay for their murderous rampage." Christophe had said.

'But what is he doing to find Philippe?'

'He says there's a need to proceed with caution. The police hope that those who have him don't realise who he is. If it became known that he's a police officer, then the Almighty alone knows what they would do with him or to him.'

'Futile, futile, futile,' Louise said angrily. 'Of course they *know* who he is! His photograph was splashed all over the media when he was awarded his double promotion after Berlin. These are not some illiterate Bedouin tent-dwellers from the far-flung reaches of Saudi Arabia. These are savvy home-grown assassins with their devil-inspired ideology. They know *exactly* who he is and that's why they took him with them.'

'But that's why he left his ID and his Sig under that girl's body. He realised he was alone, and in danger, so he tried to conceal his identity.'

'Who except a police officer wears a leg pouch with a revolver in it?'

'A criminal, perhaps? They might think that.'

'No, they won't, my dear,' Louise said, shaking her head for emphasis. 'But we don't have to wait for the police to act; we could do something ourselves.'

'Such as?'

'We could advertise. Discreetly, of course, in some of the newspapers. And offer a large reward, for Philippe's safe return.'

'They don't want *money,* Louise – they want *revenge.* They want to punish the West for God-alone-knows-what we're supposed to have done.'

'Because we're Christian,' Rosa said sadly. 'And we believe our Lord is loving and kind.'

'Maybe. But know this Louise; I will not be party to anything that places Philippe's life in more danger than it is already. We must allow the police to do what they feel is best.'

'And in the meantime…?'

'In the meantime we pray that new information is garnered as more witnesses are questioned, and that very soon Georges Martin will be well enough to be interviewed. He's an experienced police officer; I'm sure his information will be significant. But now I really do need to go home.'

'Why don't you stay with us tonight, my dear,' Louise said. 'I don't like to think of you being alone at this time.'

'But I'm not alone. There's a demanding little cat waiting for me to take her for a walk before she shreds our curtains and settees.'

'She could stay too. I'm sure Brodie would be happy to share his basket with her again.'

'Another time, Louise,' she replied, gathering up her belongings, 'after Philippe's home with us again. Oh, and one more thing. Christophe said none of us should speak to the media, not even a response if they ask how we are feeling; don't say anything at all. Not a single word. Understand?'

Louise and Rosa, who was still sniffling, nodded.

There followed five minutes of hugging, kissing, and more hugging, before they would let her leave. After she had finally untangled herself from their embraces, she turned quickly away so they wouldn't see her tears.

'Keep the Faith,' she said, as she opened the apartment's door. 'And remember General Foch's famous quotation.'

'General Foch?'

'Yes – he after whom this Boulevard was named.'

'Long forgotten, I'm afraid, m'dear.'

'Never mind. He said, "the most powerful weapon on earth is the human soul on fire."'

'And do you believe that?'

'Yes, with all my heart.'

She blinked as she was immersed in the sunshine as she left the apartment building and reached quickly for her sunglasses. Carole, and her white Renault were waiting for her; it was a welcome sight after the barely-contained emotion of the last hour or so.

'How'd it go?' She asked.

'As well as could be expected, I suppose. No, perhaps a little better than that. Is there any news?'

As she spoke, she switched on her phone. There were seven missed calls and a similar number of texts. She sighed as she scrolled down the lists. Thomas Jefferson Aitkens had phoned three times, but it was his text that caught her attention.

I know what's happened and want to help. Still have contacts in the US who will assist. I'm more mobile now. May I visit you? Intentions strictly honourable. Tom x

'Not bloody likely,' she muttered. 'Not when I'm vulnerable and alone.'

'Sorry?'

'Just thinking aloud, Carole. Now please take me home, as fast as you can.'

Then she quickly sent a reply.

Thanks, but no thanks, Tom. I have all the help I need right now.

And that, for the time-being, was definitely that.

TWELVE

She walked into their apartment, removed her shoes and slumped into the nearest chair. Kitty, who had been doing an urgent crossed-leg dance in the hall immediately jumped into her lap meowing loudly.

'Yes, I know sweetie, you need a walk, and you need it right now.'

The feline scampered off to the kitchen, retrieved her harness then dragged it behind her to drop it at Meg's feet.

'Subtle, so very subtle, Ms Moggs. Give me five minutes to recover then I'll take you for a lovely walk in the park.'

The cat immediately resumed her crossed-legged jig.

She sighed and put her shoes on again.

'Okay, you win – let's go right now.'

She lifted Kitty into the elevator, pressed the button and they speedily arrived at the ground floor. The afternoon concierge greeted them warmly but asked no questions. She cautiously opened the outside door and looked around. *No sign of any parasites,* she thought gratefully. *Carole must have scared them off this morning.*

They headed briskly towards the small park close to their apartment. Kitty pulled her towards a patch of soft earth near a stand of leafless trees and began digging furiously. As she turned away to give her some privacy she caught a glimpse of a man on the opposite side of the park retreating behind a bush. *Hmm, looks like Moggs is not the only one answering an urgent call of nature.*

The sunshine was welcome, and there were others in the park; nannies pushing prams, toddlers escaping from their mothers as they chased after birds, and a few dogs on leads. The cat tidied up her toilet area and bounded back to her considerably relieved. As she re-attached the harness she thought she glimpsed the mystery man again but could not be sure. *Blood-sucker or worse? Or have I caught the paranoid bug too?*

Suddenly her phone buzzed. Private number. She hesitated for a few seconds then answered.

'Jacques, is that you?'

'Yes, Madame. How are you and the feisty furry one enjoying your walk?'

'How did you...? Where are you?'

'I'm about to join you on your bench in the sun.'

Then he was standing in front of her, offering his hand. She would have none of that formality, not from Philippe's colleague and friend. She jumped up, threw her arms around him and hugged him. Then, to the surprise of both of them, her tears began. She sobbed until it seemed there were no more tears left to shed. Jacques was bewildered, *what have I done to cause this reaction?* He wondered. He patted her back gently but still she clung to him.

Eventually she released him, full of apologies.

'So sorry, Jacques, I didn't mean to embarrass you. It's just that… seeing you here without Philippe, I just… It's been a pressure-cooker kind of day, and…'

'No need to concern yourself, Madame, I understand. I have some news for you…'

'Good or bad,' she interrupted quickly.

Jacques hesitated.

'Neither, really… just er interesting.'

The capable, experienced police officer knew the importance of not raising false hopes in situations of this nature.

'I've seen Georges and spoken with him.'

'I thought he was being placed in an induced coma. How is he?'

'He's making progress now so no need for the coma option, although his head aches and he has an ugly bruise and swelling where the rifle butt hit him. My visit was er *irregular*… I managed to con one of the lads on duty to take a break while I had a few minutes alone with him.'

'And?'

'He says the chief ordered him to stop the car to let him out, otherwise he wouldn't have left him alone in that location. But by the time he'd parked the car – the first corner being further away than they had realised – things had changed and the boss was in danger. Georges became very upset at that point; he could see the danger escalating, but he couldn't get back in time to help. He feels he failed the chief at the most critical moment of his life.'

'He mustn't feel that way. We know Georges would never desert anyone in a time of danger.'

'That's what I told him, Madame; exactly that. As he ran across the rue towards 'La Belle Equipe' he saw the door open and a heavy-set man, dressed in black, raising a weapon ready to fire at the boss. Georges shouted a warning, the chief attempted to draw his revolver but something went wrong. Georges fired at the gunman, but can't be certain he was hit. The last thing he remembers was the chief falling to the ground. He thinks he was wounded in the upper arm near the Humerus, but he's not sure; everything happened so fast, he says. Then came the heavy blow and Georges was out for the count.'

'The Humerus…I don't know where that is,' she said weakly.

'It's a large bone that connects the elbow with the shoulder; it supports many of the arm's functions. It's one of the longest bones in the body.'

'Oh. What arm does Georges thinks was hit?'

Jacques paused.

'I regret… It was his right arm.'

'The gunman, at close range… he could have… But he didn't. Why? Louise was right; he recognised Philippe,' she said, thinking aloud.

'Indeed. That's what Georges believes and I agree with him. The gunman made the choice to *disable* the boss, not kill him.'

'Will you come back to the apartment for a cup of coffee now? I need to get Moggs home.'

'*Non merci*, Madame. I must be off too.'

'Why were you doing that spy stuff routine earlier?' She asked as they strolled towards the street together.

Jacques looked embarrassed.

'I had to make sure there were no reporters or photographers around. I'll leave you here, in case I missed any of them.'

'God bless you Jacques, you're a good friend.'

'And you, Madame, and you. Michelle and I lit a candle for the chief at our church last night and we will light another tonight. And every night, until he is safely home again.'

'*Merci,* Jacques. *Au revoir.*'

'*Au revoir,* Madame. Oh, I almost forgot! Madeleine has been found.'

'Madeleine?'

'The old street lady who the boss tries to help. She usually lives under one of the bridges of the Seine.'

'Oh, yes. I remember her. Philippe took me to meet her recently and she was greatly attracted to the silk scarf I was wearing.'

'She was wearing it when I saw her this morning; she told me you had given it to her.'

'I did. Where's she been? I know Philippe turned Paris inside out looking for her, but without success.'

'She wouldn't say: perhaps she doesn't remember now. But she's anxious to see you, Madame.'

'Me? Why?'

'She wouldn't tell me that either. Do you wish to see her?'

'Of course. I know how much Philippe cares for her; he'd do anything he could to help her and so would I. But her English is even worse than my French. I'd need an interpreter.'

'At your service, Madame,' Jacques said with a little bow. 'Shall we say Monday morning, if nothing worse happens in the meantime?'

'The worst has already happened, Jacques; we have nothing more to fear. So Monday morning it is.'

Saturday 14th November 2015
A rural area of Belgium,
precise location unknown

> *I am poured out like water,*
> *and all my bones are out of joint.*
> *My heart has turned to wax;*
> *it has melted within me*

When he awoke that first morning, he had no idea where he was, or whether it was night or day. Every part of his body was pulsing with pain but his arm caused him the most grief; it was throbbing with a relentless beat in sync with his heart.

The previous night one of his captors, who seemed to have some rudimentary medical knowledge, had – without the benefit of anaesthesia, or any attempt at sterilisation as far as his patient was aware – painstakingly, and with considerable pleasure, dug out the bullet with his cruel little knife. The bullet had indeed come close to breaking his Humerus bone but had chipped a piece off it instead. Despite the excruciating pain he had remained conscious for most of the time. Then the ersatz doctor applied pressure to stop the bleeding, bandaging the wound with strips of old cloth before giving the arm a savage twist as a parting gesture.

Well, if they don't kill me, the Sepsis surely will, he thought ruefully.

They wanted him to writhe or scream or beg for mercy, but he would not. *I will not show them any weakness,* he repeated in his mind over and over; *do not be afraid, I am with you… do not be afraid, I am with you… yea though I walk through the valley of the shadow of death…* Until at last he mercifully lost consciousness.

The respite didn't last very long; a bucket of cold water thrown over him brought an end to his brief sojourn in the pain-free zone. Then the questions began, accompanied by a hefty slap if he refused to answer or if they didn't believe what he had said. And that became the pattern for the next three days. Question – slap… question – slap. Sometimes with an open hand, other times with a closed fist and several twists of his damaged arm.

At times he managed to put himself into another space during an interrogation. He recalled his initial meeting with Meg and the intensity of his attraction to her. And the unforgettable experience of giving themselves joyously and completely to each other for the first time. He traced the cool, smooth contours of her body in his mind and evoked her natural scent.

Those interludes were of immense comfort to him. Other times the relentless pain from his arm goaded him in and out of consciousness. Once he saw a long tunnel with a bright light at the end. And he heard the distant sound of beautiful music, while a siren voice whispered 'come, come.' Then there, near the far end of the tunnel, he saw his beloved father. He was smiling and serene, but he did not beckon him. The vision abruptly vanished when his interrogator, the burly shooter, began shouting again while slapping his face to bring him back to reality.

At one point the torture unexpectedly ended; it seemed that an argument had broken out between his captors. Later, to his surprise, he heard an English voice for the first time. A precise, perfectly enunciated, English voice. It was a voice he thought he recognised. Or was he hallucinating again.

'You must stop now, otherwise you will kill him,' the voice said.

'So what?' Replied a heavily-accented voice, also in English, spitting enthusiastically for emphasis.

'Then all your efforts on Friday night will have been in vain.'

More heated discussion, but in Arabic.

'Okay, okay,' said the one with the accent. 'Give him the… er *medicine* now.'

They pulled his head back and forced the liquid down his throat.

'Drink, infidel dog – drink! You must not die yet; we have plans for you.'

It made him cough but the taste was strangely palatable. *If this is actually poison,* he thought, *so be it. Now I lay me down to sleep, I pray the Lord my soul to keep; if I should die before I wake, I pray the Lord my soul to take.*

But he had not died in the night and now the persistent pain in his arm made him long for another dose of whatever it was that they had given him. Then came the three knocks on the door. This was the signal for him to tie the blindfold across his eyes again before the door was unlocked. Failure to comply would have consequences, he knew that already: twisting his wounded arm was a favourite punishment for even small infractions of the rules.

'Water – please some water,' he said as someone entered the room. His plea was not answered; instead his hands were tightly tied again and he was dragged a short distance into what he presumed was the main room.

He had not seen all of them; only the one who had shot him, and his accomplice who had dragged him inside the restaurant afterwards. The first man was his chief inquisitor and torturer: Maigret had sufficient experience of mentally deranged criminals to realise that this one enjoyed inflicting pain. There had been a battered black van waiting near the rear door of the restaurant. Before he was hauled inside a crude foul-smelling blindfold was placed across his eyes and firmly secured while his hands were tied in front of him. And those restrictions had been left in place during the days. At night, as he was thrown into the little cell-like room in which he slept, his hands were untied so he could take the blindfold off himself.

The room had obviously been used by someone before him; there was a lingering smell of stale sweat and other body odours on which he chose not to dwell. It had a small washbasin in one corner with a primitive dirty toilet next to it. There was a window with opaque glass, and beyond that bars. At first he thought he was in a cellar, but then he heard the occasional sounds of cars or farm machinery and sometimes the mooing of cows.

As for the rest of his jailors, he had only heard them speak occasionally. At these times he tried to establish who was who. And, more importantly, who was top dog. He thought it was probably his inquisitor, but he was not sure. He decided to assign code names, the more easily to identify them. *But have I heard all of them speak?* He asked himself. *I don't even know how many of them there are. Four? Five?*

'Not yet,' said the gruff voice, who Philippe had already named The Psychopath. 'Questions first, water later.'

'No! Water now!'

The psychopath strolled across the room – ten steps his captive estimated – and retrieved something. He sauntered back to Maigret, grabbed his hands and placed them on the table in front of them. Then he brought the hammer down hard – as though he was cracking a walnut – missing the little finger of his left hand by what seemed like a fraction of a centimetre. Despite himself, he jumped with fright.

'Next time, the whole hand gets it,' the psychopath said cheerfully, 'which will make arse-wiping very difficult for you. And, as I said before, questions first, water later – maybe. Or even some food.'

But his questions were elementary; laughably so, his prisoner thought.

'In what prison are our comrades being kept,' was one such.

'I don't know.' That earned him both an angry slap and a punch. He *did* know. Not names; but that captured Islamists were kept in numerous prisons all over the country for security reasons, and to prevent further radicalisation.

'How much will the police pay for your return?'

'Nothing. The Republic does not negotiate with terrorists.'

He prepared himself for the slap or punch but it did not come. The next moment he knew why. The smell came first: the smell of burning flesh. Then the intense pain. The psychopath had burnt him three times – dot, dot, and longer dot – with his cigarette on the inside wrist of his injured right arm.

'Liar! Liar, liar, liar! You say France does not negotiate but we know it does; quietly, and through go-betweens or back-channels, as they are called. So for you – how much? Maybe we don't insist on money. What do you think of that? How about twenty of our boys for you? A fair exchange – is it not?' And so the questions continued.

They really were ridiculous questions. Not even the usual war time opening gambit of 'name, rank and serial number'. *I was a crime of opportunity for them, wasn't I? And now they have me they don't know what to do with me.*

'Give him some water,' another voice said, in French. 'We are not animals. And if he should die…'

Ah, the Worry-wart speaks, Philippe thought. *He's been quiet for so long I thought he might have left.*

'I agree. It's in our best interests to look after him properly.' That was the precise English voice again who Philippe had already decided to name The Posh Boy.

There was another; he was The Geek. He hardly spoke, being too intent on hacking either the computer system or the radio network of *Police Nationale*. Apparently he suffered from IBS – irritable bowel syndrome, because he farted a great deal, both nosily and pungently, much to the annoyance of his colleagues. *So that's four,* he thought. *The psychopath, the posh boy, the worry-wart, and the geek. Is that all? Or have I missed someone? Or does the worry-wart double as the medicine man? I remember that he didn't utter a word as he dug out the bullet.*

On the fourth morning of his captivity, after a good night's sleep, courtesy of the mixture they poured down him before he was consigned to the room where he slept, he came to a decision.

There are only two ways out for me: suicide, or escape. Yes, I suppose suicide is a form of escape but it is a little too final for me, so I choose the second option. But how? He asked his subconscious. Well, for a start, stop drinking the stuff they give you at night. *But it eases the pain,* he protested. Yes, it does. And do you know why? *How could I?* Don't try to con us, Phil, we're your subconscious and what *you* know, we know. *So?* It's a drug – and you've known that from the beginning. How long do you think it will be before you're addicted? *They force me to drink it – how can I not take it?* Think of some excuse or cough it up when they pour it into you. Tell them you'll take it later. *They won't buy that!* They might; you've been compliant so far. And anyway what have you got to lose? *But I need it!* So – you're well on the way to being hooked already! Want to be a morphine junkie and lose everything that's important to you? *It can't be morphine.* Of course it is. It's the same synthetic junk they give the misfits and petty-crims when they don the suicide vests. You know that! The post-mortem blood tests have proved it time and time again. And from the way you slept last night we've come to the conclusion that they're upping the strength every night.

'By the Grace of the Lord, I'll do it.'

'What was that?' It was the geek, farting his way backwards into the room wearing an inadequate mask. *Hmm, just as I thought, a skinny young guy with a wispy beard. I think he was the one who kicked me when I was on the pavement at the back of the restaurant. Him I could probably take, even with one arm in a sling.*

'I've come to a decision,' he said. 'Now I'm going to tell you everything you want to know about police operations in Paris. But only if… if you stop forcing me to drink that stuff at night.'

'The pain will be far worse without it.'

'Yes, I know,' he sighed. 'But it makes me forget things. My brain's turning to mush.'

'I'll tell the boss,' the geek said. Then he left the room.

THIRTEEN

Monday 16th November 2015
Paris, 6th Arrondissement

As it happened, the feisty feline proved to be a god-send. If it hadn't been for her twice daily walks, Meg would not have left the apartment for the rest of that weekend. She preferred to be alone, seeing no one, speaking to no one. But the cat insisted and so they walked. And each night she lit candles for her love's safe return with tears in her eyes and fell asleep hugging his pillow, while the cat purred contentedly in her nest of his bedclothes.

The phone calls came, and the texts, all asking the same thing: *has everything calmed down in Paris now, and are you and Philippe OK?* To which, without actually lying, she invariably replied in the positive – with a few exceptions. But she told no one, not even members of her own family, that he was missing. Some of their friends had seen media reports of injuries among *Police Nationale* personnel, including one account of a senior officer having been seriously wounded and they feared it might have been Philippe. It was of course Inspector Georges Martin. But although neither she, nor anyone in

Christophe Saint-Valéry's Department, made any attempt to correct that wrong impression, they had not planted the story themselves. The media had simply put two and two together and come up with the wrong number.

As she was getting ready for Jacques arrival her phone rang.

'Madame Maigret?' She did not immediately recognise the voice.

'Yes.'

'It's Giles de Montfort; we met recently at my sister-in-law's…'

Giles de Montfort, also known by some as the Spawn QC. What can he want with me?

'Yes, we did. Although you said we'd met before at one of Angie's summer parties.'

'Correct.' There followed a longish pause which she found unnerving.

'You phoned me Giles, so what can I do for you?'

'Indeed.'

Another pause.

'I… I have a… er *reason* to come to Paris in the next day or so to see a rather wayward client who… well – that's for another time. I wondered if we might meet. Fleur's coming with me; did you know she works with me now?'

'No, I didn't.'

'Well, she does. Her law degree from Oxford gives her the cachet to accompany me into Court as my junior, even though she's never actually practised.'

'Good for her.'

'Yes. Er, now this is where the terrain becomes a little more – shall we say... er – *rugged*. And that calls for a degree of *circumspection*. I'm aware of the difficult situation in which you find yourself...'

'Really? How?'

'Courtesy of Fleur's erstwhile fiancé who seems to have been recently reinstated; at least temporarily. He has been asked by a friend of yours, a certain plod who hails from north of the border to render whatever assistance he can.'

'I understand.' *Translation; Chief Inspector Clive Scott, of the Met Police, born to Scots parents in Berlin but largely raised in Edinburgh.*

'My client has a list of offences as long as one's proverbial, for which the French are desperate to see him locked away for the rest of his natural – should that prove possible.'

'What's he done?'

'Without betraying my lawyer-client obligations I can say, with a fair degree of confidence, that he's committed just about every offence in the statute book.'

'Yet you choose to defend a man like that?'

'Why not? He's entitled to a fair trial and a good defence, no matter how black his character might be. But leaving all that aside, my client has also offended – grievously offended – in England. And some of those offences were, so he alleges, committed *prior* to those in France.'

'Let me guess; he'd prefer to be tried in England because he believes English courts are a soft touch compared with those in France.'

'Without prejudice, that's what he believes. He also believes he has a bargaining-chip to play: he says you've mislaid something of great value to you – totally irreplaceable, in fact – and he claims to know something about its possible whereabouts.'

'But does he really?'

'That's the purpose of my visit to Paris. I need to ascertain whether he's bluffing or if he really does have useful information.'

'And if he does?'

'Then we'll all be happy.'

'Hmm. When do you and Fleur arrive here?'

'Thursday morning, via EuroStar. We'll be staying in central Paris somewhere. I'll text you the details if I may, after our arrangements have been confirmed.'

'Of course.'

'*Au revoir,* Madame.'

'Meg, please.'

'Very well, *au revoir,* Meg.'

Jacques arrived early, as she knew he would, but she was already downstairs waiting for him. If the concierge thought it strange for a police officer to be escorting Madame Maigret when he hadn't seen her husband since Friday, he didn't give any indication. He probably assumed, as did so many others, that Chief Superintendent Maigret had been wounded and was in hospital.

After their initial greeting they both remained silent for the drive to the Seine and the bridge where

Madeleine and her companions – or *nos autres Amis* – our other Friends, as Philippe referred to them – had made their home. Contrary to public opinion not all the homeless people in Paris are drug addicts, or drunks; many, like Madeleine, have some form of mental illness or long-term emotional damage. Failed marriages, sexual or physical abuse – often both or some other trauma that had delivered them into their vulnerable state.

As they drew closer to their destination Jacques asked what she had in the bag she was carrying. She opened it and lifted out one of the two bottles of red wine so he could read the label. He whistled in surprise.

'Er, Madame – how did you choose this wine?'

'I reached into the wine cupboard and picked up the first two bottles.'

'But are you sure the chief would want to part with them? It's an excellent Merlot and quite expensive.'

'I'm sure it; is my Monsieur always drinks the best wine.'

'Well then, perhaps...'

'And I tell you this, Jacques: if any of these other friends of ours has useful information about where Philippe is, or *how* he is, then I will happily buy them cases of the stuff. *Comprendre?*'

'Understood, Madame. Completely understood. And I will happily be your delivery man.'

Jacques parked the car as close to the Seine as he could and they began to walk. It was another clear November day, with an azure sky and a gentle breeze.

It's a lovely day, yet I'm aware of the dark cloud hanging over my head, she realised. *It hits me when I open my bedroom curtains each morning and it doesn't leave until I fall asleep. I know its various names; grief, fear, anger, anxiety, helplessness – but mostly it is a paralysing sense of loss. What if I never see him again? What if he's already lost to me? How could I go on without him?*

They walked in companionable silence for some five minutes until they saw the little group of people who they were seeking. Madeleine saw them too, and hurried to greet them. Meg was relieved to find that she was now using a walking-stick. When they met she took her hand and kissed it. Then she began to weep.

'Chère, Madame, je suis vraiment désolée.' Jacques prepared to translate. She touched his arm.

'Thanks, Jacques; I know what she said. 'Merci, Madame Madeleine.'

As they walked towards the rest of the tribe, she whispered to Jacques.

'She knows he's missing, doesn't she?'

'Maybe. I think she knows *something*. Or perhaps she's having one of her strange days.'

'Ask her, please.' He did, and a rapid conversation ensued, very little of which she understood.

'She says she has something important to show you. It is something that the brother of Gervais found.'

'Gervais?'

'Yes. Gervais Allard, the elderly man whose body was found in the Seine recently.'

'Oh yes. I remember him; poor man.'

They met up with the rest of the group and introductions were made again out of consideration for those whose memory had not stood the test of time as well as others, and the rickety old chair ritual was once more observed.

This time it was Louis who dusted it with a theatrical flourish before she was invited to sit, although he was not an itinerant. Apparently he had been accorded this honour because of his recent bereavement: his resemblance to the gallant Gervais was remarkable.

Jacques produced the bottles of Merlot and battered old cups and mugs were rapidly proffered, while he played the role of both sommelier and waiter. She glanced at her watch; it was only 10.45 am. She shook her head when he approached her. It seemed too early, and she doubted the provenance of the beaker she had been given. He quickly whispered that it would give offence if they didn't drink, so she held out her cup.

Madeleine stood, preparing to make a toast, and her heart missed a beat, fearing what she might divulge. She need not have worried.

'*Aux vieux Amis*' she said – to old Friends – and they raised their glasses some with tears in their eyes, while Meg silently added, 'and lovers'.

After a few minutes of this geniality Louis made his excuses and went deeper into their refuge, appearing soon after with an expression of gravity on his face and something white in his hands. A hush descended on the group like the moment of denouement in a mystery play.

Without a word he approached her, his hands steady and, with a courtly bow, gave her the little handkerchief-wrapped parcel as though he were offering her the Holy Grail itself. She opened it a fraction and then gasped. It was a ring: a solid gold ring, a ring she would recognise anywhere and at any time. It was the ring she had placed on Philippe's finger the day they were married. The next thing she remembered was Madeleine wafting a fan in front of her face and Jacques anxiously offering her some more wine.

'Is it… Madame, is it…?'

'Yes,' she said, pressing it to her lips, 'it is. But how?'

Then Jacques was angrily interrogating Louis in fast, furious French. *'Vuleur! Scélérat!'* he shouted.

'Don't hurt him,' she cried. 'Ask him what he knows!'

'Merci, Madame,' Louis said, in surprisingly good English, although clearly unnerved. 'I am not a thief, nor am I a scoundrel. If this… if he will release my arm, I will tell you everything.'

'Very well, sir. Jacques, find him something to sit on, while he tells his story. And apologise to him before you do it.'

A shabby travel trunk of ancient vintage was speedily produced from the depths of their stronghold and Jacques lugged it into the sunshine. Louis and Madeleine sat down on it, side by side. Then, as a further act of contrition, Jacques refilled Louis' cup. He took a healthy draught from it and then began his defence in a mixture of English and French. If she didn't understand something he said she looked enquiringly at Jacques who whispered a translation.

This is Louis' account.

On Friday night – the night when all of Paris seemed bereft, I was waiting in a doorway not far from the back door of 'La Belle Equipe'. There are a number of bars and eateries in the area and I knew that on most nights – but Fridays in particular – at the end of the dinner service the kitchen hands transfer the surplus food into containers to give to the needy of the quarter. We – my widowed sister and I – are not so poor, we have a roof over our heads, for which we thank the Father Almighty, but the rent has increased and we had to pay for our brother Gervais to have a good Christian funeral. God rest his soul.

Around 9.30 on Friday night I heard the gunshots. Pop, pop, pop they went at first. Then there came the loud bursts of rapid gunfire; semi-automatics, or something of that kind. After what seemed like a very long time everything went quiet, and I wondered if it was safe to make my escape. Damn the food, I thought. Better to eat bread and cheese than die here. But I was still afraid to leave. What if the bastards should see me?

Just as I was summoning my courage I heard three more pop, pop, pop shots, like at the beginning, so I stayed where I was, with my heart thumping so hard that I thought I might be having a seizure. Then everything went quiet again. A few moments later I heard the sound of the restaurant's door opening. That door always sticks a little, so it makes a grating sound. I moved back further into the doorway and kept so still I could hardly breathe. But I could see clearly: and I saw a bearded man dragging another man along the ground by the collar of his jacket which was open. The man on the ground had blood on his face and down his shirt. Very much blood and his face was very pale.

The man with the beard let go of the other man as he opened the van parked right near the back door. At that moment the injured man fumbled something in his hand then turned towards me. I recognised him from the photographs in the newspapers. I must have moved slightly – the surprise of recognition, I suppose. He looked straight at me and nodded as if to say, 'yes, I am who you think I am.' Then, while still looking at me, he turned to one side – which I could tell by his face caused him great pain, and without making a sound dropped something in the gutter.

Suddenly another man appeared from the restaurant, not nearly as big as the first one: he had a beard too, but a thin scraggly one because he was young. He gave the wounded man a kick to his shoulder and he groaned and closed his eyes. Then scraggly beard shouted something to the other one, who produced a torn piece of cloth or an old scarf and tied it around the wounded man's eyes. Oh, and I think it might have been then that they tied the man's hands together, because they were tied, but I can't remember exactly when that happened. Please forgive me; some of these things remain tangled in my mind. The next minute they had tossed him in the back of the van and driven off very fast.

Not too long after that I heard the police sirens and the screech of their brakes and I knew it was safe for me to leave. I went immediately to the gutter and found what the... what he had placed there. It was this very ring, wrapped in a white handkerchief. There was more blood on it so I took it home and my sister washed it so Madame would not be upset when I returned it to her with the ring. I hope I didn't do wrong.'

Bugger, thought Jacques. *We could have done with that unwashed proof of life.*

'Did you happen to see the numberplate of the van, sir?' He asked Louis in a very civil way.

'No, Monsieur. I did try to read it but it was covered with dirt and mud.'

I'll just bet it was, Jacques thought, *those devils knew exactly what they were about and all the tricks of their bloody trade.*

'Never mind, you've given us an excellent account of how events took place that night. Well done, and our grateful thanks to you.'

After the complete silence in which Louis' account had been heard there was a collective sigh, then spontaneous applause while Meg hugged and kissed him many times. They stayed perhaps half an hour longer and then made their farewell with many embraces and a few more kisses. As they walked back to the car, she spoke.

'You know Jacques, this ring had never left Philippe's finger since the day it went on. And there's only one reason I can think for him to have removed it on Friday night.'

'So it wouldn't be stolen by the terrorists, Madame?'

'No. It was so I would know – *we* would all know – that he was still alive and fighting.'

When they reached the car Jacques asked if he should deliver the case of Merlot that afternoon.

'Leave it until the morning and I'll come to the wine store with you, with my credit card.'

'No need, Madame. The lads at HQ will pass around the hat and we'll have enough for many cases.'

'That's very kind of you and the lads but I suggest you take them a case at a time; we don't want to completely wreck their livers, do we?'

'I fear that ship might have already sailed, Madame.'

They were both quiet on the drive back to the Maigret apartment each immersed in their own thoughts; although Meg noticed that Jacques seemed increasingly fidgety the closer they were to the 6th. When they arrived he cleared his throat, and spoke hesitantly.

'Madame Maigret, I er… I regret that I must.' He took another breath to steady his nerves. 'I regret. I regret that I must ask you. It is… you see. I must…'

'Let me help, Monsieur. You need to ask if you may take Philippe's ring because it is evidence. Correct?'

He nodded, considerably relieved.

'And so you may: but only from my cold dead body.'

'Understood, Madame – *completely* understood.'

FOURTEEN

Wednesday 18th November 2015
Rural Belgium

'I understand you finally want to cooperate,' the psychopath said.

'Yes, but first I have some conditions.'

'Listen to him,' he said. 'He's as good as blind and shackled yet he tries to set conditions.' His colleagues muttered their agreement. 'Go on then, I could do with a laugh.'

'Firstly, my shoulder needs a change of dressing. There's an almond smell.'

There wasn't, but he knew it was only a matter of time before there was: twenty-four hours was his estimate.

'Fair enough. It will be done.'

'Right now?'

'Soon. What else?'

'After five days I stink! I need a bath and a shave. I also need a toothbrush and paste. And a change of clothes.'

'Look around you – we don't do shaving here. Oh, I forgot, you can't see, can you? And as for the clothes, the ones we have would be too short for you.'

'Don't you have a spare thobe around for when you go to the mosque?'

'Well, well. The infidel knows more than we thought. A thobe indeed – not for the likes of you! What do you think?' He said in an aside to one of his gang.

'No point in allowing him a bath if we don't give him clean clothes; they pong as much as he does.' It was the posh boy speaking.

'Hmm. Do you have an old thobe that might do?'

'I have one I bought for my father that he may use, but it will still be too short.'

Now that's interesting, thought Maigret. *The psycho defers to the posh boy. But why?* Because he's higher up the totem pole, you Muppet, his subconscious replied. He's not a camel-jockey like the rest of them. *I have never, ever referred to any Arab as a camel-jockey,* Maigret protested. *And I never would.* Oh sorry, Phil. We think we're getting interference from the posh boy: that's certainly what he's been thinking. *What? Is that even possible?* Search us mate, we don't have all the answers; far from it!

'And that's another condition: I want the blindfold removed – permanently – and my hands untied.'

'If we do that you will see us. Then we will have to kill you.'

'You'll probably kill me anyway. I saw you and the kid with the scrawny beard at the restaurant on Friday night.'

'Hmm. What do you think?' The psycho said to the posh boy again.

'Well, to be honest Haz, I was going to suggest the bath myself. He really does have a frightful pong. But as for the rest of it, well it's a risk and a trade-off, isn't it? If we get quality Intel from him… it would be worth it. And in his condition I don't see how he could overpower all of us.'

'Hmm. And where would he go if he did? He doesn't know where he is.'

'Precisely.'

'Okay, you can have a bath. But we have no spare toothbrushes so you'll have to use your finger. And your hands will be untied, but the blindfold stays until we test the quality of the info you give us. And if, at any time, you remove the blindfold, I will shoot you. I won't shoot to kill, just to leave you permanently disabled. A knee-cap job perhaps – a favourite of the IRA in previous fights – so you never walk again. Or maybe I'll knock out a few vertebrae, which will have the same affect; you already know how accurate I can be at short-range. Do I make myself clear?'

'Yes, perfectly. The blindfold remains for the present. And the change of dressing?'

'That will be done now.'

Maigret laid back in the deep bath luxuriating as the hot water washed over his skin. It felt good, very good, although the need to avoid getting the arm dressing wet was a hindrance. He massaged his aching wrists and relaxed for the first time in days. His wound looked clean according to the quack medico, and seemed to be healing well. He had no idea if this was true, but it certainly felt more comfortable. He had asked for some kind of antiseptic to be poured over the area before anything else was done, but his captors said they had none. When he informed them that alcohol was a suitable alternative he was told firmly that they spurned alcohol; against our religion they said. *So no alcohol but torture and mass murder of women and children is okay? What a strange morality this religion adheres to,* he thought.

'Hurry up in there,' the worrywart called, knocking on the door, 'the boss has questions for you.'

'Five more minutes, please. I'm trying to wash my hair.'

'Okay; but no longer.'

Washing his hair was certainly difficult with his physical restrictions, but he was really buying time. *What can I tell them without compromising my sworn ethics and the safety of my fellow officers? What I say has to sound credible, otherwise...* Hello, it's us again. We seem to be getting more interference from the posh boy, his subconscious interrupted. *What's he saying?* He says you should be creative; think back to your recent activities in Berlin but transpose them to a Parisian setting. *No – I don't want to think about Berlin! I want to put that whole episode in a box and throw it in the deepest part of the North Sea.* You are such a fool, Phil. Meg loves you; she's shown that many times. What happened in New York all those years ago has no significance for her now. And neither does Tom Aitkens: he's yesterday's man as far as she's concerned.

He reluctantly left the warmth of the bath, dried himself as best he could, and donned the thobe. Although too short it at least ended within sight of his ankles and it was clean, albeit with an eau de moth-balls scent. He knocked on the bathroom door.

'I'm ready to come out but I need someone to help me tie the blindfold on again.'

'Okay, I'm on my way.' It was the worrywart again.

'Well, look at him now,' the psycho exclaimed as Maigret was guided back into the living room. 'The thobe really suits him; he's an attractive fellow, isn't he?'

'Haz… you promised,' the posh boy said.

'Did I? I don't remember. I'm only human, after all.'

What the hell does that comment mean? We're not sure, but we don't like the sound of it. *What's the posh boy thinking?* He's worried, not thinking much, but he just called the psycho an animal. And quite frankly we think that's flattering him; sub-human would be a more accurate description. *Are you telling me everything? You know something, don't you? How can you keep information from me? You're my subconscious.* Stay cool, Phil. Subconscious FM is going off air now for scheduled maintenance. *Wait – wait!* But there was no reply.

'Now then, time for the question and answer session to begin,' the psycho said. 'Someone get him some coffee and decent food, we need to keep up his strength.'

He will probably start with some easy questions – ones to which he already knows the answers – so he can test if I'm telling the truth. I may have to compromise sometimes, for the greater good, Maigret thought. He was right.

'Where are the headquarters of *Police Nationale* in Paris?'

'36 Quai des Orfèvres.'

'And police numbers in Paris?'

He might know the answer, but I need to be creative now.

'It *was* around 150,000 but we've been increasing numbers year upon year. I think it's probably somewhere around 300,000 now.'

'Good, good. How many *Brigades Centrales* in Paris?'

'Those numbers have significantly increased too. There were formerly six, but must be around eleven or twelve now.'

'What is the *Brigade criminelle* responsible for?'

'The Criminal brigade – or BC, also known as 'la Crim' is the oldest police division. They deal with homicides, kidnapping, bomb attacks and investigations involving famous personalities.'

'What is the BRI?'

'The BRI is the research and intervention brigade, an elite intervention unit specialising in hostage taking, very serious cases of armed robbery, and catching dangerous gangsters.'

'Hah! So they'll be the ones looking for you, my fine fellow – won't they?'

'I doubt it. In fact I doubt that anyone even realises that I'm missing yet.'

'But you're a celebrity, aren't you? Of course they'll be looking for you.'

'Really? Have you seen any mention of me in the newspapers? Have any feelers been put out for my release? Any ransom offered? I assure you they will have far bigger concerns than me after on the carnage on Friday night.'

And so the cat and mouse game continued. After an hour Maigret was confidently creative. New divisions were created; personnel numbers hugely exaggerated, and the *Gendarmerie* was added to the concoction in extravagant numbers. So was the equipment the French army had at its disposal; tanks, rocket-launchers, attack drones, weapons of every kind were bandied about in numbers designed to shock and repel on a grand scale. In fact, Joseph Goebbels, Reich Minister of Propaganda in Nazi Germany would have envied his finesse.

'Take him back to his room now,' Haz said an hour later, 'he needs to rest. I'll have further questions for him later – and maybe a surprise or two.'

'Please remember your promise.' The posh boy reiterated.

'And *you* should remember who is in charge of this operation because it is certainly not you!'

Maigret had no real idea of how much time passed before the knock on the door came again. It might have been an hour or so, or it might have been far longer. His father's watch had been taken from him, together with his 'vanilla phone' on the night he was captured. They were welcome to the phone; it would yield no helpful information. But he did grieve the loss of his watch, both for practical as well as sentimental reasons.

He heard the psycho railing at someone as he and the worrywart approached the main room.

'Call yourself a computer expert, do you? You've been tinkering around on your damn computer for days now, but have you hacked into the *Police Nationale's* system yet – no you bloody haven't. Useless – that's what you are. A stinky little rodent not worth the waste of a bullet!'

'Boss, it takes time,' the geek protested. 'It's a police computer and it has all kinds of security built into it most of which I've even never seen before…'

'Doesn't it have a back door? I thought all computers had a back for emergencies, or something like that.'

Hmm. Looks like the belligerent bully knows as much about computers as I do, Maigret thought. *But maybe this gives me an unexpected opportunity.*

'If I might make a suggestion…'

'What!' The psych shouted.

'Why go in the back door when you could more easily go through the front?'

'Not possible, boss. Don't listen to him, it's a trap,' the geek warned.

'No trap, I assure you.'

'Then how?'

'I give you my police ID number, he keys it in and the door opens; it's as simple as that. It won't give you access to any of the classified material, but it will allow you to state what you want in exchange for my release.'

'Don't listen to him. The number he gives you will be a duress code, or something like that. And it will immediately reveal our location.'

'No, not immediately. If he's online for a minute, or thereabouts, there won't be time for a trace to be made. It's an eight digit number.'

'Hmm. An interesting proposition. I'll think about it.'

Wonder why he's not conferring with the posh boy, Phil? *Oh, you're back again are you?* Yes, scheduled re-boot successfully carried-out while you were napping and we're ready to assist now. *Why hasn't he asked the posh boy for his opinion?* He can't – the boy's gone. *What? How can he be gone?* We don't know, but he's not here. Do you notice anything else – like there being a different atmosphere in the room? *I thought that was probably the geek who has IBS.* Not *that* kind of atmosphere, you Muppet. A cut it with a knife atmosphere. We're telling you: the worrywart and the geek are dead scared, and the posh one's gone! Say something. Ask the psycho what's going on.

'Is everything er… okay?' He asked tentatively.

'Never better,' was the succinct reply.

'What you have decided? Will he key in my ID number or not?'

'No. He's working on another angle right now.'

Ask him about the English kid, Phil – it's important.

'Do you have more questions for me?'

'Not yet; we're having some downtime and I'm reading the newspaper.'

'It's very quiet. Is your friend from across the water here?'

'You're asking too many questions, infidel: that's my job, not yours.'

'Where's the lad from across the Channel?' He persisted.

The psycho laid down his newspaper, walked across the room, and slapped him. Then he put a revolver to

Maigret's temple. It was cold and hard. Next came the sound of the weapon being cocked and the cylinder revolving; he held his breath and steeled himself for the impact. Instead there was a click: the chamber was empty.

'Next time there will be a bullet in it,' he said, as he returned to his paper.

Crikey, Phil – that was a close-run thing! Don't ask him any more questions. *I wouldn't have asked him the ones I did if it hadn't been for you lot!* Steady on mate, we're doing our best to help you.

The rest of that strange evening passed in the same way. The geek worked diligently on the computer with no apparent success, while the worrywart fiddled nervously with his prayer beads. Food came and went; a tasty mix of middle-Eastern fare, served with various flatbreads and fruit juice. But the silence continued. After he'd eaten Maigret leant back in his chair and began to nod off.

'Sleepy again, are we?' The tormentor asked.

'Yes, it seems I am. I think I need a burst of fresh air.'

'You'll have that tomorrow morning. Best you sleep now.'

The worrywart led him back to his room. He laid face down on the bed and stretched his body to its full extent. *No pain,* he thought sleepily, *just a wonderful feeling of complete relaxation. I don't think I could move a muscle if I tried.* Within five minutes he was asleep. He didn't hear the door open twenty minutes later. But shortly afterwards he felt the weight of a body on top of him.

Over the course of the next hour or so the psycho, with deliberate, excessive savagery, sodomised him twice. Maigret was aware of what was happening but could not move or cry out: paralysed by a combination of drugs added in precise proportions to the fruit juice he had enjoyed.

'We'll make a convert out of you yet, Maigret,' he said as he finally left the room.

FIFTEEN

The screaming started the instant the worrywart entered Maigret's cell. He rushed back to the main room screaming 'he's dead, he's dead! You've killed him, boss. What did you do to him?'

'Nothing. We just enjoyed some physical fun together.'

'But he's not moving and his bed's covered in blood. You must have gone too far this time.'

'I admit I might have been a little over-enthusiastic, but he *was* my first police officer; who could blame me for being excited?'

'I tell you he's dead. Come and see for yourself.'

'Okay, if you insist.'

They walked quickly into the bedroom and examined him together.

'He's not dead. Feel him; he's warm and he has a pulse.'

'It's a very weak pulse,' the worrywart said anxiously, feeling the neck pulse and then the wrist.

'Just stop the bleeding and he'll be fine.'

'I don't think I can. Something's ruptured inside him – that's obvious from the colour of the blood.'

'Pack him with plenty of gauze or some other dressing and wait half an hour or so and see what happens.'

'But if the bleeding doesn't stop, or he dies? What then?'

'Then we'll have to get rid of him, and remove every trace that he was ever here,' the psycho said matter-of-factly.

'How?'

'We'll move the van as close to the back door as possible, then heave both him and the mattress in it. Afterwards we'll take a drive to find a remote place to dump him.'

'What's with the damn ruckus?' The geek, who had been in bed said as he entered the room.

'Oh… blessed Father Abr… What's wrong with him? Is he dead?' He asked, taking in the full horror of the scene in a single glance.

'Not far off,' the worrywart said grimly. 'I can't see him lasting the night.'

'We have to get rid of him now,' the geek said. 'The English kid's not back from his walk; he's been gone for hours, and that makes me nervous.'

'Don't worry – he's solid. He'll be back soon.'

'I don't think so, boss. I have a really bad feeling about this,' the worrywart replied.

'You have a bad feeling about everything!'

'I agree with him, boss,' the geek said. 'And it's safer to do it now under cover of darkness than risk it in the morning. It's time for us to move on anyway; we've been here too long already.'

'It seems I'm out-numbered,' the psycho said. 'Okay – let's start packing up now. We'll dump him and move on.'

Thursday 19th November 2015
Scotland Yard, London

First thing that morning Chief Inspector Scott received a phone call from a puzzled Scotland Yard telephonist.

'What is it, Janet?'

'Chief Inspector, there's a man on our helpline asking to speak with you.'

'Who is he? What's his name?'

'He won't say, sir.'

'Some crackpot, like as not.'

'I don't think so. He's phoning from somewhere outside of the UK. I could tell from the signal when I answered.'

Clive groaned.

'Okay, put him through.'

'Listen, don't speak,' the voice on the other end instructed. 'You know me – or you should at least recognise my voice. Do you?'

'No. And I have limited patience and too much work. State your name and business or be gone.'

'I've… I've been set up and I'm far from home.'

'By whom?'

'The people where I work; you know who they are, you arranged the job.'

'Wait a moment. Did I meet you in…?'

'Yeah. You were with your Gallic friend and it was very nearly a real blast.'

There was a gasp from Clive.

'Know anything about his current whereabouts…?'

'I know where he was last night.'

'Okay – cards on the table. Did you have any involvement in what occurred in Paris on Friday night? Yes or no.'

Silence followed.

'Hello? Are you still there?'

'I'm here,' the caller said. 'I'm thinking. The answer's not as simple as yes or no.'

'It is for me!'

More silence.

'How well do you know the Musée des Beaux-Arts in Brussels?'

'I've been there.'

'How soon cane you get there?'

'Three or four o'clock this afternoon if I catch the right Eurostar.'

'Brilliant. I'll meet you near the Bruegel painting; the one with the boy having a nasty fall. I'll find you: I'll tell you everything then. In the meantime, know this; *I was at all times, following orders.* Where I went and what I did, was because of those orders, no matter what you may have been told. Now give me your private email address and I'll send some rough map coordinates. You'll have to do the rest. But make it fast; they might be on the move soon.'

Scott did.

'Wait! His situation?'

'Extremely grave. Be careful who you trust. Definitely not the Belgian authorities; the signs are they've been compromised. Speak to our mutual friend's closest allies – no one else.'

There's really only one person I can trust, he thought. *And that's his missus.* He was surprised to find that his hands were shaking and his heart felt like it was ready to burst through his skin. *Calm yourself laddie*, he thought. *There's a lot riding on your shoulders now; you'll be no good to anyone if you don't keep a cool head.*

'Good morning, Clive,' She said as she answered her phone. 'Any news?' That was the question she always asked.

'Not sure yet. First I need to speak urgently with Christophe, the police minister. Do you have his private number? I don't want to go through the usual channels.'

'Why not?'

'It's a sensitive issue; a police matter. That's all I'm prepared to say.'

'I have Christophe's number but it's for our personal use. I'm not sure I should...'

'Do it – do it right now for Philippe's sake.'

So of course she did.

Christophe answered his phone on the first ring, expecting that it might be Meg. Instead it was a UK number which he didn't recognise.

'Minister, I'm Chief Inspector Clive Scott of the Met Police in London. If you follow the coordinates that I'm about to send you they should lead you to your missing officer.'

'Philippe M…?'

'Yes. But time is critical: he was in that particular area last night but he may not be there much longer. It looks like it's a rural part of western Belgium, not too far from the French border. An old farmhouse or some other rustic building.'

'How did you get this information?'

'I can't say. But I trust the source and I believe it's accurate.'

'Send me the coordinates now.'

Scott did. Ten minutes later his phone rang; it was the Minister.

'Chief Inspector, a squad from Strasbourg will be on the way shortly. In the interim there will be helicopter reconnaissance of the entire area and rolling liaison with the ground troops.'

'Then pray, as I will, that they find him in time, Minister. *Au revoir.*'

'*Merci et au revoir,* Chief Inspector Scott.'

The team from Strasbourg eventually located the Belgian farmhouse. It was immediately sealed off and a search was made prior to the arrival of a specialist forensic team from Paris. There was evidence of recent occupation and a hasty departure. Evidence too, of hacking devices but no computer.

No Philippe Maigret either. However, in the room where he had slept the forensic squad found some fingerprints and a few drops of his blood. More blood was found outside the building near the tyre-tracks of the vehicle the jihadis had used. And, in the bathroom, the most important clues of all: some strands of his hair, stuck in place with dried soap on the under-side of the mirrored wall cabinet, and some clear fingerprints too, missed in the panic of the gang's departure.

Clive Scott arrived in Brussels on the EuroStar before 3 pm. He checked into his hotel, and left in good time for his meeting in the Musée des Beaux-Arts. It had been necessary to obfuscate when explaining his need for urgent travel to his superiors. *I've missed my calling,* he thought on his short walk to the Musée. *I should have been a diplomat; or a politician.*

He had deliberately arrived early to verify that the Musée was operating normally on all levels: no indication of masked assassins lurking in dimly-lit corners ready to pounce. And by this cautionary approach he made his way to the masterpiece that is 'Landscape with the Fall of Icarus.'

Controversy had eddied around this work for some time: who had actually painted it? For a long period it was attributed to the leading artist of Dutch and Flemish Renaissance art, Pieter Bruegel the Elder. But following technical examinations in 1996 that name was considered unsafe; maybe the painting – thought to have been painted in the 1560s – was a good early copy of Bruegel's lost original, by an unknown artist. However, more recent technical research had revived the question and the composition is definitely thought to be Bruegel's work now.

I don't give a damn who actually painted it, Clive thought, because whoever he was, he was a genius: *a momentous event is taking place and no one notices it! A boy who just wanted to fly is drowning; unseen and unsung. It's the human affliction. We're always so engrossed in our mundane affairs that the extraordinary moments which change the course of history go unnoticed. An archduke is assassinated in Sarajevo and it precipitates a world war in which 20 million die and a further 21 million are wounded. But how many people witnessed that moment and recognised the significance? Or the consequences.*

'One would have thought that since his name is in the title we'd have seen more than his spindly legs flailing about in a splash of water in the lower right corner,' the voice behind him said, causing him to jump. 'Don't turn around – you know who I am.'

'It's lucky you have a job; you obviously wouldn't make a living as an art critic. The painting is not about Icarus *per se*. It's about *us* – missing the moment or the point, time after time because we never learn. That's why the painting's entitled '*Landscape* with the fall of Icarus' and not 'The Fall of Icarus'. BTW, what the hell are you supposed to be in that getup? The beard looks as phoney as a two-bob watch.'

He laughed.

'The beard's *real,* Clive. I've been bumming around Europe for months now; I used whatever gear I had at hand for the rest of the disguise.'

'Yes, I heard you'd wandered off the reservation. How do you want to proceed with this malarkey?'

'I thought we could be strangers who have chanced to meet in front of a famous painting; so while we pretend to discuss its composition, I could tell you my sad story.'

'Sad?'

'Yes – very. Of course you know my code name?'

'Yes, Icarus, I do. I thought I might have recognised your voice but couldn't be certain until you suggested our meeting place – then the proverbial dropped. But what's at the top of my agenda is how you know where Maigret is.'

'I suppose you know that according to the people for whom I work…'

'MI6…'

'Yes, and that's the last time that label will be used. Okay?' Clive nodded. 'So, according to the afore-mentioned, there are two scenarios; either I've gone rogue or I'm dead.'

'Yeah, those are the options I've heard.'

'In a few moments pretend to accidentally bump into me as we move closer to the painting. I want to drop something in your pocket.'

'Okay – now?'

'Yes.'

'Got it?'

'Yes. I can feel that it's a watch.'

'So it is, but no ordinary watch. It's the watch that belonged to Maigret senior; apparently he gave it to

Philippe almost on his death-bed. It's of great sentimental value to him.'

'And you somehow managed to steal it? You'd only be able to do that if he was dead! You killed him, you bastard.'

'Calm down, don't draw attention to us. I'm no thief. I took the watch for safe-keeping, and now I've passed it on to you for the same reason. But perhaps I should start from the beginning of this saga.'

'I wish you would. And you had better make it convincing otherwise you won't leave this gallery alive.'

(Jamal Ahmadi, British born, Arabic speaking, university educated, former radical Islamist, escaped from his murderous comrades on the eve of their planned Berlin atrocity and with Philippe Maigret, Clive Scott, and others saved many lives, including those of the German hierarchy.

In the aftermath of those momentous events, neither the British nor the German authorities relished the idea of putting him on trial; the fallout from which might have devastated both countries' security service. Then Clive came up with a creative solution: set a thief to catch a thief. In other words, give a reformed jihadi a significant position at MI6 to develop strategies to thwart the unreconstructed from carrying out their deadly intentions.

That was how Jamal Ahmadi disappeared. A new back story was created for him, and a new name provided. That name must remain secret; enough to know that his code name subsequently became Icarus. Perhaps, given that the plot in Berlin involved a massive bomb, Phoenix might have been more appropriate. But what's done is done; and that is one of Clive Scott's granny's sayings.)

'This is my story. I will abbreviate as much as possible, and I may, or may not decide to answer questions when I've finished. Some months ago, a person considerably senior to me, gave me some confidential orders. They were so secret that the meeting at which he gave them took place in an obscure brasserie well away from our usual place of business. The orders were not in writing: it was made clear to me that they were off the books. In fact so far off that they were out of the library and several blocks away. With me so far?'

Clive nodded.

'I was given a credit card in a false name and told that there were ample funds at my disposal. My remit was wander around Europe, attending mosques, picking up information, and attaching myself to whatever suspect groups I encountered. And that was how I met an evil little cell of insurgents in Antwerp and subsequently travelled with them to Brussels. There were three of them; the boss was a particularly nasty thug, all too handy with his fists, the other two were more in the weird category. One was a constantly worried little guy who had some medical training – goodness knows how, or where – and a computer guy who had an industrial strength flatulence problem.

Before I left London an impressive criminal history was concocted for me: radicalised at University, engaged in subversion and criminal activity – petty theft, dodgy investment deals. And yes, I see your raised eyebrows, Clive: you're thinking my real history was far worse and it was – but that was then, and this is now. Anyone checking on me would soon find that I'd spent time in Saudi Arabia and other Middle Eastern hotspots where I was considered a useful asset for the cause. The insurgents must have been aware of my fabricated status because they were fairly deferential towards me. Early last week they told me they some business in Paris. I asked if I might tag along but they said I couldn't; I should wait at the farmhouse where they left me and they would join me in a few days.

At this point I should confirm that I remain a Muslim: a *true* Muslim and I do not accept or approve of the direction in which these death-obsessed apostates have taken my faith. Thus I have sworn to oppose them whenever, or wherever I come across them. Understand?'

Clive nodded again.

'Before I left London, my handler informed me that he had liaised, in a non-official way, with a number of security organisations in Europe and they all agreed that following the Charlie Hebdo outrage something far bigger and more deadly, was a distinct possibility. Hence my role. Therefore, to answer your question when we spoke yesterday, I had no prior knowledge of what was to happen in Paris on Friday night. I did however, have knowledge *after* the fact, as the Americans would say.'

'Good God – how?'

'Because when they returned to the farmhouse in the small hours of Saturday morning they brought a wounded Maigret with them.'

'How badly wounded?'

'Bad enough, an upper arm wound; he'd lost a lot of blood. The weirdo with the medical experience treated him after a fashion, but I didn't like the way things were going, as far as he was concerned.'

'He was tortured?'

'Yes. I didn't know what to do to help him. Should I blow my cover; compromise everything I'd done in the past months? I was unarmed, and they had a veritable arsenal at their disposal. That's why I decided to leave last night.'

'The man who gave you these orders – what was he like?'

'Average height; unremarkable appearance. Light brown hair and a neat moustache. He was in his late forties or early fifties, I thought. Oh, and he wore some kind of regimental tie.'

'You didn't question his authority, or the orders he gave you?'

'No, not for a second. Looking back I can see how flattered I was that someone like him would even know of my existence, much less offer me an assignment, especially one of this nature. He was from the higher echelons, while I was a newbie, there for only a few months, working in the Arabic section in the basement. I was totally blinded by hubris, Clive, and, as the ancient Greeks knew all too well, hubris is inevitably followed by nemesis. But I'd heard mention of his name within the service and he was credible. I did not doubt that he was genuine.'

'Now you think otherwise?'

'Yes. A week ago I found that my ATM card had been cancelled because it was over-drawn. That could not have been correct. I've kept a record of all monies spent and there's no way that I spent upwards of 10,000 Euros in three months.'

'Don't be too quick to judge yourself; you were dealing with a pro. I guarantee that this was not his first escapade. How do you contact him?'

'I don't. He phones me at the same time twice a week. At least that was the arrangement; I haven't heard from him since I discovered my credit had been withdrawn.'

'You've been set-up.'

'Well and truly. But why – to what end?'

'Before I answer your question you need to tell me his name.'

Jamal looked uncomfortable.

'I can't.'

'Sure you can. It's the only way I can help you.'

Another awkward pause.

'How about we find a coffee shop somewhere and have a relaxed chat about things?' He said finally.

'How about I walk out of here right now Sonny-Jim and leave you completely out in the cold.'

'Alexander Duncan,' he said reluctantly. 'Do you know of him?'

'Better than that; at the time he was recruited by the spooks he was a police officer. Sandy Duncan was a Dundee man, a fine, decent man. I knew him well. So well in fact, that I was invited to deliver a tribute at his funeral some years ago!'

SIXTEEN

A farmer found him that frosty morning as he drove his horse and dray to market with some chickens to sell. It might have been expected that the squad of French police stationed in Strasbourg should have found him, but they didn't, although they had conducted a search covering a wide radius from the farmhouse. Their usual deployment was to protect the official seat of the European Parliament and associated entities such as: The Council of Europe; The European Court of Human Rights; The Centre for information on European Institutions; Lieu d'Europe; European Consumer Centre; Infobest and, presumably, Uncle Tom Cobley and all!

But to be fair to the French there were sensibilities involved; they didn't relish their intrusion into another country's territory, especially Belgium which had suffered so much trampling over her sovereign soil by foreign armies in recent history.

Nor did the French police have the same advantage as the Belgian farmer who chanced to witness a slight movement of the tarpaulin covering the local compost heap. As he watched, intrigued by the sight, an arm flopped out from under the covering. He stopped his horse and moved cautiously towards the pile. Then he heard a faint moan followed by '*Aidez-moi – Aidez-moi!* Help me – help me.'

He may have been a farmer living in a rural hamlet but he certainly had a mobile phone and he immediately put it to use. While he waited for the emergency services he did his best to help the stranger. He gingerly rolled back the tarpaulin and made his own assessment of the man's condition. Blood-spattered, unshaven, facial cuts and bruises, eyes closed, scarcely able to breathe: life hanging by a thread, he concluded.

Next he carefully lifted the cover at the other end and was surprised to find the man was barefoot and wearing a robe that finished before mid-calf level. It looked like an Arabic garment of some kind, yet the man appeared to be European. He returned to his original position and moved the covering back a little further. *Pale, parched skin – a long slender body: an egg-shell man, so fragile that if I touched him he would crack into pieces.* So he used speech; soothing, kind words instead of touch.

'Dear Monsieur, I do not know what has happened to you, but please stay alive if you can. The ambulance people will be here soon and they will help you more than I can. As you could see, if you opened your eyes, I am no longer young. The Lord willing I will celebrate my seventieth birthday in the spring.'

In the distance he could hear the first faint sounds of the siren. At the same time he realised that the man's breathing was becoming even more laboured. Without knowing why he began to say *Hail Mary, full of grace pray for us sinners now and at the hour of our death.* He knew his prayer was not word perfect – he was, after all a long time lapsed – but to his surprise the man opened his eyes and smiled feebly.

'*Je ne suis pas encore mort,*' he whispered. Then, for good measure, he said it again in English, 'I'm not dead yet: thanks to you, Monsieur le Grand-père.'

I am poured out like water,
and all my bones are out of joint.
My heart has turned to wax;
it has melted within me.

The emergency room doctor at the country hospital looked at the patient lying on the trolley in front of him, scratched his head and despaired. Where to start first was the problem. With the help of a patient care assistant or orderly as they were once known, the patient was moved into an examination room then transferred to a treatment table.

A young nurse bustled in and wrinkled her nose in disgust.

'Doctor he stinks – and there's something crawling in his hair! He needs a bath.' She had already judged him to be a derelict, a drunk, or a drug addict. Or possibly all three.

'Nurse, *first we save his life,* and then perhaps we can consider the niceties of a bath,' the doctor said through almost clenched teeth. 'This man is as close to death as anyone I've seen in thirty years of professional experience who was still breathing. Someone's been praying for him; that's the only explanation. And if you can't stand the smell rub some peppermint oil under your nose, wear a damn mask, and find some air freshener – otherwise get out and send me someone who can help. Understand?'

'Yes, Doctor,' she said meekly, hurrying out of the room and retching into the nearest bin.

'Why is my nurse vomiting the bin outside?' the Sister demanded as she entered the room.

'Because she's bloody useless; she'd rather talk about smells than help a man who is more dead than alive. Why do you keep sending me these untrained people?'

'She's neither useless nor untrained; she's just young and new. You should be more patient with these fledging nurses, Doctor.'

'As you are?' He scoffed. 'I've seen you reduce them to tears more times than I can remember. But never mind that; get me a recorder of some kind. I want to itemise the man's injuries as I go; it cuts down on the damned paperwork afterwards.'

'The nurse will bring one when she returns. What have you given him so far?'

'Well, as you can see, I've put both an anti-biotic and a saline drip in his arm. And just now I gave him 2 mg of morphine. Check with me before you give him any more. In his state 2 mg is probably all his body can tolerate, anything stronger and we risk killing him. Now, fetch me some scissors please, so I can cut him out of this robe he's wearing. I need to determine the extent of his injuries. Oh, but first remove the dirty bandage on his upper arm so we can see what the wound looks like.'

She did as instructed, carefully and expertly. The patient did not move, but both of them were horrified. A deep, angry wound was revealed; the skin near it had a cluster of tiny blood spots that resembled pin-pricks and there was a faint almond smell. *The early signs of Sepsis,* they both thought, *but hopefully the anti-biotics will constrain it.*

'If I'm not mistaken that's a bullet wound, treated by some bloody butcher. Too late for sutures; just give the area a good clean and put a fresh dressing on it while I cut him out of his clothes. You'd better stay with me Sister, I need your skill now; not the hindrance of some damn acolyte.'

The doctor expertly cut through the cloth a third of the way, then exclaimed in surprise.

'Hell's teeth! This poor man has four more bullet wounds – all old ones, and cigarette burns on his body, wrists and arms. He's been tortured and it happened recently.'

'Perhaps he's a criminal or a spy.'

'Hmm. Maybe.'

'His clothing suggests the Middle-East and he might be growing a beard. But my nurse was right: he's filthy.'

'You'd be filthy too if you'd been dumped on a dung heap overnight. He's been babbling stuff in French and English. I think he's European.'

The sister shrugged.

'He still might be middle-eastern some people in that region speak two or three languages.'

'Yes Sister, but I doubt many of them recite fragments of the Hail Mary *in extremis*. Okay, no more serious wounds I can see on his front, now let's carefully turn him on his side.' They did.

'Oh – Sweet Mary…' The sister cried, crossing herself. 'What's been done to this poor soul?'

'He's been violated… sodomised, and in a very brutal manner; the force of the assault has caused internal bleeding. Someone has packed his anal cavity with various bits of old stuff in an attempt to stop the blood surge. Check his vital signs for me before I go any further.'

'Pulse thready, blood pressure jumping around…'

'Keep an eye on the monitor while I try to remove the dressings. God alone knows what might happen when I do. Steady, steady…' The patient moaned, and then cried out. 'Sorry friend, I'm being as gentle as possible.'

When all the material had been removed the doctor was relieved to find that no fresh blood loss was visible. He cautiously lubricated the area with an anaesthetising emollient, then stood back and breathed a sigh of relief while regretting the day, many years earlier, when he had forsworn cigarettes.

'Now he needs a transfusion – and as quickly as possible.'

'Crossed-matched…?'

'No time. Two units of whole blood and right now! There's no telling how much blood he's lost; the packing inside him was saturated with dried stuff. Then into intensive care for the foreseeable. Oh – and the emollient should be re-applied every two hours during the day, but not at night – it's important that he sleeps then: the body knows how to heal, given half a chance. And, when you think he's up to it, a sponge bath followed by a haircut and delouse. A shave too, if you have the time.'

Later that day the local constable came to interview the patient having heard about him via both the ambulance crew and the local grapevine, but was told that he had been sedated. He was a decent man, that officer, but one not overly troubled by intellect or imagination: it did not occur to him that it might be a good step towards formal identification for some fingerprints to be taken. In any event he assumed that Maigret was a vagrant, and there were so many of them to the euro these days that another one barely made an impression.

However, his superior was a different make of man. Young, ambitious, and well-educated. As his officer related the circumstances of his visit and the appearance of the patient, a memory stirred. A discreet Europol message, received days ago, for station heads only, concerning a missing police officer from Paris. He scrolled back until he found it. The more times he read the description of the missing man, the more convinced he became that, unlikely as it was that someone of importance would be found in his little cabbage patch, he just might have been.

With scarcely a word to his colleague he hurried out of the station and sped off to the hospital. As he entered he bumped into the A & E doctor who was preparing to go home for lunch.

'So who is he?' The doctor asked.

'An itinerant probably, no one you need be concerned about; there's no indication that he's dangerous.'

'Come off it Armand, don't try to con an old hand. I can't remember the last time we had two visits from your station in the same day. What's going on?'

'I'm not sure. But I'll give you a tip; take very good care of him. Give him your five-star service and keep him under lock and key. Oh, and invent some plausible explanation for why I'm showing interest in him.'

'Like what?'

'I don't know! You think of something; you're the doctor.'

'Okay, I get the message. Follow me.'

'Get rid of the nurse,' the officer whispered as they entered the room. 'And make sure we're not disturbed.'

He stood at the foot of the bed, studied the patient for a few minutes, and shook his head. *This ashen husk of a man can't possibly be Chief Superintendent Maigret of Police Nationale Paris,* he thought, visualising the photograph that had accompanied the Europol notice. *Or can it?*

'Doctor, how tall do you judge him to be?'

'Er… 190 cm or thereabouts.'

'Do you still have his clothes and shoes?'

'He was barefoot when he was brought in. As for his clothes they might have been burnt already. I had to cut him out of the robe thing he was wearing.'

'Any distinguishing features? Birth marks, moles, tattoos or scars?' He asked as he set about taking the fingerprints.

'Do bullet wounds count? He has four old ones and one quite recent.'

The police officer's heart missed a beat or three. *I do believe it's him. It has to be – it might be. Shite – who would have thought it?*

He hurried back to his station, informed the constable that he could take the rest of the day off, and ran the fingerprints through the computer.

'Come on, come on,' he muttered impatiently as the computer went through its scanning wizardry. Then finally the match signal sounded.

Prints identified as those of Chief Superintendent Philippe Maigret, Police Nationale Paris.

'Oh God – oh God!' He yelled to the empty walls and ceiling, 'I'm going to be famous! What the hell do I do now?'

He phoned a fellow officer in Mons; they had done their basic training together. When he told him of his discovery his friend whistled.

'Are you absolutely sure?'

'Yes. Fingerprints don't lie, do they?'

'They can sometimes be *made* to lie; only the blood never lies.'

'It's him, I'm sure. What should I do now, Marcel? Do I contact Brussels or Paris?'

'First of all, calm bloody down. Secondly, play this one absolutely by the book; something like this could make or break your career. Thirdly, if you read the fine print at the bottom of the Interpol alert it will tell you exactly what to do in the event of a positive identification.'

And so it did.

Four hours later a helicopter arrived from Paris. It was unmarked and innocuous, but it carried an illustrious cargo. Two surgeon-specialists at the zenith of their careers, the pilot, and Christophe Saint-Valéry the Minister of Police.

They swept into that rural hospital in a cloud of protocol while the staff stood back in something approaching religious awe and the modest A & E doctor regretted that he had no cap to doff.

Instead he led them to the patient's room. Then something remarkable happened. The Minister looked at the figure lying in the bed, gasped and nodded 'oui.' Then he fell to his knees, rested his head on the bed, and wept for his friend. After a few minutes he composed himself, stood to his feet and kissed him on his forehead and cheeks.

'Pardon gentlemen,' he said, to no one in particular. Then speaking directly to the doctor said, 'please make the patient ready for travel; he will return to Paris with us.'

'If you move him he will die. Minister, look at him carefully. Do you see who is standing behind him?'

'There's no one.'

'Is there not? Look again, sir. I can see a figure very clearly: but then I've had this experience before.'

'What are you babbling about, man?' One of the Parisian doctors said. 'The Minister's correct – there's no one there!'

'I've seen the Angel of Mercy many times, and at first I thought it was she. But I was wrong. This one's no gentle ministering Angel releasing a soul from suffering. This one's the black-hearted devil of death and he's wearing his grotesque rictus smile.'

'Doctor…'

'Do you know what that smile is saying? "This one's mine" – that's what. Move this poor man who has suffered so terribly already and the fiend will win. And I tell you this, as God Almighty is my witness and my judge, you'll have to kill me before you do it.'

SEVENTEEN

'How long, Doctor?' Saint-Valéry asked.

'Before he can be moved?'

'Yes.'

'If he survives the night... I'll know more in the morning. But I can't see it happening for at least a week and even then it will be risky.'

'Understood. In the meantime, he needs protection. What is the police strength in this town?'

'Two.'

'What!'

'You saw it from the air. It's a village, really not much bigger than a hamlet. We have two police officers; a sergeant and a constable.'

'Then why is your hospital here?' One of the Parisian eminences asked.

'It was an army hospital during the war; afterwards someone important decided it should be converted rather than demolished.'

'Doctor, would you have any objection to us examining your patient.'

'Yes, I would. As you can tell he's been sedated, and I see no purpose in disturbing him, especially as he was in delirium when admitted. However, in a spirit of shared compassion, you may – if you wish – read his file.'

The two doctors and the Minister conferred for a few minutes.

'Thank you Doctor…?'

'Defoe – Lucas Defoe.'

'Thank you, Dr Defoe. And yes, if we may see his notes that would be appreciated.'

The doctor passed his clipboard to the Minister and watched their expressions change as he and the two specialists read the full horrific account of what had been inflicted on Philippe Maigret.

'Oh, my Lord,' Saint-Valéry gasped after a few minutes of complete silence during which Dr Defoe took the opportunity to check his personal pulse rate. 'He's a married man… he has a wife. How can I tell her about this… this horrific degradation?'

'If you're asking for my advice, why tell her anything at all?' The pragmatic doctor said. 'He's entitled to complete confidentially, as are all our patients. In my opinion she need *never* know.'

'But… for their future relationship…'

'Let the future take care of itself; this man may not even survive the night. But if he does, allow him to stay quietly here while he heals. I give you my word that he will receive the best treatment we can offer. No need to think about anything else at present. But I must have a name for him; I presume you don't want to give me his *real* one.'

'You presume correctly, Doctor. Invent some innocuous name and occupation. Suffice it to say that he is a decorated police officer, and more than that he is my friend. What happened to him has been done precisely because of *who* he is, and *what* he is and that, in the year of our Lord twenty-fifteen, is an abomination. But now he must be protected at all times; we need a cordon around the hospital.'

'With respect sir, that might attract the wrong kind of attention.'

'Then an armed guard outside his door, twenty-four hours a day. And the *Rijkswacht/Gendarmerie* discreetly patrolling the perimeter from tonight onwards. How does that sound to you, Doctor Defoe?'

'Perfect.'

'Then it shall be done. I'll arrange it on our flight to Paris.'

'You can do that so soon?'

'I believe I can; your Police Minister owes me a favour or two and it's time for him to pay up.'

Before he left he took a business card out of his top pocket, turned it over and wrote quickly on the back.

'My personal contact details for you, Dr Defoe. If there's any change in his condition phone me immediately – day or night – otherwise a routine update from you at around the same time each morning would be greatly appreciated. Is that acceptable to you?'

'Yes, sir.'

'Now I like to spend some quiet time alone with my friend before we return to Paris. I trust that's acceptable to you gentlemen?'

They all indicated that it was. He stayed an hour longer with Philippe before they left the hospital.

For most of the time he had prayed: the patient slept peacefully.

Christophe actually made two important phone calls on the return flight to Paris early that evening. The first was to the Belgian police minister, who readily agreed to the twenty-four hour protection of an important, but anonymous, patient in the country hospital, even though he was intensely curious.

'If we are to guard him surely I have the right to know who he is, Christophe,' he protested.

'And so you will, Antoine, just as soon as he's back on his native soil again.'

The second phone call was to Chief Inspector Scott's mobile. To his surprise he discovered that the detective was in Brussels.

'Have you found him? Where is he?' Scott said.

'Wait a minute, Monsieur, what are you doing in Brussels?'

'Minding my own business,' was the terse reply.

'Hardly. I doubt Scotland Yard's territory includes Belgium.'

'I'm waiting for a Eurostar to take me back to Blighty; I've decided not to stay overnight. Now tell me about Philippe; was he generally in the area of the coordinates I gave you? Tell me that and I'll divulge something significant to you.'

'Very well.'

What followed was a very clear summary of the circumstances of Maigret's discovery. No detail was omitted, but neither was a single extraneous word included. This was Saint-Valéry's forte: the ability to provide a precis of any incident or indeed, any ministerial report, without omitting a single relevant detail. That was how he had been given his first ministerial position when he was barely thirty, and it also explains why, no matter what shade of political power was installed in France, he was always retained. Unfortunately Clive Scott had not been similarly blessed by his Creator.

However he was a good listener; so he absorbed the Minister's account without interruption, except for an occasional gasp of horror, usually accompanied by the use of the word *'bastards'* – delivered with great venom – as the full extent of Maigret's treatment was disclosed to him.

'*Bastards, bastards!*' He said angrily as Christophe finished his narrative. 'They tortured him.'

'Yes, indeed they did.'

'Was there anything more…?'

'I've already confirmed that he was tortured – isn't that bad enough for you? It certainly is for me.'

'It's something I gathered… never mind from whom. I worried that there might have been something… more er *personal.'*

There was a long pause on the other end.

'There was. He was assaulted in an extreme act of sadistic abuse.'

'Dear God – you don't mean…?'

'I'm afraid I do. The doctor treating him was very frank.'

'Which one of them did it?' Clive asked.

'We don't know. But we will find out; the doctor was able to retrieve some DNA.'

'Then let me fill in some of the blanks for you, Minister.'

Clive related the circumstances of his phone conversation with Jamal and their subsequent meeting at the Musee des beaux Arts. It was a rambling, sometimes imprecise account: he was a volatile, emotional man, although he attempted to control that aspect of his personality.

'So just to be clear. Some months ago, this Icarus was sent on some kind of wild goose chase around Europe by a man who you know for certain has been dead for years. Is that the gist of it?'

'Yes.'

'In the course of this tour he infiltrated a small group of discontents who later played a major role in the murderous events in Paris a week ago. Correct, so far?'

'Yes.'

'But he took no part in the atrocity as during that time he was sequestered in an old farmhouse in rural Belgium?'

'Yes.'

'*Conneries!* I don't believe a word of it!'

'No, not BS, and I can prove it. He gave me the watch that Philippe's father gave him before he died. I have it with me now.'

'Obviously the man was fully complicit and stole it.'

'No, I believe him when he said he took it when he escaped to keep it safe for Maigret. And I tell you this; I watched him very carefully while he related his story and I believed every word of it. Besides, there's what he did for the cause in Berlin at great risk to himself. He was telling the truth, I'm certain of that.'

'If that's so, why didn't he choose to return to London with you tonight? Especially since we're expected to believe he has no access to funds now.'

'He's determined to track down this bunch of swine. It's personal for him now because he witnessed some of what they did to Maigret. He says he can support himself as he's done before by translating Arabic into English and vice versa. Apparently there's quite a market for it in Brussels these days.'

'I'll just bet there is! Some parts of Brussels are a cesspit of radicalisation from what I hear,' Saint-Valéry said.

'I didn't ask you how his missus took the news that he's safe and well; she must have been jubilant.'

'She doesn't know yet.'

'What? You told me before her?'

Christophe sighed before he answered.

'I know Meg; in fact I've come to know her very well since she and Philippe were married. She's a lovely woman in many ways, but she can be formidable when she's fired up about something. If I told her we know where he is she would hold my feet to the fire until I gave her his exact location. I don't want her to know yet.'

'Why not? Where's the harm?'

'If she knew she'd be there in a flash; I don't want her to see him in his present state. I saw him and I doubt whether I'll ever get that image out of my mind. He may be safe but he's very far from well.'

'And if he should, God forbid, die in the night? What then?'

'Then I'll have to live with that…'

'The hell you will! If you don't inform her as soon as you land in Paris I'll tell her myself.'

'Please don't Clive. I promise I'll do it first thing tomorrow morning, straight after Dr Defoe has given me an update.'

Central Paris
Thursday 19th November 2015
(late evening)

Clive reluctantly agreed but he need not have worried. Mere hours after Christophe walked through his own front door his phone rang. It was Dr Defoe.

'Sir… I regret to advise you…'

'No – do not say it!'

'No, no – you misunderstand. The patient is alive, but he became distressed a while ago and then the haemorrhaging began again. I have managed to stop the surge but I fear that a pattern is developing and the time might come when I won't be able to control it, no matter what I do. He needs specialist attention; I'm a country doctor, not an experienced surgeon. There's a specialist clinic outside of Zurich where I've referred patients before; it has an excellent reputation. They will take your friend if you can arrange a flight.'

'I thought you said it was too risky to move him…'

'It still is. We're in the lesser of two evils territory now. The situation is under control at present but if he should go into hemorrhagic shock: that's a life-threatening condition.'

'When do you suggest, Doctor?'

'First thing in the morning; he's sleeping now so best not to disturb him. I'll stay with him for most of the night, and I live only ten minutes away from the hospital; he will have an experienced critical care nurse with him at all times during my absence.'

'Very much appreciated, Dr Defoe. Please have him prepared for a medevac flight at 9 am tomorrow and advise the Zurich clinic accordingly.'

'Will do, sir. Thank you and good evening.'

As that call ended, he pressed his speed dial. Bernard, his office supremo – he of the naughty cornflake on the cheek infamy – immediately answered even though he was by that time relaxing at home.

'Minister?'

'Bernard, I need you to organise another medevac flight from Paris to the same part of Belgium as today, arriving 8.45 am to transfer a patient to a Zurich Clinic. I'll be on that flight and will have precise details by then. I'm not sure how long I'll be away so best to cancel my appointments for the next few days. And I want one of our top high-speed police drivers to get me to Orly in the morning.'

'A helicopter sir, like the one earlier today?'

'Yes.'

'The condition of the patient?'

'Grave. Make sure the medevac has all the necessary life-saving gear on board that might be needed, and the personnel to administer it. Now get moving.'

He poured himself a generous measure of whisky, took a few sips, and steeled himself for the most difficult phone conversation of all. He picked up his phone and pressed the Maigret residence number which went straight to message mode. Meg answered her mobile by the second ring. He knew exactly what she would say; it was the same words whenever he called her.

'Oh, Christophe… any good news?'

'There's news, m'dear. Some good, some not so good. Philippe is safe but he's been er… hurt.'

'Where is he, when can I see him?' She whispered before the sobbing began. 'Thank you Lord, thank you Lord,' she repeated.

'He will be in a clinic in Switzerland sometime tomorrow morning,' he said, choosing his words carefully. 'But he will be in intensive care and I'm not sure visitors will be allowed. We'll know more after he's been admitted and examined. I just wanted to give you the news as soon as possible.'

'Are you telling me everything you know, Christophe?' She asked between sobs.

'Of course I'm not. But I am telling you as much as you need to know. Can you be content with that for now?'

'Will you at least promise me that he's safe and well?'

'He's definitely safe, but that's all I can promise at present. I'll call you again tomorrow sometime. In the meantime, please inform Louise Maigret and give her my kindest regards.'

Clive Scott's EuroStar departure from Brussels was delayed because of emergency track maintenance. As the train's imminent arrival was finally announced, his phone rang. It was Jamal and he was excited.

'Clive, I've seen them! Or rather, not them actually but the van they were driving, and I'm certain the three of them were in it. I followed as long as I could but on foot it was impossible, even with the traffic holdups. However, I know their direction of travel and I have an idea about where they might be headed.'

'That's a good start, Jamal – well done. Are you armed?'

'What? Me armed? Definitely not! I'm supposed to be a spy, not a damn assassin.'

'Well, I guess that makes me an assassin by your definition. I'll change my ticket and meet you in the coffee shop where we went after the Musee as soon as I can. Looks like I'll be staying overnight in Brussels after all! And I have some news of my own: Philippe Maigret has been found. He's safe now.'

'His condition?'

'Not good. He's in a hospital. I don't have any details.'

'Er, was he hurt? I mean…'

'You know he was! You were there when he was tortured.'

'Yes, I was. And it was terrible... but was there er anything else?'

'Are you asking me if he was...?'

'Yes. Yes, I am. Was he?'

'He was.'

'Oh – blest Father Abraham. That lying bastard! He promised me that... I showed him, *proved* to him from our sacred writings that it was anti-Islamic... an *abomination* to force another person into sexual activity against their will. And he promised... he actually promised me...'

'You know which one of them did it?'

'Yes. It was that bloody maniac Haz! I saw the way he looked at Maigret now and then. But he promised me. He actually *promised me.*'

'You knew his predilection for men?'

'Not necessarily men: forced sex... sex with savagery and violence... that was his preference. But he said he would change – *he swore it.* And I reminded him of that oath, but he... what a fool I am to have believed he would ever, *could* ever, change. Or that he even *wanted* to try.'

'Tell me this; did Haz know who Maigret was from the beginning?'

'Oh yes, he knew. He recognised him from the photos in the newspapers. And he wanted to humiliate him, he told me that himself. "Cut the rich cop down to size", is what he said. I should have read the signs better.'

'Don't be too harsh on yourself, laddie. You did what you could, and it is thanks to you that Maigret was found. We will track down this miserable excuse for a man and when we do…'

'What then, Clive…?'

'Never-you-mind. Just know that if I had my way he would never see the inside of a Court of Law, nor have the chance to boast about what he did to Maigret.'

'But how likely are you to get your way?'

'We'll see. He replied enigmatically. 'Now, forget we ever had this conversation – understand? It *never* happened.'

EIGHTEEN

British Embassy,
8th Arrondissement, Paris
Thursday 19th November 2015

The day that Philippe was found Meg had her meeting with Giles de Montfort and his niece. They arrived from London that morning and settled into their plush accommodation in the British Embassy in the fashionable 8th arrondissement. Fleur was not impressed by the grandeur of the surroundings or the fact that Rue du Faubourg Saint-Honoré is one of the most famous streets in France.

'The Brit Embassy is among the best-known architecture in Paris,' Meg admonished. 'Many people would be delighted to receive an invitation to stay here.'

'Maybe, but I'm not one of them; it has the stench of luxury in the face of poverty about it.'

'Spoken like a true champagne socialist. You're only a few doors down from the Élysée Palace for goodness sake.'

'Have you been inside before?'

'No, not the Embassy. But I've been to a Reception at the official residence of the Ambassador, the Hôtel de Charost just down the street, that's another historic building. Bought by the Duke of Wellington after he was appointed to the Court of Louis XVIII. It previously belonged to Princess Borghese who went into exile on Elba with her brother, Napoleon Bonaparte. But they ran out of money; hence the sale of the building.'

'Fascinating,' Flo said faking a yawn. 'We're certainly a long way from Hampstead, Dorothy!'

Meg laughed.

'You might as well give in; I'm determined to give you a history lesson while we wait for Giles. Where is he by the way? And how are things with you and David?'

'Oh, Quinn,' she sighed. 'How to explain the phenomenon that is David Quinn? He's brilliantly deliciously wonderful, and utterly bloody annoying.'

'That's an oxymoron, isn't it?'

'Of course; but he's *my* oxymoron and it's likely I love him. As for Unc, another irritating man, he's been delayed at the prison where he's meeting his crim client. Some ruckus about a prisoner being knifed in the showers or something.'

'By his client?'

'No, not him. He was, probably for the few times in his life, an innocent bystander. Unc said he'd be with us in about half an hour. Would you like a glass of wine while we wait?'

'I thought I was invited for afternoon tea.'

'Nah – I feel like a chilled glass or two of Sancerre. Are you up for it?'

'Maybe. It's not as though I have anything else to look forward to tonight,' she said without thinking.

'Philippe is still in hospital?'

'Er… yes. But I hope he'll be home soon.'

'Time to come clean love; he's never actually been in hospital has he?'

'Of course he has. Why would I say he was, if he wasn't?'

'Listen, my dear: the jig is up. London's rumour-mills have been grinding overtime with talk of a missing senior French police officer, and every time I've phoned you since… since Friday night I could tell you'd been crying. He's missing, isn't he? And no one knows where he is, or even if he's…'

'Oh Flo…' Then she began to cry, just as Giles de Montfort arrived.

'What's going on here?' He asked. Flo quickly whispered an update to him and he immediately ordered a superior bottle of French wine.

'Let me help,' he said gently. 'This is what I believe: Philippe Maigret has been missing since Friday night and neither you nor the French Government have any idea where he is. Correct?'

'Yes.'

'What are the authorities telling you?'

'Christophe, the Minister of Police, phones me every day and says almost the same thing. They're making discreet enquiries, they've offered a substantial reward through a third party, or parties, but nothing of any substance has surfaced yet. See this ring?' She asked, showing them the gold ring on the middle finger of her left hand. 'This is Philippe's wedding ring, and I know more about the circumstances by which it was removed than Christophe Saint-Valéry ever will.'

'Then why don't you tell us, m'dear?'

'Very well, I will.'

She related the story of how Louis Allard had been waiting at the back entrance of 'La Belle Equipe' on Friday night hoping to score some free take-away when the dinner service finished. When he heard the first bout of gunfire he took cover in a nearby doorway and waited for it to end. After a long interval of silence, just as he was preparing to leave his hiding-place, he heard three more shots in rapid succession, so he stayed where he was safe. Then everything went quiet again. A little while later he heard the sound of the backdoor opening and moved further back in the doorway where he wouldn't be seen but could still watch. And what he saw was a large bearded man dragging another man along the ground by the collar of his jacket. This man had blood on his face and down his shirt. A lot of blood, Louis said; his hands were tied and he was very pale. Then a younger man, with a scruffy beard appeared and he kicked the man on the ground in a callous way. The older man let go of the man for a moment to open the door of the van parked at the kerbside. The injured man held something in his hands before glancing in Louis' direction. He immediately recognised him: it was Philippe! He moved involuntarily – "the surprise of recognition, I suppose" – was the phrase he used. With that movement Philippe looked directly at him and nodded to confirm that he was who Louis thought he was. Then he turned to one side, obviously in pain, and quietly dropped something in the gutter. Shortly afterwards the thugs blindfolded him, tossed him in the back of the van and drove off at high speed. A little later Louis heard the sound of the police arriving and knew it was safe to leave. He went immediately to the gutter and retrieved what Philippe had left there. It was his wedding ring inside one of his handkerchiefs which was saturated with blood. So dear kind Louis took the handkerchief home and his sister washed it so I wouldn't be upset at the sight. And I wish with all my heart that they had left that blood where it was: it would have been more precious to me than all the rings in the world!'

There was silence for a long period after she had finished her account. Flo was on the edge of tears from both the story and the way Meg had kept herself so tightly under control while she told it.

Giles was similarly moved. This woman has been to hell and back and she's still in torment. *What to say to comfort her?* You're the celebrated wordsmith QC. Can't you think of something? His inner voice said.

'Courage under fire,' he said without realising he had spoken. But whether he meant Philippe or Meg not even he could have said for sure.

'What?' Fleur said, stifling a sob.

'Why don't you tell us how your visit to the prison went?' Meg asked, aware of his predicament. 'Useful or otherwise, Giles?'

'Hmm. Later, not now; I have some questions for you. Firstly, do you trust – implicitly trust – that Louis was speaking the truth? And if you do, on what do you base that belief.'

'Less of the QC interrogation and more of the regular human-speak if you don't mind, Unc.'

'Sorry. Old habits…'

'I trust Louis' story because I heard him tell it and his sincerity was obvious. He wanted to *help,* that was clear. Maybe he felt that by doing so the police would more carefully investigate his brother's murder.'

'Wrong place, wrong time, most likely.'

'You might be right. Philippe says these street people see and hear far more than we realise as they criss-cross Paris each day.'

'I don't know anything about this murder; could either of you enlighten me please?'

'I can. I've been mulling over many things in my mind in recent days. It seems that a number of unusual events took place in a fairly short space of time, and I'm always intrigued when that happens.'

'Coincidence?' The QC queried.

'If they actually exist.'

'Do they not?'

'For the love of my sanity tell him what happened and let him make up his own damn mind.'

'Okay. As soon as we returned from London we were

informed of two things: Gervais Allard's body had been found floating in the Seine, and Madeleine, his close friend and fellow street wanderer, was missing. Philippe turned Paris on its head looking for her but she seems to have resurfaced only *after* Friday night's attacks.'

'Gervais was drowned?'

'It's possible. All I know is that his throat was cut and then he was thrown in the river.'

'Madeleine – did she disappear before or after Gervais was murdered?'

'Philippe thought afterwards. He felt she might even have witnessed what happened to him.'

'So she did a runner.'

Giles winced at his niece's use of the vernacular. And *criminal* at that.

'How old was the poor man?'

'Mid-seventies, we supposed; always hard to tell with people who have been living rough for years.'

'Hmm. I can see why you're intrigued. Is the wine not to your taste? You've hardly touched it.'

'I'm sure it's fine, I'm just thinking.'

'Well I can drink and think at the same time, so fill 'er up,' Flo said, indicating that her glass was almost empty.

'About what?' He replied, ignoring her.

'About whether your client gave you any useful information today. After all, that's why we're here, isn't it?'

'Yes, yes indeed. I'm not sure whether it was helpful or not. I'd put him in the fantasist category, really. A modern day Walter Mitty, perhaps.'

'Walter who?'

'A character in a short story written by James Thurber a long time ago, Flo. He was a meek, mild man who lived a colourful fantasy life. He imagined himself as a pilot, a surgeon, and even a cheerful killer.'

'It all ends in tears, I suppose.'

'It ends the way it should; you need to read the story – it's brilliant. A work of genius, in my opinion.'

'Indeed. However, my client is definitely no genius; he may have trouble telling the difference between the truth and a lie, although he did spin a fascinating tale.'

'Go on then, spill the beans.'

'I can't – there's such a thing as lawyer-client privilege as you are well aware. I'm not prepared to risk disbarment to satisfy your curiosity.'

'There must be *something* you can tell us, Giles. Can't you redact as you go?'

'I've been working on that from the time I left the prison, but I'm still unsure.'

'Get on with it, Unc! Surely your belief that he's a fantasist liar militates against an accusation of default of privilege?'

'An interesting argument but not one I'd like to put to the test.'

'Well, here's another angle; if you don't tell, *we* won't tell. Right, Meg?'

'I'll pretend I didn't hear that comment.'

'Agreed,' replied the wife of a distinguished police officer. 'We'll stay schtum.'

'What? Why did you say that? Why use a German word at this time?'

'I suppose I've watched too many old war films.'

'Why do you look so weird, Unc?'

'Never mind, it's not important. And neither was the bizarre story my client told me about a mysterious man who had infiltrated our security service. But of course he offered not a shred of proof; which renders his account useless as far as him being tried in an English court is concerned. And that, you may remember, was his aim. Although he obviously knows his Greek mythology.' He added as an after-thought.

'What?' The women exclaimed.

'Well, he must; he said the mole's code name was Icarus.'

'Impossible!'

'Yes; totally impossible,' Meg agreed, finally taking a swig of her wine.

'I think one of you should explain to me exactly what's happening here.'

'After you, Meg. You out-rank me by marriage.'

'No, no, dear girl – please, after you.'

'But I insist…'

She took another generous drink.

'The fact of the matter is… er I have *some…* knowledge of the person with the code name Icarus and so it seems does Fleur.'

'Yes, I do. And I can tell you he's no foreign spy: he's as true-blue as… as… Yorkshire pudding.'

'What?'

'Hardly. Wasn't he born in Birmingham?'

'Okay, time out everyone,' the QC said. 'Have I,

perchance, wandered into the Mad Hatter's tea party? Some straight talk now; at least from *one* of you.'

'The explanation is simple; it's known as pillow-talk.'

'Post coitus conversation, Unc.'

'Am I to understand that you two come by confidential British Security information simply because of the men with whom you sleep?'

'Got it in one.'

'But we don't *usually* pass that information on to anyone else…'

'Oh well that's alright then!'

'It's just that you seemed to be…'

'In danger of barking up the wrong tree so we absolutely *had* to tell you.'

'God help us,' he said, massaging both his temples simultaneously. 'Is honour dead? Has rectitude regressed? What happened to the *loose lips sink ships* refrain of former days?'

'Ancient history.'

They sat silently drinking their wine for a time, while Giles digested the women's revelation.

'My client said something strange as I was preparing to leave. A phrase in German, which I didn't understand, that's why I queried your use of the word schtum earlier, Meg.'

'What did he say?'

'Wait a minute.' He shuffled through his papers. 'I wrote it down somewhere – yes, here it is. He said "Denn die Todten reiten schnell".'

'I don't know what that means.'

'Same goes for me.'

'That is precisely why I phoned my dear brother Robert, the only one in our family who has a smattering of German, and he knew what it meant. It's a famous phrase from an old German poem, also used by Bram Stoker in his Dracula story. It means *Because the dead ride fast.*'

'Jeepers. And what's that supposed to signify do you suppose?'

'Bram Stoker,' Meg mused. 'What's in a name? It's actually *all* in the name, isn't it? Bram sounds mysterious, maybe even *sinister*, as befits the author of a famous *Gothic novel*. But when you learn that his real name was Abraham, as was his father's, then everything changes; he's suddenly benign, like an Old Testament patriarch, the founder of a new nation.'

'So?'

'So maybe the opposite also applies. Ask yourself; how could a man with a name like Henry Livingstone be anything other than beyond reproach?'

'Henry Livingstone? Now that's definitely a coincidence. Dear old Rob said he'd had an unexpected visitor earlier today: a man whose name was Henry Livingstone. Rob said he'd visited him before, some weeks ago as far as he could remember.'

'And?'

'The thing is he claimed to be a friend of Rob's, but now he says he doesn't believe they'd ever before that first visit.'

'But Dad has his good days, and then there's the

other kind. We can't really trust his memory.'

'Perhaps we can. You said at the time that you'd never heard Rob mention this man before.'

'I don't claim to know all his friends.'

'But if he's not a friend why is he visiting him?'

'Oh, I can explain that. Rob says Livingstone was very interested to learn about the process by which he devised those cryptic crosswords over so many years. He wondered from whence his inspiration came, and how he chose the clues.'

'Oh Lord, Flo. Remember your Dad's weird repetitive babbling to me while you were organising the afternoon tea that day? He was obsessed with the fox being in the hen-house and chaos and…'

'*Sturm and drang. Turmoil* – and on a massive scale.'

'Exactly! I think Henry Livingstone is terrified of what Rob might know; or *might* eventually remember.'

'But he doesn't know anything. He's my lovely old lad who is suffering from early dementia.'

'And yet he had no difficulty in translating what *Denn die Todten reiten schnell* means, which just happens to be what Giles' client said at the end of their meeting. Giles, I think your client might have earned his right to trial in England.'

'Are you saying that you think this Livingstone character could be the MI6 mole?'

'No. I'm saying that I most *definitely* believe he damn-well is!'

NINETEEN

'And Icarus – who is he?'

'Not for your ears, Unc. Just take it from us that he's genuine and has nothing to do with Henry Livingstone or your crim client.'

'Do you agree, Meg?'

'Yes. But now I must leave. Philippe's mother has not been well these past few days and I need to visit her on my way home.'

'She knows he's missing?'

'Yes, and she's distraught, but trying not to show it. She's an amazing woman.'

As the door was opened for her to leave she had an after-thought.

'When you see your Dad the next time, check the drawer in the little cabinet next to his armchair,' she whispered to Flo.

'Why?'

'To see if there are more pills there following Henry Livingstone's latest visit.'

'If you suspect he planted those you found before, Quinn and I got rid of them.'

'Yes, you told me. But maybe they've been replaced. I don't trust this Livingstone character; I think he's up to mischief.'

'What kind?'

'I don't know, but weird things seem to happen when he's around. Ever heard of the Deep State, Flo?'

'No. What is it, some kind of new relaxation therapy?'

'Er... not exactly. Ask David, I have a feeling he might know.'

'More pillow-talk information?'

'No, something Tony Blair said when he was Prime Minister, about not underestimating the Civil Service's belief that it's their job to actually run the country while resisting any changes proposed by "here today, gone tomorrow" politicians.'

'That sounds subversive.'

'Of course it is. That's why it's called the Deep State.'

'Something similar to the dark web?'

'Quite possibly; didn't we think Henry Livingstone looked like a civil servant?'

'We did. I'll quiz Quinn when I'm back in London.'

'Does he still have the photo of Livingstone from the CCTV at Willows Glen?'

'I'm sure he does. Want me to send it to you?'

'Yes. I'd like to take a second look at this bod.'

After this exchange they made their final farewells then she stepped out into the less rarefied air of the Rue du Faubourg Saint-Honoré. She was surprised to find

Carole standing on the pavement near her car, waiting for her.

'Is Christophe Saint-Valéry having me followed, or is *Police Nationale* operating a taxi service these days?' `

'Just following orders, Madame. The Minister doesn't want you harassed by the usual media rabble.' Meg looked around quickly. 'Oh don't worry, I've already checked and anyway the vicinity of the British Embassy is usually a reptile-free zone. Where to now – home or somewhere else?'

'To the Avenue Foch first Carole, if that suits you; I can make my own way home afterwards.'

'Do you see a meter in this vehicle, Madame?'

'No.'

'Well then – I'm to take you wherever you need to go. And if necessary I'll wait all night in the Avenue Foch until you are ready to go home.'

'Don't you have a home to go to yourself? Or a husband and family?'

'Yes to all three, but this is my job and they understand. I also have a very accommodating mother-in-law.'

'As do I, and that's who I'm visiting now; she's not been very well since…'

'I understand. Avenue Foch, here we come.'

They heard the sirens long before they arrived at Louise Maigret's apartment building: in fact the ambulance was only minutes ahead of them.

'Oh, it's stopped right in front of her building. Please God it can't be she who needs it.' But it was.

In a matter of seconds Carole slammed on the brakes, leapt out of the car flashing her police ID to the ambulance crew and began questioning them in volatile French. They responded in the same vein before two of them rushed up to the front entrance and went inside.

'Can I go up to her apartment?' She asked the remaining paramedic as he finished speaking into his phone.

'Pleased to wait here, Madame. My colleagues will help her and she is not alone, there is another lady with her upstairs.' he replied in English.

Rosa, she thought, *and thank Heaven for that – she adores Louise.*

'It's a suspected heart attack,' Carole explained. 'They're giving her nitro-glycerine and oxygen; they will bring her down after she stabilises.'

'Will they allow me to go to the hospital with her?'

'I'd like to see them try to stop us!'

'I want her taken to the American Hospital.'

'Why?'

'Because… because I know someone who was a patient there for a long time; it's a very good hospital. Louise has private health cover I think that's what she would want.'

'Very well. When the paramedics are ready to leave I'll make sure they take you with them, and I'll follow. Is that acceptable, Madame Maigret?'

'Yes, thank you. However I intend to stay overnight at the hospital. I won't leave her until I know all's well.'

'That should be no problem.'

'It will be if *you* stay too. I don't want you to do that; please tell your superiors that I insist you go off duty once we reach the hospital.'

'You might need me to translate…'

'Not at that hospital – that's another reason to take her there.'

'Then I'll stay until I know that *both* of you are okay. Agreed?'

'Agreed; one hour, then home you go.'

She was half-sleeping in a chair next to Louise's bed when Christophe made his late night phone call to tell her Philippe had been found.

'There's news, m'dear. Some good, some not so good. Philippe is safe, but he's been er… hurt.'

'Are you telling me everything you know?' She asked between sobs.

'Of course not! But I am telling you as much as I can reveal. Will you be content with that for now?'

'Can you at least promise me that he's safe and well?'

'He's definitely safe, but that's all I can promise now. In the meantime, please inform Louise Maigret for me and give her my kindest personal regards.'

'I'm in the hospital with Louise now. She's had a heart attack.'

'Oh, God. So that's why you've been whispering. What are the doctors telling you, and what treatment has she been given?'

'She had an ECG soon after she was admitted. It seems her heart's strong but the beat is sometimes irregular. There's a consensus that one of her arteries might be blocked but her heart's not behaving as anticipated if that were the problem so they're puzzled. They've decided on rest and recovery for now because of her age. Depending on how she is in the morning they may insert s stent.'

'Do they know who she is?'

'Yes, they know her name.'

'That's not what I meant. Is Carole still with you?'

'Yes, she's in the corridor outside.'

'Please get her for me. No, better yet take your phone to her.'

She did. And another animated conversation ensued, albeit conducted in hushed tones on Carole's part, ending with her repeating "oui Monsieur, ce sera fait" numerous times. Meg had heard that phrase enough times since her marriage to know that it meant 'yes, sir, it shall be done.'

'What does he want you to do?' She asked a subdued Carole as she returned her phone.

'Er… er, the Minister wants er…'

'You to make the doctors aware of the patient's importance? Is that it?'

'Yes. And he also wants to stress that no effort or expense should be spared to guarantee her comfort and recovery.'

'Well off you go then, better tell them right away.'

She smiled.

'I told them as soon as we arrived.'

'Not about Philippe's absence, I hope.'

'No. I said that he was er… away at present and that you were the patient's next-of-kin. I also gave the Minister the names of two of the doctors treating her and he will speak to them himself to make sure that nothing reaches the media. And he also said that, no matter how much you objected, I'm to stay until you're ready to go home.'

'Hmm, we'll see about that!'

A little after midnight Louise Maigret stirred uneasily in her bed and cried out "Où suis-je?" – "where am I?" several times.

'Ssh, Louise, you're in the hospital and I'm here with you so there's no need for you to be concerned.'

'Oh, dear girl. I was having the most wonderful dream. I dreamt that Philippe had been found and that he would be home soon.'

Was it a dream, or did her subconscious hear some of my conversation with Christophe?

'It wasn't a dream. Christophe phoned with the good news while you were sleeping. Philippe is safe and all is well in our world at last.'

'He's safe? He's really safe?'

'Yes.'

'But where – and how?'

'I don't know any details; this seems to have happened very recently. But details don't really matter, do they? The important thing is that he's safe and we will see him soon. Now, please go back to sleep; we need you to be completely well when he comes home.'

'Deo gratias,' she said, turning over and snuggling down in her bed again. 'Deo gratias.'

Friday 20th November 2015
Zurich. Afternoon

The dangerously ill Maigret, and his almost exhausted friend, Saint-Valéry, eventually arrived at the clinic near Zurich. They were hours later than expected, the delay due to atrocious weather conditions. The patient had been sedated prior to the flight: the Minister was surreptitiously tranquilised post-arrival by means of a large whisky with a little extra *je ne sais quoi* – I don't know what – added to ensure that he would also rest. Not standard medical practice to be sure, but that clinic had admitted and treated enough stressed captains of industry and their anxious kin to know what worked best most of the time.

Zurich, the largest city in Switzerland, located at the north-western tip of Lake Zurich, and the capital of the canton of Zurich. The twenty-six cantons being the federal states of the Swiss confederation. It is a hub for railways, roads and air traffic which are the busiest in the country. It was founded by the Romans who named it Turicum: in 1519 it became a primary centre of the Protestant Reformation in Europe.

This bustling city is also one of the world's largest financial centres and home to many fiscal institutions. Many of Switzerland's research and development centres are concentrated in the Greater Zurich area

215

where low tax and useful subsidies persuade companies to establish their headquarters there. It is ranked among the ten most liveable cities in the world, together with Geneva and Basel.

It follows then, that the clinic to which Maigret was referred by the astute Dr Defoe was well-funded up to the hilt, and highly regarded. In fact there was no better – or even *halfway-equal* – medical establishment in the whole of Europe to which he could have been admitted.

The planets must have been in some peculiar configuration that November. No, not the supposed alignment for the arrival of the Age of Aquarius: that fizzled out in disenchantment as the last drug-addled hippy left San Francisco towards the end of the last century, but something perhaps more poetically justified.

Before dawn that day the Belgian police, following a tip-off from an anonymous source, raided a property in the Molenbeek area of Brussels: an impoverished area with a high immigrant population, rising crime rate, cultural intolerance, and a recognised Islamist breeding ground for many years. One of the attackers in the commuter train bombings in Madrid in 2004 lived there, and so did the French citizen who killed four people in the Jewish Museum in Brussels ten years later. Some people even referred to it as The Islamic State of Molenbeek, and consider it a no go area for the law-abiding.

A brief, but vicious battle erupted as the heavily-armed police entered the building. The two men there were given the opportunity to surrender but they, seemingly high on drugs resisted, preferring pseudo martyrdom instead. When the gun battle finally ended both were dead. Then the police made a curious discovery; a third man in another room, dead too but not shot by either police firearms, or those of his cohorts. Two bullets from another weapon; one to the head, one to the heart. An execution carried out by someone who clearly knew what they were doing, was the assessment of those police officers. But it was the weapon used that fascinated them; it was a semi-automatic German Luger, vintage 1939 – 1945, which used superb brass-cased ammunition. A relic of previous conflicts which would undoubtedly prove untraceable even if found: unusual weapons invariably had their serial numbers removed.

The victim was similarly problematic despite his fingerprints being on their database. By general agreement his name was Haz, or Hazariah; surname unknown, nationality debatable, but wanted by Europol and several Middle-Eastern countries for previous atrocities in addition to the assault on 'La Belle Equipe' in Paris.

'It's a pity that brute will never stand trial; we might have cleared up some cold-cases if he had,' one of the officers remarked.

'Nah,' replied his colleague, 'a waste of time and money, this way is best.'

'If we think like that we are no better than they are.'

Later that same Friday, Clive Scott and Jamal returned to London via the EuroStar. It had taken considerable persuasion from Clive to convince Icarus that he should leave Brussels: part of him believed he had more counter-terrorism work to do in Europe. That part was his heart; but in the end his head won that battle, expertly assisted by Clive who proved that since his mission had supposedly been instigated by a man known to be dead, it was quite obviously invalid.

'But where do we go from here and what do we do next?' He asked Clive as the train gathered speed.

'First London, to connect body and soul together again. Then we reunite you with MI6, and track down the devious bastard that sent you, on a false prospectus, straight into the lions' den.'

'And then?'

'And then we ask him why he did it.'

TWENTY

Friday 20th November 2015
The American Hospital, Paris

Louise Maigret's health was greatly improved that morning; a good night's sleep and the knowledge that Philippe was safe had wrought the miracle. Her doctors decided that she was well enough for an angiogram to be performed: a stent was later inserted in an artery near her heart.

Meanwhile Meg took the opportunity to have a quick breakfast in the hospital's coffee shop. She was enjoying an excellent re-fill when her phone rang.

'Meg? It's Tom Aitkens. Please don't hang up I need to speak with you about…'

'Why would I?'

'Because you sent me a somewhat terse text the other day…'

'It wasn't terse, it was *succinct*. And I was under a great deal of pressure at the time.'

'You didn't trust me when I offered help.'

'Perhaps I didn't trust myself. Anyway, that's water under the proverbial now. What do you want, Tom?'

'I wondered if there was any news.'

'There is and I'm pleased you phoned because I need to ask you about Switzerland.'

'Sorry, did I miss something?'

'Or more specifically, what do you know about specialist clinics in Switzerland?'

'So that's where he is? What happened to him?'

'I don't know. The Minister was short on detail when he phoned last night. All I was told is that he was safe but injured, and that he would be in a clinic in Switzerland today. But I don't know which one.'

'Hmm. Interesting. Do you know how or where he was found?'

'No.'

'Hmm. Not fit enough to travel as far as Paris from wherever he was located, so Switzerland was closer. Either that or the treatment needed is so specific that Switzerland was the best option,' he said, thinking aloud.

'Maybe.'

'Zurich gets my vote. Somewhere in the vicinity of Zurich.'

'Why?'

'Because there's so much filthy lucre sloshing around Zurich that their clinics lack for absolutely nothing. You name it, they've got it: doctors, skilled surgeons and state of the art medical equipment. If you'll let me help I'll make more enquiries. Will you?'

'Yes. Thank you, I'd be very grateful.'

'Okay. I'll get right on it, then back to you ASAP.'

'Wait – do you speak any German?'

'What, me? No, not really; I'm American in case you've forgotten. Why?'

'I wondered if, given your former association with the CIA…'

'Homeland Security, dear heart. *Never* the other bunch of desperados.'

'Yes, sorry, my apologies. I wondered if you'd ever come across the phrase Denn die Todten…'

'*"What ails my love? The moon shines bright; Bravely the dead men ride through the night."* It's Rossetti's translation of an old German poem.'

'The English Pre-Raphaelite?'

'That's him; and the precocious young smart-ass did it when he was sixteen. I studied it at college; my first degree was Liberal Arts.'

'So who's the smarty-pants now?'

'Touché. And before you ask, that's almost the limit of my French. But take some advice; don't repeat that phrase in public again. Nor the initials, in fact *especially* not the initials.'

'DDTRS why…?

'Dear God – what did I just say? You have probably heard of a right-wing political party in Germany, the AfD – Alternative for Deutschland? Although it was very new it narrowly missed gaining a seat in the Bundestag in the election two years ago.'

'So?'

'So the AfD has a number of rivals. The main one's located in Chemnitz, previously known as Karl-Marx Stadt when it was part of East Germany. After the Berlin

Wall came down it seems that Chemnitz underwent a kind of gradual conversion to the extent that a quarter of the population now supports the right of politics. And they're especially wary of the wave of non-white or non-Christian migrants arriving in the country at present.'

'A fertile breeding ground for the right?'

'Indeed; the tip of a dangerous iceberg. The group whose initials you recently mentioned and which I won't repeat, is gaining considerable support from what I hear.'

'From whence do you hear this?'

'From having my ear to the ground, not official sources.'

'Hmm. But why this old poem, and those initials?'

'Read the runes, honey. It's the message about certain people moving fast; *dead* people. *Long dead people!*'

'Not the... head honcho in previous times?'

'The very same; the old house painter himself. May he *never* rest in peace or anything remotely like it.'

Not long after this conversation ended, Carole arrived together with Rosa, who would stay with Louise while Meg went home for a shower and a change of clothes.

'Ready to leave, Madame?'

'I will be, just as soon as I've checked on Louise's progress.'

'Already done, we asked before we came to find you. Everything went better than expected, she's in recovery and will be returned to her room in an hour or two.'

'That's wonderful news, thanks. Now I'm ready to leave when you are.'

Soon after they set off for the 6th her phone rang again. This time it was Christophe with an update.

'We arrived at the clinic safely after a long delay due to the rough weather. And now he's having another blood transfusion.'

'Another – when was the first? And where?'

There was a pause before he replied.

'This is what I can tell you at present. He was found in rural Belgium, in a poor condition and suffering from exposure. He was taken to a small hospital nearby and soon after arrival was given an emergency transfusion because of considerable blood loss. That's all I can say now.'

'No, you could tell me where he is and how soon I can see him.'

'I wish I could, but it's not possible.'

'Not possible? May I remind you, Monsieur, that I'm his wife?'

'That fact is not disputed, Madame. I will phone again when there's more that I can disclose. For now please be assured that he's safe, comfortable, and receiving the best possible treatment.'

'How long before I can see him?'

But he had already terminated the call.

She uttered some uncomplimentary words about the Minister which drew a snigger from Carole.

'He's not really a heartless beast, Madame. He has limits to his authority as do all Government officials.'

'Forgive me my dear, I was just venting my frustration. I know he's a good man and an even better friend. You couldn't help hearing our conversation; do you have a translation for me.'

'Translation? But sir was speaking English.'

'Of course he was. But how about a police-speak translation? Any thoughts? Strictly off the record naturally, and never to be repeated outside of this vehicle.'

Carole thought for a few moments.

'I believe, in circumstances such as these, it is not abnormal for... er victims of crime to be kept... er *isolated* from their relatives until such time as...'

'Dear God Carole, if you go on this way I'll need a translator to translate what you've said. Plain speech, if you please and remember that our conversation is not being recorded therefore it will remain private.'

'I understand. Sorry, Madame.'

'And that's another thing. Why won't you use my Christian name, as I've invited you to do more than once?'

'It would not be appropriate. It's a question of etiquette.'

'And Philippe? How do you address him when you cross paths at HQ or elsewhere?'

'I say Chief Superintendent Maigret, or sir.'

'I give up! Please continue with your take on what the Minister said.'

'As soon as he's well enough they will debrief him before his memory is er compromised by conversations with his family. He'll have a great deal of useful information.'

'Thank you. Although I'd have thought that all the sedation he's been given might do far more harm to his memory than speaking to me would.'

'I tend to agree.'

'This process could take days, couldn't it?'

'Yes.'

'Well I'm not prepared to wait that long, as I will tell the Minister the next time he phones.'

They arrived at the Maigret apartment building but the last ten minutes of their journey had been in silence; each preoccupied with recent events.

'Shall I wait for you here, Madame?'

'No. I have some phone calls to make. I'll be in touch when I'm ready to leave. Or I could take a taxi – whatever is easier.'

'Please text me, I won't be far away.'

Saint Luke Clinic, near Zurich
Friday 20th November 2015

When Philippe Maigret finally woke the day was almost over and it was early evening. His throat was sore, his mouth parched, and his vision blurred. And, for the second time in a few days he had no idea where he was.

'Water.' He whispered.

A hand guided a glass with a straw towards his mouth and he slurped it quickly.

After the second glass, his eyes began to focus.

'You're back! Welcome to the first day of the rest of your life, old friend,' a familiar voice said.

'Christophe?'

'Indeed it is,' he replied, kissing him on his forehead and both cheeks. 'You've had us worried; you really should resist your tendency for spontaneous tourism. How do you feel?'

'Like I've been in hell and I'm only just out on parole. Where am I? Where's Meg? I need to see her.' As his eyes did a further re-set he looked around the room. 'I'm in a hospital – in Paris? How did I get here? And why do I have a cannula in my hand? My body aches everywhere, and my bum hurts. Oh God – my anus hurts and my rectum is on fire!'

'You're in a clinic near Zurich,' Christophe said, pressing the help switch. 'We arrived here by a medevac flight.'

'From where?'

'Belgium. The patient's in need of pain relief,' he said into the monitor.

A nurse hurried in, took Maigret's temperature and felt his pulse. Then she gently turned over his hand revealing a small button in the palm.

'Press the button three times please,' she said.

Maigret did and the relief was immediate.

'When the pain begins press it just as you did then. But do it as *soon* as it begins; don't wait until the pain becomes severe. And don't worry; the button delivers a precise amount which means an overdose is not possible.'

'What is it?'

The nurse hesitated.

'Morphine. You had an intricate operation soon after you arrived to correct an internal er irregularity. The procedure went very well, but the pain will come and go – in waves – for the next day or so. When you feel it starting press the button three times immediately to get on top of it: don't let the pain win. And I repeat – this system delivers a precise measure, therefore it's not possible to have too much.'

'Do you know anything about my recent er experiences, Christophe?' He asked as she left the room.

'Yes. In fact I know a great deal. I read the Belgian doctor's notes at the hospital. Dr Defoe was… quite meticulous.'

'And my wife?'

'Nothing really. She knows that when found you were half-dead with exposure and that you had an injury that required a blood transfusion. But that's all.'

'Is she here?'

'No, she's in Paris. I'm sorry to tell you that your Mother had a problem with her heart. Everything's fine now, but she remains in hospital and Meg's with her.'

'Oh, Lord. Which hospital?'

'The American Hospital.'

'Why there?'

'I think it was Meg's decision.'

'I need a phone. They stole my vanilla version and my father's watch.'

'Your watch is safe, Clive Scott has it.'

'Clive? How?'

'It's a long story. Let's order you something to eat and I'll tell you everything.'

'Not hungry. No food until after I've spoken to Meg. Give me your phone, Christophe.'

'I can't, you know that. Full debrief first – that's the established procedure – most of which you wrote.'

'Yes I did, and I was wrong. To deny contact with a loved one after a trauma is cruel and unhelpful. We should at least allow a short phone conversation for reassurance, if that's requested.'

'Hmm. Private or monitored?'

'Private, of course; it's the only option. Anything else would add grievance to injury. Now give me your bloody phone!'

'You always were an uncompromising bastard,' he muttered, handing over his phone as he spoke. 'The exact location must not be disclosed until after the completion of the debrief. Understood?'

'Yeah, yeah – I know the drill. And that stipulation needs to be changed too.'

'Hmm… We'll see. Now I'll give you five minutes of privacy while I arrange some food for both of us. Agreed?'

'Agreed. And thanks.'

At that time Meg was speaking with Sergeant Jacques Laurent, a valued member of Philippe's squad. He had heard a whisper on the police grapevine that his chief might have been found and had phoned for confirmation.

'Yes, he's definitely been found, and he's safe in a clinic in Switzerland. You can tell Georges – how is he, by the way – but no one else for now, please.'

'Georges is doing well, Madame, and he'll be all the better for hearing the good news.'

After a few minutes they ended their conversation. As they did her phone rang again. She answered it quickly as she could see it was from Christophe.

'More news?' She asked before the caller spoke.

'Darling, it's me. And it's wonderful to hear your voice again.'

As he spoke the feisty furry one leapt into her lap rubbing her face against the phone and purring loudly.

'Oh… oh… my love…'

'What's that noise? It sounds like you have a tractor next to you.'

'It's Moggs; she's telling you how pleased she is to hear from you. She's been a nightmare since you… Oh – say again that it's you, I'm afraid I'm dreaming. I can't believe it's really you!'

'It's no dream, darling. Are you crying?'

'You know I am. But that's good because they're happy tears this time. How long before I can see you or you are home with me?'

'I'm not sure. But you can be certain that it will be as soon as possible.'

'The debrief?'

'Yes, but I'll get that over in two days, if I can.'

'So you can't travel yet? What has happened to you, love?'

'I had... an operation some hours ago which was er successful, but I believe I'm to be kept under observation for a few days.'

'An operation?'

'Yes, it was a... procedure really, to repair a few concerns that the doctors had. It's all fine now.'

'I know the fanatics hurt you. Your blood was found at the restaurant. Oh, and I have your wedding ring; Louis returned it and that meant so much to me.'

'Louis?'

'Yes, the elderly man who was standing in the doorway at the rear of 'La Belle Equipe'. He saw you drop your handkerchief with your ring inside in the gutter. He recognised you.'

'Oh God bless him! I thought he knew me but I couldn't be sure. So my ring is safe and my father's watch too. And that's wonderful.'

'I don't have your watch darling, just your wedding ring.'

'Yes, but that's okay; Clive Scott has my father's watch.'

'He does? He phoned me asking for Christophe's private phone number but I'm not sure what day that was.'

'You gave it to him?'

'Yes. He said it was to help you.'

'Did he indeed? Interesting. I think some of the puzzle is beginning to take shape.'

'Puzzle? I don't understand.'

'Neither do I, but I will soon.'

At that moment Christophe entered the room.

'Time's up,' he whispered, tapping his watch for good measure.

'I have to end now, darling. I'll phone you again tomorrow.' He looked pointedly at Christophe as he spoke. He raised his eyebrows but said nothing. 'Until then, take care of yourself, and know that I love you and I always will – come what may.'

'I agreed to one phone call. For *reassurance.*'

'Did you? Well that's another restriction that we need to change. In fact I suspect we may have to re-write the whole damn post-trauma debriefing manual. Now where's the food; I'm absolutely starving. And by the way, exactly what part did Scotland Yard play in my discovery?'

TWENTY-ONE

Saturday 21st November 2015
Saint Luke Clinic

'Now down to business,' Christophe said, as they finished their breakfast the next morning. 'Or would you prefer to take a little nap before we begin to debrief?'

'I'm fine. I've been sedated or sleeping for days! I'll let you know if things change,' Maigret said, pressing the button on his palm three times.

'Very well. First the formalities. This debrief is taking place in the Clinic of Saint Luke, greater-Zurich on Saturday 21st November 2015 at er – 11.45 am. Present are Christophe Saint-Valéry, Minister of Police and...'

'Chief Superintendent Philippe Maigret. Hold on; are we being recorded?'

'Of course, you know all debriefs are recorded.'

'So this room's bugged and has been from the time I woke yesterday?'

'No. The recording started when I said "now down to business".'

'I don't see any recording gear.'

'Nor will you.'

'Then how?'

'It's being transmitted via my phone to an outside source. And when we've finished speaking the recording will end. It's the new technology.'

'Hmm.'

'Tell me what you remember of that night a week ago.'

'I remember… a lovely young woman dying on the pavement outside a restaurant… her name was Marianne. And there was no one to mourn her, except me…'

'But before that, where were you?' He asked gently.

'Oh… yes. Before that Georges Martin and I were on our way to the concert hall…'

'The Bataclan?'

'Yes. While en route we were diverted to the Rue Charonne; the restaurant 'La Belle Equipe' was under attack. We could hear the gunfire and grenades while we were still a fair way off. When we arrived we drove slowly down the rue; there was a group of people standing in front of the restaurant 'Septime' next to the one attacked. There were bodies strewn on the pavement and across the tables where the people had been dining. I insisted that Georges stop the car… I countermanded the orders we had been given. He protested but I was adamant. I take full responsibility for what happened next.'

'Go on.'

'People had been slaughtered. Blood everywhere. Running relentlessly down the gutters: a tidal wave of innocent blood. I thought someone might still be alive

– that's why I made Georges stop. But the first people I examined were dead; as those bystanders had said they were. I identified myself as a police officer, produced my ID and said they should return to 'Septime', secure the doors and wait for the squad cars that were on the way.

From the corner of my eye I saw a slight movement: it was Marianne with a gaping wound near her liver, her sweet face masked with pain. I couldn't… I couldn't stop the blood… but I tried… dear God *how* I tried! I hurt her… even while trying to help. Why wouldn't the blood stop? Jesus – why? I knelt beside her and held her in my arms… she just closed her eyes… she was gone. I… I felt then that my entire life had been a sham… a miserable obscene failure. If I couldn't save Marianne then what was the point of my existence? I lay down beside her and railed at the Almighty for not saving her life while begging him to take mine instead. I think I stayed like that for a long time cursing the heavens while mourning a girl I didn't even know. Then I heard Georges call out to me. A warning. But it was too late.'

Christophe looked carefully at his old friend. Face drawn and pallid, yet glistening with perspiration; blank eyes sunk back in their sockets. Memory or morphine? Which had done the most damage? He knew they had to stop.

'Let's have a coffee break now – shall we?'

'No, not yet – just a little longer. I don't want to be asked to relive that scene again.'

'Okay.'

'At the same time as I heard Georges' warning the restaurant door opened. He stood in the doorway and looked at me: I knew I'd been recognised. But I must go back – I must retrace my steps. After Marianne died I laid her down on the ground and covered her with a tablecloth. As I did my Sig fell from the inside pocket of my jacket. That had never happened before; I felt it was an omen – a *potent* omen. I tucked my ID and the Sig under her body: she was soft and warm. I was still kneeling on the ground when the door began opening. I tried to get my revolver out of the leg pouch but my hands wouldn't work properly; I fumbled and it fell to the ground.'

'That's enough now, Philippe.'

'Not yet – just a little more. When the door opened and he recognised me, I realised that I was, in that very moment, looking into the face of absolute evil. He smiled as he raised his weapon. We were so close that I could smell his stinking body: he could have killed me and I thought that was his intention. But instead he smiled again – an ugly smirk – and deliberately aimed at my shoulder. I believe he meant to break it but perhaps he was distracted because all he managed was to remove a piece of the Humerus bone.'

'How's the wound now?'

'I'm still aware of it but it's no longer painful, just tender.'

'That's good. Now you really must rest. I have already debriefed Inspector Martin: there's no need for us to rake over old ground. Coffee first, then you need to relax. Have a nap, if you can. I might decide to do the same; we both had a late night.'

'What about Clive Scott and his part in this account?'

'All in good time: we will delve into that matter this afternoon.'

Philippe, who had been sitting in his bed propped up on three pillows during the entire debrief, slid down under the covers and within a few minutes was soundly asleep. His coffee remained untouched on the cabinet next to him.

When he finally woke, Christophe was sitting in the chair on the window side of the bed as he had been during the interview; however now he looked unusually dishevelled.

'How long did I actually sleep and what happened to you in the meantime?'

'Over three hours: it appears I became so relaxed that I slid off the chair right in the middle of a vividly sensual dream and hit my head.'

Philippe chuckled.

'Oh dear, that's a pity. I mean the disrupted erotic episode, not the bump on the head.'

'It's all very well for you to find it amusing. You had the luxury of a bed, not an uncomfortable chair that's probably done irreparable damage to my back.'

'It can't have been *too* uncomfortable…'

'Well it damn-well was! Now, do you want some lunch?'

'Not sure.'

'How about a bowl of chicken soup and a toasted ham and cheese croissant?'

'Isn't that rather a clash of cultures?'

'Maybe, but it's what I had and I enjoyed it. Do you want it or not?'

'Okay. And a beer or a glass of wine.'

Christophe left the room and returned a few minutes later.

'It's on the way, minus the alcohol. Not permitted for the next few days.'

'Because of the morphine?'

'Who knows? Hospital personnel are a law unto themselves; best not to give them any backchat.'

'Will you tell me about Clive's involvement while I'm eating? It will save time.' He said as the food arrived.

'Yes, that's a good idea.'

'Right down to business again,' he repeated for the benefit of the recording.

'On Wednesday morning Chief Inspector Scott received a phone call, via Scotland Yard's helpline, from a man who declined to give his name. At first Clive assumed that he was a crank and was inclined to hang-up except for the telephone operator's comment that the call was from outside the UK and the caller had asked for him by name. Clive didn't recognise the voice although the caller thought he should, so he told him to state his business or desist. At that point he said he'd been set-up and was far from home.'

'Set-up by whom?'

'The very question Clive asked. The caller said it was the people for whom he worked and that Clive had arranged the job for him.'

'The posh boy! Didn't I think his voice seemed familiar? Of course it was him.'

'Sorry?'

'There were three in the gang that abducted me at the restaurant. I saw the leader – a swarthy beefy man, and a weedy young fellow with a scraggly beard, but not the third man who drove the van. Then I was blindfolded and I had to remain that way for the duration, except when I was locked in my room. So I never saw the third man nor the one who was waiting at the place where I was held. To keep track of them I gave them nicknames. Where was I kept?'

'Deserted farmhouse in Belgium. But tell me about the posh boy. Why did you give him that name?'

'Because he had an English accent: very precise, polished and with Oxbridge tempi.'

'Oxbridge?'

'Educated at either Oxford or Cambridge University: RP – received pronunciation.'

'I see; I've learnt some new words today. So he was the posh boy – what about the others?'

'The beefy one was the leader. I couldn't decide whether he was a sociopath or a psychopath. In the end I chose the latter: unfortunately it transpired that I was right. The English lad called him Haz – but only once or twice.'

'And the other two?'

'The worrywart and the geek. The worrywart, although he seemed anxious about everything – I could hear him constantly fiddling with his worry beads – had some medical training. I believe he patched up my arm, yet he also enjoyed inflicting pain. The geek was their tech guy. He tried to hack into the HQ's computer and probably my phone too. But they'd have learnt nothing from it even if he'd succeeded. He had a terrible case of flatulence; irritable bowel syndrome I presume.'

'That brings us back to how Clive played a major role in your release.'

'How?'

'When he eventually realised who the caller was, he asked him if he knew anything about your whereabouts. Not actually mentioning your name as it was not a safe line. He said he knew where you had been the previous night. At which point Clive asked him directly if he'd played any part in the attacks in Paris. Instead of answering the question he suggested they meet that afternoon at the Musée des Beaux-Arts in Brussels, near the Bruegel painting; the one depicting Icarus falling to earth.'

'Jamal Ahmadi, code name Icarus, who MI6 presumed had gone rogue had resurfaced to ask for Clive's support.'

'Precisely.'

'He said he would reveal everything when they met, but made it clear that he had been following orders. Then he asked for his email address so he could send some coordinates of your possible location. He told Clive to act quickly as the gang might bolt when they realised he'd gone. He added that your situation was dire, and to be careful who he trusted because Belgian security was probably compromised. "Speak to our mutual friend's closest allies – no one else" is how he ended that conversation.'

'So Clive phoned Meg to get your private details then he contacted you.'

'Yes, and I sent a helicopter and a squad from Strasbourg but you'd already been moved. They found the evidence you left in the bathroom and your blood on the floor of the room in which you slept.'

'But in the end it was an old Belgian farmer who saved my life! Who'd have imagined it possible?'

'The Almighty works in mysterious ways…'

'Indeed.'

'Before we end this session, I'd like you to take a look at something for me,' he said, delving into his briefcase on the floor near his chair.

'What?'

'A report from the Belgium police about some killings that took place in Brussels in the early hours of yesterday morning. They thought we might be interested.' He passed the document to Philippe who read it quickly.

'Any post-morten photos?'

'Not yet, but we'll get them very soon. Is it them? And did you take note of the weapon used to kill their leader?'

'Yes. Although I didn't see of all them there's no doubt in my mind that this is the gang who took me. The weapon's unusual. Interesting.'

'An antique German Luger. A war souvenir, probably. Has someone done you a favour?'

'How the hell should I know?' He said angrily.

'Philippe – no one, least of all me, will point the finger at *anyone* as far as this killing is concerned.'

'The media will, once they know a German war relic was used for him. And the survivors from the 'La Belle Equipe' raid will be interviewed. Who knows what they might contribute? Nothing remains private for long these days – you know that. And the more that people try to hide the details, the more the media will dig away until they know everything – or think they do. I might as well stand on a soap-box in the middle of La Concorde and inform the whole world that I was raped! Why the hell did you tell him anyway?'

'Who says I did? Jamal was certainly aware of Haz and his sexual deviancy. He wanted to help you but was unarmed; that's why he left the farmhouse. Clive's an honourable man; he will not betray that confidence. Stay calm, my friend. The serial number on the Luger would have been removed long ago: even if it were found identification would be impossible. Why would you imagine that Clive had any involvement in what happened in Brussels anyway?'

'Because I know his father served in the British Army of the Rhine in post-war Berlin. He's sure to have brought a souvenir or two home with him; they all did from what I hear.'

'A coincidence: which proves absolutely nothing, as any first year law student would tell you.'

TWENTY-TWO

After she left the Embassy Giles and Fleur retired to their respective rooms; he to write a report of his meeting with his client and she to ponder more about her father and his supposed connection with Henry Livingstone. Saint or sinner? Why should he be either; wasn't everything multifaceted now?

Her shoes hit the floor with a satisfying thud and she stretched comfortably on the bed, the better to think. When Meg made her confident assertion that Livingstone was the MI6 mole she had been inclined to dismiss it as nonsense, but the more she thought about it, the more likely it seemed. She followed the train of her thoughts starting at possible, travelling past unreasonable, then on to quite-likely, most probable and undeniable until finally she reached her destination: complete *certainty*. Why else did he always arrive at Willows Glen unannounced, his excuse being that he had just been in the neighbourhood or passing through? And why was Rob ambivalent about whether or not he knew him? Yes, her lovely old lad had dementia but that usually affected his short-term memory more than anything else. Would he really forget an old pub friend? *Not bloody likely*, she thought. *So what's Livingstone's game? What's in it for him? There must be some benefit, unless he's a crackpot which was quite feasible.*

In desperation she phoned Quinn whose mind, she had reluctantly accepted, was sometimes more finely-tuned to rational thought than hers.

'Quinn! I need your help.' She said peremptorily.

'Sorry? Did you not mean "good afternoon David, man of my dreams, husband-to-be, I miss you and can't wait to be held in your manly arms again"?'

'Yeah, yeah – what you said, you Edwardian-throwback loony. And besides all that I need your help.'

'Speak, beloved. Unburden your soul to me.'

'Have you been reading Keats again?'

'I may have been palely loitering in his general direction whilst ailing because of your absence.'

'More likely an excess of pale ale last night. Out with the lads were we?'

'I'd plead the fifth but for the fact that we don't have a written Constitution.'

'No, but the Magna Carta gave us the right to trial by jury which one of us might need very soon if you don't sober up and listen to why I need your help.'

'It is late afternoon and I'm as sober as a… No, let me put that another way; light of my life, how may I help you?'

'Listen without speaking, while I tell you everything.'

He did; he was usually a good listener.

'So – what do you think of all that, David?' She asked when she finished.

'David is it now? You must really need my help this time, Fleur-flower.'

'Well?'

'If you'd told me this yesterday, I'd have said it was pure invention from a woman under incredible pressure. Any news on Philippe yet?'

'No, but she finally admitted that as we thought, he's missing and never was in hospital.'

'I hope he's still alive.'

'He survived the assault on the restaurant that much we know, but the creeps took him with them when they left. They'll try to ransom him I suppose, but no approach has been made yet.'

'The French won't be telling Meg everything they know. They'll be operating through every back-channel they can find. They can't afford to lose a man like him; he's too valuable to them.'

'He won't tell them anything.'

No, he won't – and that's the danger; they might inadvertently kill him in the extraction process, Quinn thought.

'But to return to your story, sweetheart. I'd have dismissed it yesterday…'

'But not now?'

'No, not now. I visited your dad this afternoon. He was having a good day; only wandered off the lucid path once or twice, but otherwise he was almost his old self. And yes, I found a few more assorted pills in his cabinet drawer which I removed while he wasn't looking. Then Giles phoned with a query about some German phrase and while he was occupied I looked through the small pile of books Rob had on top of the cabinet. And that's when I made a discovery; a folded letter between the pages of one of the books. It was from the Jericho Publishing Company in Leipzig enclosing a cheque which was four months old.'

'I don't understand. Jericho's in central Oxford. I know it well, as do you. Leipzig's in Germany, isn't it?'

'Yep. It's about a two hour drive south of Berlin in what was formerly East Germany.'

'But what connection could this company have with my dad?'

'The very question I asked myself at the time. I'd have quizzed Rob but unfortunately he went off on a little path-meandering after his conversation with Giles.'

'In former times he had contracts with a number of newspapers who published his crosswords, but they were all in the UK as far as I know. I don't remember him being published in Germany or anywhere else in Europe.'

'Nor was he it would seem, until recently. When I went home I phoned Jericho Publishing and after some unethical verbal footwork, persuaded them to answer a simple question: what was their cheque in favour of Robert de Montfort – as yet uncashed – actually for?'

'What did they say?'

'They said it was a Royalty payment for crosswords they had been publishing throughout Germany for the past year or so.'

'But dad hasn't been able to create any crosswords for ages.'

'Exactly. Then they told me that these were er… how did he put it – *the vintage crosswords*. The vintage *cryptic* crosswords, to be precise, as the Germans always try to be. Or, as the helpful gentleman to whom I spoke said, "der Jahrgang", which I think means the same thing.'

'What was the value of the cheque?'

'A little over ten thousand Euros.'

'What? For one crossword puzzle?'

'No, you haven't been paying attention, love. Jericho had been running his puzzles in both fortnightly and monthly magazines all over Germany. That cheque was a Royalty payment for the previous quarter. Apparently the Germans greatly enjoy Rob's work. But the most significant part of my conversation with the helpful Herr was that this cheque was just the most recent in a series of cheques they'd issued to Rob. So the question now becomes…'

'What happened to the previous ones?'

'Exactly. And here's another question; how long has it been since your dad visited Germany?'

'Yonks. At least five years, I'd say. So?'

'So who negotiated and signed the contract with Jericho Publishing? His agent, maybe?'

'No, his agent died years ago and after that Dad acted for himself. Of course Giles helped him with the finer legal aspects, but that was all. Dad had a good idea of what his creative work was worth by then; he named his price and usually that's what he received. What the hell's been going on?'

'At a rough guess I'd say that someone's been impersonating Rob and signing contracts in his name while collecting the Royalty payments. But something must have gone wrong with the last payment and it ended up with the right person instead of the fake.'

'He's been scammed, the poor old lad. It's intellectual property theft – what bastards!'

'Or worse.'

'What could be worse than that?'

'How about cross-border fanatics and spies?'

'Henry Livingstone included?'

'Absolutely. I asked the German Herr with the unprounceable name if he'd actually met Rob, and he said he had. Then I asked him if he could describe him. Roughly of course, since he had only met him once. "Oh no," he replied, "I've met Herr de Montfort many times; he usually delivers the new batch of crosswords himself. His German is very good, very fluent". Does that sound like your dad?'

'He knows some German but he's definitely not fluent by any means.'

'Exactly. Nor could he be described as being medium height, solid build, with brown hair, a moustache and a devotee of Regimental ties.'

'Dad's almost six feet tall; or he used to be. And he's rather on the lean and hungry side these days.'

'Perzactly. So that brings us to the nitty-gritty. I understand that earlier this year Rob went walkabout for a few days. Why didn't you tell me, love? Why did I have to hear it from Meg?'

'Er… well… it was in March and things were a little rocky between us at the time if you recall.'

'Rocky? As in you'd just ended our engagement, rocky?'

'Yes.'

'And you thought that because of our split I wouldn't care if Rob disappeared for three days? Dear God, love – don't you know me better than that? Didn't it occur to you that I might have been able to help find him?'

'I'm sorry, David; it was a terrible time for us, we were frantic with worry. I know I wasn't thinking straight and neither was mum.'

'Then he just turned up as right as rain?'

'No, far from it. That's when we noticed a huge change in his behaviour: the confusion was greater and his memory far worse. It was like he went from third gear to reverse overnight. Would you do something for me, David?'

'Of course – anything.'

'If you still have the photo of Livingstone from the CCTV at Willows Glen…'

'I do. It's fairly grainy but he's still identifiable. Why?'

'Would you send it to Clive Scott for me?'

'Why him? I showed it to some of my contacts in the security service; if they didn't recognise him, why would Scotland Yard?'

'I don't know, but Meg trusts him. And he speaks German.'

'He doesn't like me. And he's a hot-head.'

'And you're not?'

'No. I'm er… *passionate* – he's Rob Roy reimagined.'

'Nonsense. Send it to me then and I'll forward it.'

'No, I'll do it. But I expect some major brownie-points in return.'

'And you shall have them. Will you meet Unc and me at St Pancras tomorrow?'

'Yes. I want to collect those points as soon as I can.'

'Me too.'

However David Quinn did not email the photograph to Clive Scott immediately. Nor had he promised Fleur that he would, although he knew that was what she expected. However, that short delay would prove fortuitous; timing is everything in life. So while he mulled things over in his mind for the rest of the day, events were in play elsewhere to ensure that the person who most needed to see it, *would*.

How much should I divulge to Scott by way of an introduction to the Livingstone image. Very little, his subconscious warned, never volunteer any information for which you haven't been asked. *For goodness sake – we are actually on the same side!* Ever heard of turf wars, Dave? Or funding skirmishes?

The next morning, after a very good night's sleep and an indulgently late breakfast, he decided on the short and sweet approach. He sent a concise text to Clive Scott:

Good morning, Chief Inspector Scott, Fleur de Montfort has asked me to send you this photograph of a rather odd character who's been visiting her father at his nursing home. Do you recognise him? Apologies for the poor quality of the image. No trace on the usual data-bases. Sincerely, David Quinn.

When his message signalled its arrival on Scott's phone it woke him from a pleasant little nap on his Eurostar return to London with Jamal. He sighed and uttered an ancient Gaelic obscenity when he saw the sender's name. *Two clever by half,* had been his initial assessment of young Master Quinn, and he had seen no reason to revise that opinion with subsequent contact. He read the text, looked carefully at the attached photograph, and then looked again.

It can't be, he thought, glancing at Jamal, *there's no getting lucky with police work: that's constant hard slog with the occasional drop of good* fortune. *This is too easy.*

'Here, Sonny-Jim,' he said, passing his phone to Jamal, 'have a shufti at this and tell me what you think.'

He studied the image intently. His hands were unsteady as he returned the phone.

'That's him. That's the fellow who called himself Alexander Duncan when he sent me into the unknown. But he's ditched the moustache he had when I met him.'

'I'd say that moustache comes and goes as circumstances dictate. Facial hair is too easily recalled by witnesses to be long-term useful for those up to no good. He has a new name too: Henry Livingstone.'

'Do you know him?'

'No, never laid eyes on him as far as I can tell. What's the chance Livingstone's not his real name?'

'Very high, I'd say.'

'Agreed. How about the odds on him not actually existing as far as official records are concerned?'

'Same odds as before.'

'Yep. I think we might have stumbled on something considerably bigger than we imagined.'

Clive picked up his phone and called David Quinn.

'Want to join me and a friend for morning tea at the Yard around 11 am on Monday, Mr Quinn?'

'What me, the GCHQ renegade? Is this an *official* invitation, Chief Inspector?'

'Any more official and it would be written on Buckingham Palace note-paper and signed Elizabeth R!'

TWENTY-THREE

The debriefing was finished in a day and a half, although the Minister had many more questions that he could, or indeed, *should* have asked his friend. But during the process, even with the regular breaks which he stipulated, sometimes including a nap for the patient, he had become increasingly concerned about his physical and mental well-being.

As the narrative approached the events leading to the sexual assault Philippe's anxiety reached such an extreme level that he gripped the sides of his chair so tightly that his knuckles turned white under the strain.

Good God… can it be possible that Christophe thinks something in my behaviour encouraged the psycho? Does he imagine that I led him on, or indicated in some way that what he did was what I wanted? Oh Lord – I insisted on a bath! Did he take that as an invitation?

Steady on, Phil – get a grip! You're a self-confessed heterosexual. We know that and so does Christophe.

So you're back are you? Where have you been all this time?

We can't get past the damn medication and sleeping pills; *they* scramble our signal. Make 'em ease up on all that crap, Phil. If they don't you'll end up a bloody basket-case! You do realise that you have an addictive personality, don't you?

That's a damn lie – I don't!

If you say so, Phil – we only report what we detect.

Tell me about Christophe – what's he thinking? We can't read him very well. He's completely out of his depth now and overwhelmed with guilt because of what he's done to you. Oh – wait a minute. Now he's thinking his questions have done you more harm than that bastard Haz ever did.

Let him know he's wrong – he hasn't even come close!

Can't. He's one buttoned-up dude, that one. He's just closed us down again. Subconscious FM going off air for urgent maintenance and signal boost. But we'll be back, Phil. Now tell them you need a break.

'I need a break now, Christophe. And I want an immediate reduction in my sedation and other treatment.'

'Why? Don't the doctors believe you need it?'

'It's doing me more harm than good. I can feel that it is.'

At that point the alarmed chief consultant, who had been observing from an adjacent room albeit without the sound, hurried in insisting that there be no further questions until he was satisfied the patient was fit to continue. It seems that doctor was an excellent lip-reader although he wisely kept that information to himself.

That night Maigret's temperature hovered between 103 and 104 degrees Fahrenheit, while the nightmares, which the sedation had barely subdued, increased substantially. The doctors began an urgent discussion to determine what to do next, apart from increasing the intravenous anti-biotics. Did the patient's sudden decline come from physical or emotional anguish? Or even a combination of the two; that was the main subject of debate. They knew that the sodomy had occurred on Wednesday night; could the fever be the beginning of a sexually-transmitted disease? Dr Defoe had taken sufficient blood from Maigret on the day he was admitted to his hospital for use in whatever tests might be necessary later. The clinic had already carried out a forensic analysis of some of that precious fluid.

One test had been for HIV which could detect the presence of antibodies; the immune system's response to infection. None had been found. However the doctors knew that for the majority of people, HIV testing would not be accurate until four to six weeks after possible infection. And, for some it might take even longer – up to three months – for detectable antibodies to develop. This is known as "the window period". During this period, HIV tests might come back negative even though the person had the virus; HIV could be passed on to other people during that time.

'He should be isolated for a week while we embark on some experimental treatments,' one of the specialists said. 'That will hopefully allow time for the antibiotics to quell any emerging infection.'

'Have you read this man's medical file, Doctor? Shot, kidnapped, tortured, raped then left to die from blood loss and exposure on a compost heap. And now you want to segregate him while we use him as a lab rat? I refuse to be complicit in any further torture from the medical profession! Don't you remember the words of the oath we swore?'

The doctor who had made the suggestion looked mortified and no further mention of the offensive isolate word was heard.

Monday 23rd November 2015
Scotland Yard. London

David Quinn entered the building feeling like a criminal casing the Tower of London prior to stealing the Crown Jewels. Or, more likely, a youngster intent on nicking a packet of cigarettes while the shopkeeper's back was turned. He kept reminding himself that he had an *invitation* to be there, but that didn't seem to help.

He produced his temporary GCHQ ID for the benefit of the uniformed officer who approached him, adding that he had a meeting with Chief Inspector Clive Scott. The officer inspected both him and the ID with an expression that said *I don't think so, boyo!* Despite that look he was told to take the lift to an upper floor where he would be met by another officer.

When he finally arrived at the right door his knock was answered by a smiling Clive Scott who opened it looking as benign as his favourite uncle.

'Come on in, Mr Quinn. I presume you know this young man,' he said, shaking hands then indicating Jamal who quickly stood.

'Yes, I do – although not very well. How are you, Jamal?'

'Good, good – fine,' said Scott as the young men shook hands too.

Well, well, well. I do believe the old hot-head is almost as nervous as I am,' Quinn thought. *And who'd have ever imagined that was possible?*

They sat drinking their coffee in amiable but inconsequential conversation for a time then Quinn reached into his top pocket and produced the photograph of the man who was the reason for their meeting.

'Oops,' he said with a boyish grin, 'almost forgot about this grainy gem. May I introduce Mr Henry Livingstone of no fixed abode that we know about?'

'Or, as I know him, Alexander Duncan, ersatz MI6 officer, who sent me on a phoney assignment around Europe,' Jamal countered.

'Or, alternatively, Herr Robert de Montfort, as he is known in Leipzig, Germany.'

'What!' Clive and Jamal said in unison.

'A recently discovered third persona, thanks to my bride-to-be, the delectable Fleur de Montfort of Hampstead, newly returned from a quick trip to Paris with her uncle, Giles de Montfort, QC.'

At the mention of his arch-enemy's name, Clive scowled and uttered a few pithy words under his breath.

'Oh don't fret, Chief Inspector, he's well aware of his Scotland Yard alias and considers it a compliment. He says that when the guardians of the law consider him the Spawn of Satan it proves that he's doing his job properly. And that leads me to another apt disclosure. He has a client in a Paris prison who claims to know the name of an MI6 infiltrator. Interested?'

'Of course we are. Don't play games, Quinn, or you'll find yourself either in my bad books or with my boot up your backside; and neither of those options will be a pleasant experience.'

'He says the code name for this person is Icarus which, as we all know, is impossible,' Quinn said, ignoring Scott's outburst. 'As my intended and her friend, the wife of Chief Superintendent Maigret were quick to point out to Giles at the time.'

'Good God man; how do they know?'

'I'll give you three guesses,' said a sheepish Quinn. Jamal quickly leant over and whispered something in Scott's ear.

'Why can't the pair of you just roll-over and go off to sleep like any decent God-fearing man would?'

'I guess we're all different, Chief Inspector.'

Jamal attempted to stifle a laugh but failed.

'Okay, enough of the pleasantries, now I think that you, Mr Quinn, should start from the beginning.'

'I will, if I may ask you a question.'

'Ask away.'

'Are you still looking for the person or persons, who murdered Fleur's mother and grandmother? And are you aware that Fleur's father, who has dementia, disappeared earlier this year and was found in South London three days later in a confused mental state but looking physically as though he'd just been out for a stroll in the local park?'

'Good grief man. Say all that again – slowly. And one question at a time.'

'Okay. Question one: are the murders of Elisabeth Carpenter and Angela de Montfort still *active* police investigations?'

'Of course they are. Murder is murder; we don't just give up after five minutes. Although, and this is off the record, in the case of the older lady we believe that it was most likely an unfortunate accident. She's not the first person to trip and fall down the stairs in the middle of the night thus breaking her neck. Not by any means: the elderly are especially vulnerable in that regard.'

'However, her husband, Ambrose Carpenter, who I would remind you is a retired judge, maintains that far from being vulnerable she was a fit and healthy woman who walked regularly.'

` 'I know all that, but neither we, nor the Thames Valley force – who were the first on the scene – have found any indication that a crime was committed. There was no sign of forced entry, the security alarm had not been triggered, nor were there any unidentified fingerprints. And on top all that the pathologist did not find any injuries on the deceased other than those consistent with a fall. The judge is blinkered by devotion. I've seen it many times before; people can't accept that someone they loved could die from something as mundane as an accident in the home. It's always very sad, but unfortunately true.'

'So that's a no then – is it? Even if I agreed with your conclusion, which I'm reluctant to do, you surely can't believe that Angela's death was the result of a car accident?'

'Of course not. That poor woman was murdered; so drugged that she would have been unable to perform the most basic movements, much less drive a car. But that case rightly belongs to the Thames Valley force, not the Met. It's only because of... *undue political interference* that it has lobbed on our doorstep...'

'I'm aware that strings have been pulled, Chief Inspector, and I'm very grateful that they were.'

'What?'

'Hold your fire for a moment if you will, because the second question I asked is more complicated. Were you aware of Robert de Montfort's three day disappearance?'

'No, I was not. If he lived in Hampstead I'd expect the local police would have dealt with that matter.'

'Exactly as I'd assumed – and there's your trouble! What if all this seemingly unconnected business; Jamal's bogus assignment, the murders of the two women and Rob's disappearance, are all part of a conspiracy with this Livingstone-cum-Duncan character at the centre of it?'

'Impossible.'

'Is it? Then allow me to go one step further with another question: what if the catalyst for the conspiracy has been poor old Rob and his cryptic crosswords from former times? What would you say to that, sir?'

'I'd say you'd have to produce a hell of a lot of evidence to back up that conjecture, Quinn.'

'What about you, Jamal? What's your take on this?'

'I think you might be on the right track David,' he said thoughtfully, 'although I don't know why I feel that way as I have nothing to support your theory.'

'Thanks mate. Now I'd like to tell you a little story about an uncashed cheque, Jericho Publishing of Leipzig, Germany, and a fraudulent publishing contract. Oh – and a glib German speaking con-artist masquerading as Herr Robert de Montfort who you would probably know as Alexander Duncan.'

'Sandy Duncan died two or three years ago; I was privileged to speak at his funeral,' Scott said. 'This pathetic imitation of a fine, decent man is a fraud and a most likely a bloody traitor as well.'

'Agreed. And at this point I should mention that I showed this character's photo to my security service contacts when he first surfaced at Rob's nursing home and he was not known to any of them, or any other official channels I contacted. I understand that you are a fluent German speaker, Chief Inspector. Is that correct?'

'Not so fluent these days, but good enough to make myself understood. Want me to speak to the publishing people in Leipzig?'

'Yes, in due course. Although the gentleman to whom I spoke was an excellent English speaker, as many

Germans are it seems. But first let me tell you about the events that led me to him.'

When Quinn had finished his tale of the uncashed cheque, and his subsequent contact with the Leipzig company he yawned, stretched his legs, and helped himself to a piece of shortbread from the plate on the coffee table.

'I'll arrange some fresh coffee,' said a mollified Clive Scott. 'Or something stronger for you David, if you wish. And perhaps you'd like a fruit juice, Jamal or something else non-alcoholic?'

'Coffee is fine,' both men agreed.

'I have a query,' Jamal said. 'Where had the genuine Robert de Montfort been for those missing three days?'

'That is the salient question, isn't it? He was clean and tidy, yet totally disorientated and with worsening dementia.'

'Someone lifted him off the street, didn't they? They had a safe-house nearby and they kept him there while they filled him with whatever drugs they had that might persuade him to talk. And when they'd finished they tossed him back again. Now who could carry out that kind of operation?'

'Don't look at me! As far as I'm aware no one at the Met knew that Robert de Montfort existed until his wife and her mother died.'

'You're missing the point – both of you. It doesn't matter *who* did it, at least not right now. What matters is whether or not they got what they wanted from him. And obviously they didn't.'

'How can you be so sure?'

'Because of what they did next. Why would they murder Elisabeth and Angela if they already had whatever it was that they needed?'

'They were leverage?'

'Exactly, Jamal. And the tragedy is that the bastards didn't know about Rob's dementia or the harm it had done to his creative mind. The poor man probably had no idea what they were talking about or what it was they required from him.'

'The drugs they fed him accelerated his dementia?' Clive asked. 'Plus those they used afterwards to delete his memory of what had happened.'

'Precisely. So when he had to be admitted to the nursing home they realised what had gone wrong with their plans. Hence the arrival of Henry Livingstone: either to see if there had been any improvement in his condition once the drugs had left his system, or to threaten him that if he didn't cooperate his family would suffer. Or both.'

'David, this means your fiancée's life is in danger.'

'If I thought that do you imagine I'd be calmly sitting here drinking coffee? I believe that following Angela's death they realised they needed to change tack because the deaths of the women hadn't achieved anything but neither had they gone unnoticed. Any light bulbs going on yet, Jamal?'

'Maybe. Was I Plan B from the beginning? Is that why I was sent on a wild goose chase around Europe? But to what end – what was in it for them?'

'Wait a minute,' Clive said. 'Let the old boy ask a question. Did this creep give you any instructions as to where you should go and what you should do?'

'Not really. My brief was to get chummy with whatever groups or individuals I encountered who were angry, rebellious, disaffected, malcontents – especially those spouting anti-Western ideology. But wait a moment. He *did* suggest a kind of itinerary, now I think about it.'

'Which was?'

'Start in Antwerp: he said the city of diamonds was an rambunctious melting-pot, then gradually make my way by whatever means I could, through Essen, Dortmund, Hanover and so forth, until I reached Berlin. Then after that I could either follow my nose – or the contacts I'd made. And that's how I ended up in Brussels with the gang from hell! He'd suggested I stay a few days in each place depending on how er… *fertile* I judged the ground to be. There was another town he mentioned too. It was in the former East Germany; now what was the name again…?'

'Chemnitz?'

'Yes, that's it, Chemnitz. That was a pleasant, neat little town. I found no subversives there although I did find some prejudice which was confusing. I never knew whether it was because of the colour of my skin, or my classy English accent. Or maybe it was both.'

'What's Scotland Yard's interest in a small town like that?' Quinn asked.

'Well…'

'Oh, I get it. It's not the Yard that's interested; it's another part of the State, isn't it?'

'What do you do at GCHQ, Mr Quinn?'

'I no longer work at that establishment, Chief Inspector.'

'That's strange because I'd heard that you still do…'

'I may *sometimes* accept a special assignment but that's all. I'm not regularly employed there.'

'What *did* you do, when you were?'

'Data analysis, mainly. And er… other duties as directed.'

'Hah! The old catch-all phrase for the servants of the State.'

'Are these questions leading anywhere, sir?'

'Ever heard of the Alternative for Deutschland, Mr Q?'

'Yes, of course. The AfD's been on our radar for some time as are other right-wing groups across Europe.'

'You've lost me… I thought our interest was in the apostates of my Faith; the damned death-lovers like those who carried out the Paris attacks. Aren't they the very antithesis of the hard-right bods?'

'Hmm, maybe. What kind of info did you pass on to the phoney, Jamal?'

'Not much really; certainly nothing of any real significance, which is a relief because at that time I thought he was the genuine article.'

'Did he ask you about prejudice and where you'd found it?'

'Yes, on reflection, he did. But only once; and that was the last time I heard from him. The next day I discovered my bank account had been closed.'

'And?'

'I told him that I'd encountered prejudice – to a greater or lesser extent – just about everywhere I went. But I didn't dwell on it; I don't ever want to wear a victim label. Or to be forced to wear one by persons promoting their own agenda. Don't we generally feel more comfortable with people from our own or similar backgrounds? For all we know, a strand of prejudice might have been woven into human DNA before the dawn of our existence.'

'Hmm. Interesting possibility.'

'Where are these questions leading, Chief Inspector?'

'Ever heard the expression "a sprat to catch a mackerel"?'

'No, what does it mean?'

'Well, a sprat is a very small, but highly-active forage fish. The mackerel is much larger.'

'So?'

'So it follows that an experienced fisherman might choose to use the smaller fish to catch a bigger one.'

'Are you saying that the fake Duncan used me as bait?'

'You figure it out. The expression means being prepared to sacrifice something of lesser value in the hope of gaining a far greater prize. I believe that this damn chancer, far from being a terrorist hunter, was really a recruiting sergeant for the far-right mob!'

TWENTY-FOUR

Monday 23rd November 2015
Scotland Yard. London

'If you're right, Chief Inspector, then how do we catch this rat?'

'We set a trap for him; isn't that the way a rat-catcher works, Davey?'

'No, no, no! I didn't object when you referred to me as Master Quinn as though I were a schoolkid instead of a man almost thirty, or when you called me Quinn – or even Mr Q, but I won't allow you to call me Davey. That makes me sound like a bloody plumber's mate from Hackney! Not that there's anything wrong with Hackney or that job – before anyone's tempted to slap an elitist label on me.'

'Bit touchy, aren't we?'

'Touchy? If you knew my background you'd consider me the Patron Saint of Tolerance.'

'So tell us – we're fascinated, aren't we, Jamal?'

'Labels,' he said vaguely. 'Labels. That's the key – labels…'

'What are you havering about, laddie? We're on the verge of an exposé from Mr Quinn. Continue, sir.'

'Very well. Israeli mother, Christian father: hence circumcised, baptised, Bar-Mitzvahed, in that order, with a fiancée who hovers somewhere between the Quakers and the Hari-Krishnas.'

'Point taken, David. With that pedigree how do you describe yourself?'

'A bush-Baptist probably since I haven't been confirmed –yet.'

'Interesting, but I repeat; labels,' Jamal said. 'Why have we been so quick to assume that this individual is British? And why is he poking his nose into left-right factions anyway? Who made him king of Europe?'

'Or the future Führer.' Quinn added.

'Wait a minute. Wait one doggone minute.' Clive urged. 'Anyone familiar with the initials DDTRS, or as it's usually abbreviated, TRS?'

Both men shook their heads.

'It's a pop-up bunch of loopy German relics from an era we'd all prefer not to repeat – or an emerging right-wing organisation challenging the AfD, depending on whose assessment you accept.'

'Err… by any chance could those initials stand for some German phrase about fast-moving dead people?' David asked.

'*Denn die Todten reiten schnell; "because the dead ride fast"*,' Clive said. 'Now where could you have heard that before?'

'Thursday afternoon when I was visiting Robert in the nursing home. While I was there his brother, the afore-mentioned Spawn QC, phoned from Paris to ask Rob what the phrase meant.'

'And where had *he* heard it?'

'From his client in the Paris prison who wants to be tried in England instead of France. He's the one who volunteered the info that Icarus was the code name of a spy who'd infiltrated MI6. At that point Fleur and Meg revealed that they had knowledge of the real Icarus. Then, right at the end of their meeting, and apropos of absolutely nothing as far as I could tell from the thrust of the conversation, he came out with the Denn die… stuff.'

'Dear God! The further we venture into this damn swamp the more reptiles we encounter,' an exasperated Scott exclaimed.

'Yes, but it's all connected; it has to be. And here's another item to throw into the bog; how did the fake Duncan choose Jamal to send on a field trip around Europe? Better still; how did he even *know* that Jamal existed, much less that he worked for the security service?'

'He must have seen me before? But how and where?'

'Either that or he works for the same organisation…'

'We know he doesn't, certainly not in any significant or even medium-level position; none of my contacts recognised him when I showed them his photo.'

'Or your paths have crossed before.'

'How many people work for MI6? Does anyone know?' Quinn asked.

'Somewhere around three thousand, I believe,' Clive replied. 'I know they have a budget in excess of £3 billion per year.'

They sat in silent contemplation for a few minutes before Scott had his Eureka moment.

'How about this; we don't know how he found Jamal, but he did. Maybe he worked for the security service at some time, but that's irrelevant now because we know where he's been *recently*, and that's Jericho Publishing. We also know that the only crosswords he's interested in are the older cryptic ones. I'll phone the company, tell them as much as I consider necessary, and ask them to email copies of the crosswords they've published lately. Then brains-trust here...' He said, looking at Quinn, 'will attempt to decipher their meaning.'

'Forget the crosswords for a moment, and I can tell you I'm hopeless at Scrabble let alone crosswords of any kind. What do we really want to know? His *identity*. And the fastest way to do that is via his fingerprints. If he touched something the last time he was with them which...'

'Like what?'

'Like something that hasn't been washed, dusted or polished in the meantime. Then if we can't get a match on our data-base we ask Europol for assistance.'

'Sounds good to me, David. But we still need the specific puzzles to discover what kind of messages this con artist is sending to his comrades scattered across Germany and, for all we know, elsewhere in Europe too.'

'Agreed, but better ask the Jericho people to send the *solutions* too because I'll be no use whatsoever.'

'Fair enough, we can't all be good at everything; just as long as we're halfway *decent* at some bloody thing! My thing is camouflage. I'll tell them it's a missing person's case which they'll probably believe – assuming that they're innocent as far as this conspiracy is concerned.'

'Unlike the real conspirator, who as well as his other criminal activity has been also pocketing poor old Rob's royalties.'

'Indeed. And for that crime alone he'd get a hefty kick up the backside from me given the chance.' A grim Chief Inspector replied.

Monday 23rd November 2015
Louise Maigret's apartment. Paris

While that meeting was taking place in London, Meg was settling her mother-in-law back into her apartment helped by Rosa, Louise's housekeeper. She was so preoccupied with the older woman's welfare that she was startled when her phone buzzed.

'It's me, honey,' the familiar voice said, 'with some news for you regarding the whereabouts of your old man.'

'I have to take this call,' she whispered to Louise, stepping through the heritage doors and on to the balcony overlooking the Avenue Foch.

'Have company, do we?'

'Yes, in a way. So where is he?'

'Pretty-please, would have been nice but you always were refreshingly direct.'

'Get on with it, Tom.'

'As far as my sources can deduce, because Zurich

clinics are notoriously tight-lipped about enquiries from third parties, he's in the Saint Luke Clinic.'

'That's based on what?'

'A process of elimination; that clinic is the most closed-mouthed of all. Another source believes he's seen Maigret's buddy... er Christophe whatshisname, the Minister guy, going to and from from the clinic over the weekend.'

'Hmm.'

'Want me to take you there? We could storm the ramparts together. I *can* now drive as my new car's been adapted for me. But I won't; it's too far at this stage of my recovery, but my chauffeur's an excellent driver.'

'Thanks for the offer Tom, but I don't believe Philippe would want me to be indebted to you any more than I am already.'

'But you're not – he is!'

'Even so, it would amount to the same thing in his eyes.'

'The man's a fool. I should never have saved his life.'

'Please don't...'

'Shall I tell you why I did? It was because I knew that even if he *died* nothing would change; you still wouldn't be with me again.'

'And you're right. I'll always remember that amazing New York summer, but it was long ago and we've both moved on. Now forgive me, I need to make an important phone call.'

She ended the connection before he could speak and pressed a number which was answered promptly.

'*Bonjour*, Christophe. I have a yes or no question for you. Is Philippe in the Saint Luke Clinic in Zurich?'

'Yes. Do you want Carole to drive you there?'

'No, I'd rather Georges Martin did if he's well enough now, or Jacques Laurent if he's not. And I'd like to leave in about an hour. I'm with Louise in her apartment now so I'd need to go home first to pack a bag for a few days.'

'Inspector Martin is still on medical leave, but I believe he's well enough to drive you there and I know he'd want to. I have a feeling that Sergeant Laurent will be keen to tag along too. Does that suit you?'

'Of course.'

'Good. I'll let the clinic know they should expect you. One more thing; as you're aware he's still in intensive care, and... Err... well, he's... different. He *looks* different...'

'Because he's lost so much weight...?'

'Yes, that and... Well... I'm just saying that you should *prepare* yourself for the contrast. I can't actually define the change, but what he's been through has definitely er distressed more than his body. You'll probably think I'm over-reacting but I really do believe it has damaged his... er soul. Yes – that's it! What was done to him has wounded his body and psyche too.'

He has a hard edge to him now that wasn't there before. Or is it a simmering unquenched anger I sense? Either way what does it matter? I can't tell her more than I have; she will need to discover the changes for herself – God help her.

'Does that surprise you? It certainly doesn't surprise

me. How could he go through such a terrible experience and emerge unscathed afterwards? But thanks for your concern.'

Monday 23rd November 2015
Paris to Zurich

They left Paris not long after noon, Georges Martin driving, Meg sitting in the seat next to him, with Jacques, the avid map reader and navigator, in the rear. En route to the Maigret apartment the two detectives had a lively debate as to what was the best way to Zurich. There was no contest really, just two experienced drivers with their own definite opinions.

They had another agenda too: to divert their thoughts as far away as possible from the rumours that had been circulating around HQ for days concerning what might have been done to their chief during his incarceration.

That he had been tortured was accepted as Gospel now even by the most sceptical of them, but the consensus was that there was far worse yet to be revealed. And the worst thing that any of them could imagine was a sexual assault perpetrated by another man. A handful of those officers were homosexual: they were the most vociferous of all. Rape was rape: the sexual orientation of the victim made no difference they said angrily. So go tell *that* on your bloody mountain; we know it's not a widely-held belief here or anywhere else!

The female officers were aware of these discussions although they did not often take place in their presence.

When they did they exchanged wry smiles, sometimes with raised eyebrows, but said almost nothing. What was there to say? Nearly 13,000 women raped in France so far this year with little judicial or public outrage: it was too prevalent to arouse more than a tut of genteel opprobrium. Lives ruined: individual tragedies silently endured behind locked doors, closed blinds, and private tears.

The *Police Nationale* officers were also aware of the demise of the three members of the gang that had committed the 'La Belle Equipe' outrage. There were witnesses in the restaurant next door who saw those assassins shoot dead nineteen people in a matter of minutes; most of whom had been dining at alfresco tables on an unusually balmy night for that time of year. Only the irreparably-deluded would have shed any tears for those killers: the officers who attended that grisly scene most certainly would not.

Those terrorists had harmed their chief, so when the news of the killings in Brussels reached the corridors of *Police Nationale* there was muted relief and quiet satisfaction. To have given three rousing cheers then paraded around the building's perimeter shouting 'Hallelujah' accompanied by a brass band – which was their first reaction – would have been frowned upon by the higher echelons. It appears that political correctness must be observed even in the face of unspeakable barbarism.

Thus the foremost question at HQ was who had carried out the swift retribution? Most of them had heard details of the weapons used. They knew the Brussels Police had dispatched the two younger members; their weapons were standard Belgian police issue. But for the obvious leader, a truly evil piece of human detritus, a very different weapon had been chosen; a German Luger, someone's souvenir from former unhappy times. Why? To make a judicial point? Or a very obvious distinction? And where was that weapon now? At the bottom of the nearest river, some officers thought. Not a chance was the verdict of the more informed. That weapon was someone's prized possession; it will not have been thrown away, but neither will it ever be found. But as for suspects, there were very few.

One outlandish suggestion was that Christophe Saint-Valéry, a friend of their chief since their university days might have been responsible. That idea gained some currency among the junior officers until wiser heads disclosed that the Minister, who no one had ever seen holding a weapon, had been a criminal barrister before entering the political arena. But even so... some young-bloods still had their doubts.

It is 603 km from Paris to Zurich via the A5 and the distance might be covered in around seven hours, provided no detours were made. They stopped once: a food, coffee and comfort break. But during all that time she hardly spoke, except to answer her companions if they said something to her, or to choose the type of coffee she would drink. The rest of the time her thoughts were with Philippe; his physical health, and – more worryingly

– his emotional state in view of the changes Christophe had already noted.

Strange then that they managed to arrive at the Saint Luke Clinic at 6.30 pm. Of course they were in an unmarked police vehicle and a siren *might* occasionally have been used. Moreover Georges had been a trained police driver in his early career; nonetheless it was a remarkable achievement. And not one likely to be replicated in the foreseeable future.

It was dark when they arrived, as November nights are in the Northern Hemisphere. Georges parked the car in a convenient space designated 'Consultants only' near the imposing front portico.

'We won't be here long,' he said with a cheeky grin. 'Then Jacques and I will go off to find our digs and have some dinner.'

'I want you two to see him first,' she said, remaining firm despite their objections. 'And please take as long as you wish. I've been promised a room near his so can visit whenever I choose. Besides, I want to freshen up now.'

However they did not stay long; the lift carrying them arrived at the ground floor only minutes after she left the women's bathroom.

'That was quick!'

'The boss threw us out, Madame.'

'Surely not.'

'He told us to scram,' Jacques added.

'Now that I really do not believe. Scram would be too American gangster-speak for my Monsieur's taste. What did he actually say?'

'He thanked us for coming and said he'd see us for coffee at around eleven tomorrow morning.'

'That's more like it.'

His room was on the third floor: her heart was beating very fast as she walked from the lift towards the nurses' desk to ask for directions. There was unbridled *frisson* in the air not all of which emanated from her. *It looks like Philippe has acquired a new batch of wistfuls,* she thought sympathetically. *Now they're deciding whether I'm worthy of a man like him. And, as usual, he'll be completely unaware of their interest: thank the Lord for that mercy!*

He was in bed, propped up by several large pillows and looking remarkably perky as she entered the room. He smiled and opened wide his arms when he saw her. She hugged him so tightly that he cried out "mind the arm, mind the arm" – then laughed and pretended he'd been teasing. He patted the side of the bed in invitation for her to sit there but instead she took his wedding ring out of her pocket, kissed it and gave it to him.

'Do we need to have it blessed again?'

'No, you kissed it and that's good enough for me,' he replied, slipping it on his finger.

'Then I'll kiss it again now that it's back where it belongs.'

She did; then stood up, kicked off her shoes and removed her skirt.

'What are you doing, darling?'

'I'd have thought that was obvious. I'm getting ready to join you.'

'With your clothes on?'

'Oh… well er I thought I'd be cold if I took *everything* off.'

'I promise you won't…'

She quickly cast off the rest of her clothes and hopped into bed, snuggling down next to him to share his warmth.

And that's how they were when the nurse assistant entered the room an hour later to ask if they were ready for their dinner; except that by then they were – all heartache forgotten – sleeping peacefully in each other's arms. The woman retreated as quickly and silently as she could.

In the wee small hours, Philippe stirred then left the bed.

'The bathroom,' he whispered. 'I won't be long.'

Oh, dear God. I need her… But we can't… reckless… stay strong… restraint until the all-clear – whenever that might be.

He slipped into bed again and attempted to distance himself from her which was not easy in a standard hospital cot. She immediately moved closer to him.

'Feeling frisky, Monsieur?'

'Er… *moderately* so, maybe…'

'Hmm, I would say you passed moderately as you left the bathroom – we're way beyond moderately now.'

'Darling, I can't. We can't risk… Please try to understand.'

'If you need me to understand you must tell me everything, Philippe. And I mean *everything.*'

He did. Amid the deluge of their tears, clinging to her like a trembling child reliving a terrifying nightmare, he told her every last depraved detail of what he remembered from his physical humiliation.

'Now you see why I can't… we can't… until I'm no longer a risk to you. We have some bridges to cross before we can make love again, darling.'

'Do we? If that's so, then we've crossed the first bridge tonight.'

'Sorry?'

'The first bridge was Fear, and we're past that now; it can't hurt us any longer.'

'And the second bridge?'

'Trust. Then after that, there's only one left and its name is Joy. I'm ready to cross the Trust Bridge right now – are you?'

'But what if…'

'There can be no what-ifs between us love. What happens to you happens to me. I've never been especially risk adverse before and I don't intend to start now.'

'Are you quite sure about this?'

'Yes, very sure. Now what happened to your friend Mr Moderately? Is he still around?'

'He's no friend of mine! He disappeared some time ago and was instantly replaced by good old Frisky himself. But you knew that already, didn't you?'

'Yes.'

'You will be gentle – remember my arm injury.'

'That rather depends on how essential your arm might be in what happens next, doesn't it?'

'That works for me,' he murmured, drawing her closer. 'That most *certainly* works for me.'

TWENTY-FIVE

The next morning when Christophe came to Maigret's room he was surprised to see him sitting in the armchair, freshly shaved and showered, and elegantly dressed in charcoal-grey flannel trousers, a citron coloured cashmere sweater and brown English brogues.

'Well, look at you,' he said whistling, 'all dressed up but where do you think you're going?'

'Home, of course.'

'Says who? When?'

'The chief consultant, with whom I had a discussion earlier. He'll authorise my discharge tomorrow morning.'

'But you're supposed to be in intensive care.'

'Only necessary for the first twelve hours following my surgery, he said. After that it was merely to placate his overly-cautious colleagues, one of whom – to use his actual words – "suffers from a near-terminal case of an abundance of caution." He's quite certain I can continue my convalescence perfectly well at home. I told you I was a fast healer.'

'Hmm. You're also the talk of the clinic. And I suspect you've been shopping at our favourite Jermyn Street outfitters in London again.'

'Not me, Meg. They have my measurements on file, she phoned them and they sent the clothes in a matter of days. Why am I the topic of discussion here?'

'Can you truly not know? And in a hospital too – really, Philippe!'

'So a man and his wife slept in the same bed; where's the problem?'

'The nursing staff is taking bets on whether that's *all* the two of you did. On that subject take a look at this info recently received from Brussels. There are also post-morten photographs now,' he replied, passing him a sheaf of papers in a plastic wallet.

Philippe examined the photographs and then nodded.

'Are you absolutely certain?'

'Yes, without the slightest doubt. This one here is their degenerate leader Haz, a genuine psycho. This one, with the wretched excuse for a beard is the geek their flatulent tech guy, and the third one, by a process of elimination must be the worrywart who was always fiddling with his beads, who I never actually saw. Want me to write their names on the back of each photograph?'

'No, I have duplicates and I've noted the comments you made. Finished with the papers?'

'Not yet.' He thumbed through them again, followed by another time even more slowly; reading, absorbing while intoning something almost under his breath.

'If you were relying on prayer it would have been better done *before* last night's mischief, I believe.'

'He didn't have HIV! He was clean... The post-mortem results prove it.'

'Hardly *clean*...'

'How can we be sure the results are accurate? Maybe they've been degraded – not as precise as a living sample would be. How'd you get them to look for what I needed to know anyway?'

'I've done a good many favours for my opposite number in Belgium; trust me he'll be paying for a long time. But look again at the last page. Those samples were taken from *your* body by Dr Defoe on the day you were admitted to his hospital. Those were fresh, and for all medical purposes, *live*. Take my advice; don't go looking for bad news where there isn't any. Say Hallelujah and rejoice.'

'Hallelujah.'

'Amen. By the way where's your nocturnal accomplice?'

'Gone shopping. Dragooned Georges into driving her to Zurich.'

'More clothes?'

'No. She's looking for a stylish cane to keep me upright as I'm a little wonky on my pins and she doesn't want everything going mogador again.'

'What?'

'Apparently there's some unsteadiness in the way I stand or walk.'

'And er... mogador?'

'Courtesy of the Internet, Mogador is a hamlet in Surrey named after the former moniker of the Moroccan port of Essaouira. It has an elevation of about 200 metres and is one of the highest settlements in south-east England. It's just north of the M25 motorway. However…'

'What?'

'However, in the context in which my wife used the word it means something like chaotic, confused, crazy, or a total mess. That translation is from her friend Liz whose Irish mother used it regularly during her childhood. For example "sure it's all gone mogador again".'

'And all that history requires a *stylish cane?*'

'I believe Meg actually specified an *antique stylish* one…'

'Good grief man! She won't be satisfied until she's turned you into a modern day Beau Brummell; you're half-way there already.'

Philippe responded with several of the more choice Anglo-Saxon insults and Christophe laughed.

'One more thing before I *revoke* your recent promotions,' he said. 'If you're not going home until tomorrow why are you fully-dressed now?'

'I'm expecting Georges and Jacques at eleven. I thought it important for the preservation of the chain of command that they see me *clothed*, not wearing a hospital gown with the back open for all the casual curious to gawp at my exposed rump.'

'Hmm – at least that makes some sense. Now what mode of transport would Monsieur prefer for his return to Paris?'

'I'll go the same way as Meg and the lads came here. Georges and Jacques can share the driving and I'll sit in the backseat with her.'

'You'll resemble a squashed spider in a shoebox by the time you arrive in Paris.'

'It's not so far.'

'What car did they use to drive here?'

Philippe shrugged.

'A police car – a Citroen or Renault, I suppose.'

'May I remind you that I've read your medical data? I know about the numerous cigarette burns you have on your arms and elsewhere. If you imagine that I'd allow you to return to Paris in a standard issue police car, you're very much mistaken. My wife and children would never forgive me, and neither would the public. These are your options; a limousine, a helicopter, a medevac flight, or an ambulance – you choose.'

'I'll let you know, Christophe.'

'Good.' He said, as he walked towards the door. 'Oh, before I forget; if you're planning to sleep with your wife again tonight I suggest you use *her* room. I understand it has a Queen-sized bed.'

He ducked quickly and the flying cushion hit the door instead of him.

Philippe immediately used his new phone to call Meg.

'Don't panic love, we're almost at the clinic and I've found something absolutely perfect for you.'

'*Bon, bon*. Do you remember those bridges we talked about last night?'

'Of course.'

'We've just crossed the last one. I've read the post-morten reports; he didn't have the virus. In fact none of them did.'

'Oh, oh – infinite grace. What wonderful news… Thank the Lord.'

'Amen. Now there's only one question on my mind regarding tonight's sleeping arrangements…'

'Yours or mine?'

'Yes. I understand yours is bigger…'

'It is. I checked on it this morning; it gets my vote.'

'Mine too,' he said happily. 'Now how would you like to return to Paris by helicopter tomorrow?'

'I'd love it. I've never flown in one before.'

Wednesday 25th November 2015
Scotland Yard, London, mid-morning

Chief Inspector Scott was not happy. He had a throbbing headache; the result of self-inflicted wounds at a Yard retirement party the night before, while his usually tidy desk was covered with cryptic crosswords sent by Jericho Publishing. For a latent Calvinist as Scott tended to be, an untidy desk was indicative of a disorderly mind, and that he really could not tolerate.

He had been studying those crosswords all morning without any success, even though he had the solutions. He scowled when he heard the cautious knock on his door, then roared 'Come in!'

'Good morning, Chief Inspector. You rang, and here I am,' David Quinn said. 'Having problems?'

'Of course I am! Now sit down, keep quiet, and try to fathom this Jericho info while I swallow more aspirin in an attempt to get rid of this headache from hell that has been visited upon me by an unkind Fate.'

'Fate was it? Only I heard downstairs that it was twelve year old single malt. However, I'm on the case.'

After almost an hour of silence, apart from the soft shuffling of papers now and then, Quinn spoke again.

'If I might be permitted to give an opinion, sir.'

'Speak Mr Q, but softly, softly, please.'

'Head still bad?'

'On the mend, but a certain fragility has replaced the pain which I believe might disappear if I heard some good – really good – news. Do you have any?'

David sighed.

'These are typical Rob cryptics of his Sturm and Drang – or as we might say – Storm and Urge – period. They're brilliant, challenging and full of emotion and stirring conceit inspired by the late 18th Century German movement. To be more precise this society celebrated nature, feelings, and human independence: its antithesis was the enlightenment cult of rationalism. Apparently both Goethe and Schiller began their careers as prominent members of the movement.'

'And in English we would say...'

'Emotional response, experience, and religious belief trump the tradition of treating reason as the ultimate authority in religion. That's about it in a nut-shell.'

'Dear God – I wish I hadn't asked. To be clear, a bunch of harmless German eccentrics formed a faction;

where's the relevance for us in this investigation?'

'That's what I can't understand. If I were bent on forming a seditious movement to undermine or overthrow the State, I'm sure I'd find an easier way of attracting and communicating with my groupies than this arcane system.'

'Like what? You could hardly run a 'subversives wanted' advert in a newspaper, could you? And certainly not if your aim was to attract a particular type of individual.'

'Upmarket, educated, superior, and with a peculiar taste for the weirder aspects of history?'

'Yes. Now we're getting somewhere…'

'And especially if you had an overweening ambition and exaggerated sense of your own importance and destiny.'

'What? Say that again, David.'

He did.

'Oh, hell! I know – or rather, *heard* of someone like that. *Exactly* like that. And what an annoying supercilious bastard he was too by all accounts.'

Just then there was a ping on Scott's phone. He stared at the message then passed his phone to Quinn.

'Take a look at those, my man.'

'Fingerprints?'

'Yes, but not just any old fingerprints. If I'm right they're the fingerprints of a traitor and a murderer. And to cap it all, he's not even a genuine German! Now what do you think of that?'

'From Jericho Publishing?'

'Yes. Not perfect, but they'll do for our purposes: four different images of the prints on the silver frame of an award Jericho won a month ago. And, more importantly, handled by none other than the fraudulent Herr de Montfort himself. That swine might have changed his appearance, could even have had plastic surgery for all we know, but fingerprints are not so easy to disguise. They can be permanently removed of course, but that's a very painful procedure I understand.'

'Whose are they?'

'Just a moment, let's put them through the magical mystery machine to see what it reveals, while I tell you a little story.'

'You're sending to both Europol and Interpol?'

'Nah, just Europol for now; I don't think he will have gone International yet.'

He poured them both another cup of coffee from a new pot which had been nervously delivered a few moments earlier by a young trainee, intimidated by the scowl on Clive's face, then sank back in his chair and relaxed.

'There's something else I should have mentioned earlier, sir…'

'For Heaven's sake call me Clive; I've spent more time with you lately than I have with my wife.'

'It's something Fleur reminded me about last night; something Rob said to Meg on the day they visited him in the nursing home after Angela's funeral. It seems he went off on a ranting recitation while Fleur was organising the afternoon tea. Apart from the Sturm and Drang stuff he kept repeating that the fox was in the hen-house, and that the canker in the UK was not *poverty*, but *hypocrisy*.'

'*Spiritual wickedness in high places*.'

'What? Yes. So on my way here I looked up all the synonyms for hypocrisy that I could find.'

'Which are.?'

'Bigotry; deceit; deception; mockery; insincerity; fraud; dishonesty. Any of those words fit the person you have in mind?'

'All of the above, I'd say. Let me introduce you to Blake Hamilton-Burgess, former MI6 operative, cashiered out of the service four years ago for conduct unbecoming…'

'And in English we'd say…'

'Not specified, as far as I'm aware. Probably hand in the cookie jar somewhere; fiddled expenses, or large backhanders from dubious but disgustingly-rich foreign persons. Or maybe drunk and lecherous at the Christmas party: hands up a woman's skirt, that kind of thing although that's usually treated by a slap on the wrist reprimand, not prompt dismissal and loss of pension.'

'*Quis custodiet ipsos custodies?*'

'Sorry?'

'Who guards the guards? Could someone that sleazy and revolting be a Deep State traitor, Clive?'

'You bet he could! But let's get our terminology correct: the Deep State refers to the British Civil Service, not MI6 although undoubtedly there's some overlap between the two. The Civil Service assumes it's their job to actually *run* the country while resisting any changes initiated by *elected* politicians because only they protect the national interest. All complete rubbish of course, but that's their arrogance and they've been getting away with it for a long time. Those who thought the television series 'Yes Minister' was fiction were mistaken; it was more like a reality show.'

'Hmm, sounds interesting.'

'It was – in a rather chilling way. Hamilton-Burgess would have fitted right in with that bunch. I understand he's a real chameleon; smooth and charming when he chooses to be, but a tad too affected for some. I have to admit I'm wary of those with double-barrelled surnames anyway, although it seems he had a decent degree from Cambridge.'

'Ah, Clive; you can never go wrong mentioning a likely Cambridge spy to an Oxford man. Does he have MacLean somewhere in his name too? Or Philby or Blunt? Or must we be content with just Blake and Burgess? I read that Philby was protected by his former colleagues in MI6 right up to the time he jumped aboard a Soviet freighter in Beirut in 1963. Can that be true?'

'Unfortunately it is. It was not their finest patriotic period; *a generation of vipers.* They hate to be reminded of it, but we can't delete the past. They failed in their duty. It was a stain on the Service and it will remain that way until Kingdom come.'

'You like your Biblical quotes, don't you?'

'Aye. I'm not adverse to Shakespearian ones either when the mood's upon me.'

As Clive spoke a signal was emitted from the fingerprint tracer. He hurried over to the machine and read the onscreen report.

'Well lookee here! Sixteen points of reference confirm that these fingerprints are those of Blake sodding Hamilton-Burgess.'

TWENTY SIX

'How come I've never heard of this Hamilton-Burgess? And why isn't he in prison?'

'Perhaps he knows too much: no country enjoys washing their dirty linen in public. You think when people say "he knows where the bodies are buried" they're joking? The longer I live the less certain I am about that. George Blake, former double agent, was the last spy to stand trial and that was in 1961. He was foreign born and middle-class so wasn't tipped-off in time to escape as the other posh Cambridge spies were. Rank hypocrisy at work again. And the old-boys' network, of course.'

'What happened to him?'

'Sentenced to something like forty-two years in prison, which many thought was unusually harsh since he had also spied for MI6, but with help escaped from Wormwood Scrubs after serving only five years. Then off to Soviet Russia, as usual.'

They sat quietly, mulling over the inequalities of life while enjoying their coffee, before the silence was broken by Quinn receiving a text message. It was from Giles de Montfort and read:

I've come to visit Rob, as usual on a Wednesday, but something's not right here today; something out of kilter. Different woman on Reception and an unfriendly atmosphere. When I reached Rob's room the door was closed but I could hear a man inside speaking to him. Not clearly, but still there's something...
I don't like the tone of the conversation. He seems to be trying to persuade Rob to do something against his will. I don't know whether to barge in and ask him what he's about or wait until he comes out and challenge him then. All very odd and unsettling. I need your advice, David – urgently!

He passed his phone to Clive without a word. *Can I reply?* He whispered. David nodded and he did so immediately.

C.I Scott, replying Mr de Montfort. Move away from the door a little but keep it in sight. I believe I know who is with him and he's dangerous. If he attempts to leave – either alone or with Robert – stop him by whatever means you can; reasonable force pertains. Local police on the way and David and I will be there ASAP.

He returned the phone to Quinn before speaking rapidly into his own.

'Get the nearest car to Willows Glen nursing home in Highgate and establish a lockdown – front and back entrances secured. No one in or out, no exceptions. Any ARV in the area? No – incident at Heathrow? Then local force will have to respond. Yes, uniformed officers okay because of time factor, but unmarked cars if possible – two or three – and no siren; we don't want to panic the residents. I'm on my way. Any weapons at Hampstead? Well bloody find out! If they have any they'd be useful. Dangerous intruder on premises may be armed. No – *assume armed.*'

'Come on David,' he said, grabbing his coat from the hat-stand, 'you can call Fleur on the way. Tell her not to go anywhere near Willows Glen until we've found out what's going on there.'

'You think it's Hamilton-Burgess?'

'It's a dead cert. And if he's broken cover it's for a good reason else why take the risk? This is the best chance we'll have to nab the bugger and we better make sure we do.'

They hurried down the stairs, too impatient to wait for the lift then rushed out to the street where the unmarked police car was waiting with blue light flashing.

'Get in the back, David; I'm not sure we have insurance for civilians. By the way, this is Vince; he's the best and fastest driver we have on the Force.'

'Thanks, Chief.'

'Now off you go and don't make me a liar in front of Mr Quinn here. He works for that hush-hush establishment in Cheltenham.'

'Past tense Clive, I've told you that before. And please don't mention that place in front of Fleur. I've only just managed to reinstate our engagement.'

They sped off along the Victoria Embankment heading for Westminster Bridge. The traffic was beyond heavy; Quinn groaned when he saw the chaos ahead of them.

'Can't this buggy go any faster?'

'Any faster and Vince would need a pilot's licence,' Clive said, 'now stay calm and try Fleur's mobile again.'

'Just done it – still goes straight to voice-mail. Where the hell is she?'

It was a rhetorical question as all three men knew; the caprices of the female mind were as foreign to them as was the terrain of Outer Mongolia.

Thirty minutes later they arrived at Willows Glen to find the lockdown established and two uniformed officers standing guard at the front entrance while a third officer kept watch at the rear.

'He's with me,' Clive said, flashing his ID, 'where's the action? Everything under control?'

'Yes, sir. We understand the suspect was er... *apprehended* by a member of the public shortly before we arrived.'

'And the dubious dame on the Reception desk – what of her?'

'In the office adjacent to Reception being questioned by Sergeant Bailey, sir.'

'Good, good. Carry on lads.'

'Upstairs, Clive,' Quinn said as they entered the foyer, 'Rob's room's on the second floor – follow the sound of the general hubbub, I'd say.'

When they reached the second floor landing they stood silently observing the scene in front of them. Halfway down the well-lit passage was Robert de Montfort, standing in the open doorway of his room, clearly bemused but smiling. A man latterly laid-out cold on the floor was attempting to get to his feet assisted by one of the three police constables on the scene, while Giles de Montfort QC was standing in front of that man, arms akimbo, with a pugnaciously satisfied look on his face.

On both sides of the corridor other residents were also standing at their open doors in various stages of undress, astonished by the events taking place in front of them. They were calling back and forth between themselves, each adding a further detail regarding what they had witnessed. The resulting uproar was an assault on the senses.

'Bloody hell!' Chief Inspector Scott exclaimed, 'talk about *Paradise Lost*; this must be Bedlam returned.'

'Or a new Tower of Babel.'

When the throng became aware of their presence a hush fell over the area and curious eyes were fixed directly on them. Clive moved closer before he spoke and David went with him.

'Thank you, ladies and gentlemen,' he said in his finest witness for the prosecution voice. 'I'm Chief Inspector Clive Scott. May I ask that you all kindly return to your rooms now? One or two of our amiable young officers will be along later to take down your particulars…'

A titter broke out at his deliberate use of the *double entendre,* as he knew it would; he had found such an approach a valuable way to dispel anxiety many times before.

'Now, now, ladies – and please be reassured gentlemen – that your *personal details* are all that will be taken down!'

'That's a damn shame,' one of the more daring ladies remarked loudly, and further giggles followed.

'Settle down please everyone. The officers will also require your witness statements; what you saw, what you heard, that kind of thing. If you didn't see or hear anything then please just say so; there's no need for anyone to become creative. And thank you for your assistance; it will be greatly appreciated.'

The compliant old darlings did as requested, smiling and nodding as they retreated, while Scott and Quinn were thinking the same thing: *the rebellious brigade of today could learn a great deal from this generation. But they won't; they'd rather stay angry and aggressive than listen to the calm voice of reason, respect, and experience.*

'Now then,' the Chief Inspector said, 'who wants to start the ball rolling by telling me what's occurred here?'

The officers looked self-consciously at each other and shifted awkwardly in their shoes, not wanting to be the first to speak. Clive sighed.

'You there – the tall lad, you start.'

'Er… er – it was pretty much all over bar the shouting by the time we arrived, sir. This man here,' he said gesturing towards Giles, 'walloped this one here, the… er *putative intruder*, and he went down like the proverbial sack of spuds.'

'Hmm. Very succinctly put Constable, thank you.'

'If I may be permitted to speak, Chief Inspector,' Giles said.

'Not yet; your turn will come, Mr de Montfort. You,' he said, looking directly at the flustered Henry Livingstone, 'what's your story, sir?'

Livingstone attempted to tidy himself by smoothing his clothes and patting ineffectually at his hair before adopting an air of injured innocence.

'My name is Henry Livingstone. I came to visit an old friend of mine, Robert de Montfort, who I'd heard had been unwell. I found him somewhat distressed although he couldn't say why. I suggested a drive to er... Hampstead Heath to improve his mood, but when we left his room I was firstly verbally accosted by this... *thug* who then viciously assaulted me knocking me to the floor. You should arrest him Chief Inspector; the man's clearly a menace to society.'

Giles de Montfort snorted in derision.

'Total fiction,' he scoffed. 'From a charlatan and a would-be kidnapper. And to cap it all the miserable liar has a glass jaw! I hit him once – a right hook to the jaw, as per the Marquis of Queensberry – and he went down, as the young officer so colourfully declared, like the sack of rotten spuds that he undoubtedly is.'

As he spoke, Giles appraised Livingstone more critically than he had before.

'Wait a minute,' he said slowly. 'Rob, take a closer look at this spiv. Haven't we met him somewhere? Perhaps we might have even known him by a different name. What do you think?'

Robert came closer and peered at Livingstone.

'He's Henry Livingstone, Giles. That's who he says he is and that's all I know about him.'

'Are you absolutely sure, Robbie? Maybe he's made some creative changes; got rid of a moustache for instance, or perhaps his hair's a different colour or parted on the other side, but even so…'

Careful, careful, Clive Scott was thinking. *Don't lead him too far; and for Heaven's sake do not put words into his mouth, otherwise when this villain comes to trial his evidence will be contested by some smart-arse lawyer not unlike you.*

'Good God, Giles – can it be? Is it – maybe? Yes, yes it is! It's that scoundrel who was blackballed from Ambrose's Club, for – what was it? Yes, *financial improprieties*, that's it. This is that slimy Hamilton-Burgess creature isn't it? But why's he been pretending to be someone named Henry Livingstone?'

'A very succinct question, Mr de Montfort,' Clive said, 'which demands an equally concise answer.'

At that point Livingstone dramatically changed his behaviour.

'Where… where am I?' He stammered, looking around vacantly. 'How did I get here and why is my jaw so sore?'

'Laying the ground-work for the mental incompetence defence are we?' Giles said sarcastically. 'Well good luck with that option. See this?' He held up his phone, 'this is my very smart top-of-the-range assistant which has been recording the entire proceedings since you came out of my brother's room. And even before that too; inside when you were intimidating him with all kinds of…'

'Oh my God,' Rob said in a moment of pure lucidity. 'This bastard threatened that if I didn't go with him he'd take the life of my precious girl – like, oh God! Like he did to my darling Angie…' Then he began to weep.

'Let me at him!' Quinn yelled, rushing towards Hamilton-Burgess and making a serious attempt to choke him before Clive intervened.

'It's illegal… to make recording… without informing… the… person…' A coughing and spluttering Hamilton-Burgess protested.

'But not, I venture to suggest, when the person being recorded is not only suspected of involvement in a criminal conspiracy but is quite likely a con-artist, thief, intimidator, murderer: and a bloody fifth columnist who was drummed out of our security service.' Giles de Montfort said.

Just then the lift doors opened and a fresh and fragrant Fleur sashayed on to the stage.

'What's going on here? Is something wrong with Dad?'

'No, no, darling girl – all's well. No need for you to be worried about me.'

As Rob spoke Quinn felt a lump the size of Gibraltar forming in his throat. *Look at the calibre of this dear man,* he thought; *calming his daughter's fears when his heart's breaking because he's just realised that his beloved wife is dead: murdered by this bloody viper that's not fit to scrape horse shite off his boots.*

How can we best help him? Get him out of this place right now! His subconscious urged.

He walked over to Rob and put his arm across his shoulders.

'Rob, I'm not comfortable having you stay at Willows Glen a moment longer. How about you come home with Fleur and me now? We'll give you a delicious dinner with an excellent bottle of wine, and you can sleep in your own bed again.'

Robert was not the only one moved by David's spontaneous invitation. Fleur looked across at him and smiled. *Will you marry me?* She mouthed. *When?* He mouthed back. *Whenever and wherever you want. I love you, you maddening wonderful man! Are you pregnant?* He asked cheekily. She shook her head. Not *yet,* she laughingly replied.

'Come on, Daddy,' she said, 'let's pack an overnight bag for you. David and I can come back tomorrow to collect everything else.'

'Okay lads, time for us to make a move too,' Clive said. 'You, tall lad – sorry, I don't know your name, but you look like a rugby man to me – arrest and cuff the suspect, then accompany me downstairs with him in case he attempts a run for it. If he should be so unwise you have my permission to reduce him to a pile of mashed potatoes. After that it's off to the Yard for him.'

The QC looked on with amusement. *Was that instruction given for the benefit of the constable, or to warn the felon? It doesn't really matter; Glass-Jaw looks like he certainly got the message!*

'It's Jones, sir – Gareth Jones,' the constable said. 'What will be the charge?'

'Hmm. If it were up to me it would be sedition: but some clever-clogs had that crime removed in 2009.'

'If I may make a suggestion, Chief Inspector; either attempted abduction or criminal conspiracy would guarantee a bail refusal,' the QC volunteered.

'Thank you, Mr de Montfort, much obliged.' Then, turning to P.C Jones he added, 'let's settle for criminal conspiracy my Welsh *wunderkind*; I've always found that charge covers a myriad of transgressions. That okay with you, Constable Jones?'

'Yes, sir. Absolutely.'

'Good man. Meanwhile, you two lads, start your door-knocking, interviewing and witness-statement taking. But a word of caution; start with an empty bladder. You have a great deal of tea-drinking and chocolate biscuit munching ahead of you. Which you will be sure to do with kindness and tolerance, conscious of the fact that you too, will be old one day. They may also ask you questions about your love life; you'll probably find them a curious bunch on that score, so best be careful what you say. We don't want to see your faces on the front page of the tabloids tomorrow morning: I've heard the Commissioner takes a very dim view of such incidents.'

'That sounded like the voice of experience,' the QC commented as they walked together towards the lift.

'Of course it was. How'd you think I got this incredibly wise and unhealthily sized?' The chief inspector replied.

TWENTY-SEVEN

Sergeant Bailey was waiting for them as they stepped out of the lift on the ground floor.

'Where's Cruella de Frosty?' Clive asked, after he had introduced the sergeant to the QC.

'In the back office handcuffed to a filing cabinet, Chief Inspector.'

'That's a bit harsh isn't it, Sergeant? What's the charge?'

'Failure to comply and seriously unpleasant behaviour. Plus insolence and aggravated mickey-taking.'

'I see. Very creative offences; not sure they'll all stick but I like the way your mind works.'

'Err; is this the alleged intruder, sir?' Bailey asked studying Hamilton-Burgess carefully.

'Yes. Constable Jones will shortly take him to the car for a little trip to the Yard.'

'Before he does I'd appreciate a word in private with you, Chief.'

'Very well, let's move to the comfortable chairs at the other end of the room. What's this all about?' He asked as they began walking. Then he paused and called back to Giles de Montfort. 'We won't be long will you please wait for me, sir?'

'Yes, happy to so. I'm planning to stay until my family's ready to leave anyway.'

Clive and the sergeant sat down and sighed in unison.

'Now what's this all about, Sergeant? Let's start with the basics; what's this woman's name?'

Sergeant Bailey cleared his throat.

'Well, it's a question of taking your pick.'

'What?'

'The first name she gave me was Emerald Green. When I queried its authenticity she countered with the following; Daphne Devonshire, Pauline Packenham and Ruby Rochester, although I can't guarantee that's in the correct order.'

'What – no Susie Sussex or Lily Lincoln? Never mind, I get your drift. So what's her real name?'

'I don't know, Chief. She had no driver's licence, credit cards, mobile phone or keys in her handbag when I asked her to show me the contents. Absolutely no form of identification that I could find. But she did have a considerable amount of cash.'

'How much?'

'About five hundred pounds give or take, and a wad of Euros; somewhere around six thousand, I'd estimate.'

'Christopher Columbus! What did she want carrying that kind of currency?'

'I asked, but she wouldn't say. Oh, and I confiscated these, although she screamed bloody-murder when I did,' he said, handing Clive a small packet of different coloured pills.

'These are a concern; ever seen black pills before, Sergeant? How'd she get here? Is there a staff parking area?'

'No, never. There's a small space at the rear, only five cars were there when I checked earlier.'

Clive scribbled quickly on the back of his business card.

'Nip out back again, note the Registration numbers then call my driver Vince – he's D.S Crompton to you – he's waiting outside. Ask him to run them through the ANPR database to see what pops up. In the meantime I've a phone call to make.'

'Okay, Chief. There's another thing about this woman that puzzles me. No, it *troubles* me. She's very assured and confident, but there's something else too. It's like she's smiling to herself; laughing at us because she knows something that we don't. I've never met anyone like her before.'

'Now I'm also troubled. After I've made my phone call I'll interview her. Meet me in the office after you've relayed the info to Vince.'

'Will do, sir.'

As he walked off, Clive pressed his speed-dial.

'Hello? Is that you, my favourite judge?'

There was a moan from the other end.

'What do you want now, Clive?' His Honour Josh Samuels replied warily.

'Just a wee favour, Josh.'

'As ever. What?'

'Er… a blank cheque, if you would be so kind.'

'No. As I said when I indulged you recently; that was the last blank search warrant you'll get from me. And no amount of grovelling will persuade me to change my mind. Correct procedure from now on; consider that the eleventh Commandment.'

'Exceptional, exigent circumstances pertain, otherwise I wouldn't ask. Prompt entry necessary to prevent the destruction of evidence, the escape of suspects or physical harm to innocent parties.'

'Learnt by rote from the manual! You need to give me specific details or I'll assume this is another fishing expedition. What precisely is it that you suspect?'

'An illicit drug lab for starters, but I believe there's considerably more involved; maybe a conspiracy.'

'Impressive. And yet you don't know the address of the premises involved.'

'I hope to have that information within a few minutes.'

'Then call me again when you do. Meanwhile, I'll make a start on the paperwork.'

'Thanks, Josh. I'll get back to you pronto.'

As he was on his way to the office, Clive met a genial woman who looked like she might work at Willows Glen. He stopped to ask if she did and she nodded. It was Muriel, the previous matron's young deputy, and she was certainly ready for a chat.

During the course of the next five minutes he learnt that the former matron had been the victim of a hit and run accident three days earlier and was now languishing in the Royal Free Hospital having sustained a broken hip and other serious injuries. The next day, without any preamble her replacement arrived with documents which seemed to support her claim and had promptly assumed command.

'What did she say her name was?' He asked, crossing his fingers.

'Ms Alicia Beckett.'

'Hmm. Was that name written on the papers she brought with her?'

'If it was I didn't see it sir.'

Just then Clive's phone buzzed.

'Excuse me, Muriel,' he said, 'and thanks for your help. Any joy, Vince? I'm drawing blanks at this end.'

'Yes, I'd say there's something to make you smile, Chief. Most of the cars were registered to owners living in the general area, but one stood out like a pork sausage at a vegetarian barbecue.'

'Let me guess. It was from somewhere in south London.'

'Yep – SE4 to be precise.'

'Clapham?'

'Correct. And in the Old Town – the posh part. The car's registered to a…'

'Blake Hamilton-Burgess.'

'Nein, sir. The registered owner is Ms Ursula Speirs.'

'Who the hell is she?'

'I have no idea, Chief. But Sergeant Bailey wants you to take a good look at the new matron because he believes there's a familial resemblance between her and the man you've arrested.'

'Okay. I'm about to interview her now so I'll employ the famous Scott scrutiny. While I'm doing that Vince, send the Clapham address to Judge Samuels who's preparing a warrant and stress that the timing is vital. Ask him to send it direct to Inspector Moreton's phone and give him the number. Tell the Inspector to execute the search as soon as he receives the warrant; he's in command. The premises might be empty but that can't be assumed. And I want a *polite search* – no charging in like gangbusters; they should ring the door-bell, or knock and wait. If there's no answer use our keys to open the door. No rough stuff, no kicking the door down – got it?'

'Yes. Why the kid gloves, Chief?'

'Because this search is based on little more than the shifting sands of my intuition: I don't want to add injury to intrusion if I'm completely off-course. And I want regular updates of what's happening and what they've found. Also inform Matt that I need a thorough search; cellar if there is one and the loft too.'

He was about to walk back to the office for the interview when he changed his mind and returned to the front entrance where Constable Jones was waiting with the handcuffed suspect and Giles de Montfort.

'This is taking far longer than I anticipated Constable, so a change of plans now. Convey the suspect to your nick and lock him in a pleasant south-facing cell. Some Met officers will collect him later today.'

'I want a lawyer,' Hamilton-Burgess said.

'And you shall have one in the fullness of time, sir.'

'No – now! I know my rights; I've asked for legal representation and it must be provided forthwith.'

'Not so, Chief Inspector,' the QC advised. 'A delay of twenty-four to forty-eight hours would not be considered unreasonable given the complexity of the charges and circumstances.'

'Indeed. Greatly indebted, Mr de Montfort. And now, Constable, would you kindly relieve Mr Hamilton-Burgess of his phone to ensure its safety during transit.'

'You can't do that!'

'I'm afraid I can sir,' the constable replied, 'as a senior officer has given me a direct order to do so.'

'Take him out now. And for Heaven's sake get someone to spray the place with air-freshener,' Clive said. 'If there's one thing I can't abide it's the stench of treachery. And please inform Sergeant Bailey that the lockdown can be lifted; business as usual from now on.'

'Yes, sir.'

As he walked back to the office he became aware of an insistent drumbeat at the back of his mind. No, it was more like a cadence; dum der dum – dum der dum – it went, in sync with his footsteps on the floor. He stopped walking for a few moments but the cadence continued.

When he reached the office he found the erstwhile matron greatly annoyed and determined to be uncooperative.

'This is an absolute outrage! I assure you heads will roll over this, my good man,' she fumed as he released her from both the handcuffs and the filing cabinet and indicated where she should sit while he sat behind the desk.

'*Es tut mir leid, wenn Sie so denken, Madam. Ich bin nicht dein gutter Mann. Ich bin Chief Inspector Scott von der Met Police.*'

Although surprised that he had spoken to her in German, she did calm down.

'*Ich habe nichts zu sagen,*' she said.

And that was the pattern of the interview which was conducted entirely in German. He would ask her a question, and she would reply that she had nothing to say. As he pressed on with his questioning, sometimes for variation, she responded with '*Ich lehne einen Kommentar ab*' – 'I decline to comment'.

At other times they sat in silence. She didn't seem to mind, and he used the intervals for close observation of both her physical appearance and her attitude.

Sergeant Bailey must be mistaken, he concluded. *If they're related I certainly can't see it. And she's a good ten years younger than Hamilton-Burgess. But he's right about her manner, mindset and that all-knowing smile she has cultivated to great effect. Of course she's attractive – in an aloof blonde Aryan way – and she knows it. Definitely not my type though; not even if we were the last two people left in the entire Universe! But she could certainly be Hamilton-Burgess's. I think she's his paramour. So what's she doing here, exactly? Why is she content with sitting silently in this parody of an interview?*

She's killing time, you Numpty, his exasperated subconscious replied. What better way to establish an alibi than to be far away from the scene of the action in the company of a chief inspector from the Met Police? *So where's the action?* Not here. Use your loaf; you already know. *But I don't!*

Keep it up sister, neither of us moves until I hear that the search is underway.

But she was a step ahead of him.

'*Ich muss das Badezimmer benutzen,*' she said.

Oh hell! She needs to use the bathroom and so do I.

'Come with me,' he said in English. 'But don't try anything foolish; I'm armed and I'm an excellent shot.' The second part of that sentence was undoubtedly true, but Clive only carried a weapon when special circumstances dictated one might be needed.

'*Warum jetzt auf Englisch?*'

'Because your German is superior to mine. It is posh old-school and very precise.'

'Ah, but then I was born in Germany, Herr Scott.'

'And so was I, Ms Speirs. You are Ursula Speirs, are you not?'

She was momentarily unsettled by the the use of her correct name, but said nothing.

When he opened the door a flustered Muriel was lurking in suspicious proximity; obviously she had been listening. Not that she would have learnt much; unless she also spoke German, which seemed unlikely.

'The lady needs the bathroom, Muriel,' he said. 'And I could do with a visit to the gents.'

Muriel led the way and Ursula Speirs quickly disappeared into the ladies' room.

'Keep an eye on her please, and don't let her go anywhere. I won't be long. Any chance you could organise some coffee for us afterwards?'

She nodded.

'With pleasure, sir.'

At that point Sergeant Bailey appeared.

'Better make that coffee for three, Muriel; you will join us won't you, Sergeant?'

'Yes. Thanks, Chief.'

The suspect reappeared and they returned to the office yet the silence continued even after the coffee's arrival, although Clive did notice her glance at her watch again. It was the second time he'd seen her do it. Finally, with nerves jangling, he could endure the suspense no longer.

'I'm waiting for something to happen, Ms Speirs, and I'm convinced that you are too. So what is it? Or should we stay here all night?'

As he spoke, his phone buzzed. He glanced at the screen and smiled.

'And this is the something in question for me.'

'Chief, it's me,' Inspector Moreton said. 'Can you speak freely?'

'No. But I can certainly listen. Has kick-off occurred already?'

'Yes. The game is well underway. We took up our position around the corner from the premises well before Judge Samuels emailed the warrant.'

'That's good work, Matt. What's the score?'

'Totally off the board! No other way to describe it.

You need to be here, Chief; the place is a treasure trove from top to bottom. I've already had to send for another photographer: cataloguing the evidence will take days, if not weeks.'

'Our team's overwhelming the opposition?'

'No opposition, premises empty. You should see the Lab in the basement; it's a work of art – unbelievable. Someone living here must be a chemist; there's bomb-making material too which is a concern. Then there's the Fuhrer's Room.'

'What!'

'No other name for it. Walls covered with photographs, enlarged framed speeches and other memorabilia. Extensive coverage of the 1936 Olympics in Berlin too. Someone's a very big fan: either that or they're totally bonkers. There's another smaller room next to it; that has framed crossword puzzles on two of the walls. What's that about, Chief? And what's the Heracles Project? There are references to that in numerous places. Oh – and what's so special about today?'

'Stop, stop Matt! My brain's at risk of meltdown! Obviously I really do need to be there myself. What's this mention about today?'

'The 25th November is circled on every calendar I've seen so far, and there's one in almost every room. What's so significant about the date? Apart from it being a full-moon tonight, of course.'

'Oh dear God! Call-up whatever reinforcements you need – use my authority. I have to get out of here right now.'

He stood up abruptly, knocking over his chair and grabbed Ursula Speirs by the arm.

Penny finally dropped? His subconscious asked. The cadence wasn't dum der dum, you plonker. It was *full moon tonight, full moon tonight.* Don't you remember the anonymous email Jamal received? *Icarus will crash and burn before the next full moon.*

How can I stop it? Not our problem was the unhelpful reply. It's all yours, bozo.

'Cuff her again, Sergeant; she comes with us.'

'More charges, sir?'

'Oh, yes. Many more, including her deplorable taste in men.'

Clive charged ahead like the hot-headed Scot that David Quinn alleged he was, while the other two kept up as best they could. Months later he would still remember the startled looks on the faces of those who witnessed that stampede to the main entrance: mouths open like captive fish gasping for air.

Only Giles de Montfort remained calm.

'Is Quinn still here?' Clive asked, breathing hard.

'Outside, loading Fleur's car,' he replied. 'What's the matter, Chief Inspector?'

'Are there any of the uniformed lads still here? We need transport for this suspect, or should I say Hamilton—Burgess's co-conspirator. Her name's Ursula Speirs and I suspect she's his girlfriend.'

'Ich bin nicht seine Freundin. Ich bin seine Frau.'

'You have my sympathy, Madam. It seems we may be able to add bigamy to Hamilton-Burgess's charge-sheet, Sergeant. I've seen a photograph of his wife and she wasn't this woman.'

'Right-Oh, sir. I'll organise the transport if you like.'

'Good man. She can go back to your nick too, but the suspects are to be separated and kept incommunicado: the Met officers will collect both of them in an hour or two. There are additions to her charge-sheet too; criminal conspiracy, manufacture of illegal drugs, failure to comply, including the use of numerous false names. Speaking of which, I assume she's a German citizen since she was born there, but if not we might be able to add subversion to that list. *Denn die Todten reiten schnell,* Ms Speirs.'

'But that's what my client in the Paris prison said,' the QC declared. 'Doesn't it mean something about dead men riding fast?'

'Yes it does, and Ms Speirs knows all about that phrase and its particular meaning for her – don't you Madam?'

As the sergeant and suspect left, David Quinn re-entered.

'Job done,' he said cheerfully, 'we can leave as soon as Fleur and Rob are ready, Giles.'

'What do you know about the Heracles Project, David?'

'All Greek to me, Clive. What is it?'

'Very funny, but wrong time and place. I don't know. It might be nothing but on the other hand it might be… Excuse me folks, I need to make another phone call.'

Clive retreated to the comfortable armchair at the far end of the room aware that his heart was thumping furiously again.

'Is that you, Jamal? How are you?'

'Never better, Clive. What about you?'

'It's a full moon tonight – remember?'

'Sorry? Oh, the crash and burn warning? But that was supposed to happen in Brussels and I'm in London, which proves it was BS. Besides, how many people even know my code name? The warning was probably someone's idea of a joke.'

'Did you choose the Icarus name yourself?'

'What me? A lowly newbie toiling in the Arabic section in the basement? Not likely, someone far more important than me chose it.'

'Who?'

'I have no idea. I just received a memo informing me that my code was Icarus, and that was that. Can't even remember if the memo was signed. Someone probably picked it out of a hat, or from a list of options.'

'Even so… Be on your guard tonight.'

'Will do. Relax, Clive; I'm hardly likely to crash and burn in a fortress like MI6, am I? I've so much translation work to do I'll probably be here until after midnight anyway. It's some other Icarus.'

'What?'

'If it's not me, and you believe that the warning was *genuine*, it follows that it must be someone else.'

'Who?'

'I can only think of one possibility: the tall Frenchman.'

TWENTY EIGHT

Chief Inspector Scott sat in that comfortable armchair for a considerable time, hardly moving, eyes closed, but thinking, cogitating.

Maigret can't be Icarus. And he's not in Brussels either. He'll be safely home by now; he told me last night they were leaving the clinic at 10 am this morning.

The de Montfort brothers, together with Fleur and David Quinn, called their goodbyes to him and waved as they left. So did the police officers, although they did it firstly in person, mindful of police etiquette. Then blissful silence enveloped him. After a while he glanced at his watch. It was three o'clock. *What happened to lunch,* he thought. *No matter, I'm too tense to eat.*

Three o'clock in London is 4 pm in Europe, his subconscious remarked. *So – what of it?* Nothing, just saying in an attempt to be helpful.

A few minutes later, without his urging, his brain snapped into overdrive and he reached for his phone.

'Is that you, Philippe?' He asked as the call was answered after a brief delay. 'Are you in Paris now? What's with the noise?'

'Not yet, although we would have been if Zurich hadn't been struck by a massive thunderstorm again. But we're well on our way at last; the pilot just informed us that we'll be over central Paris in about twenty minutes or so.'

'Do you trust me, mate?'

'Of course. Why would you even ask the question?'

'Then listen carefully. Tell the pilot he needs to land right now. Any open field will do. But get out of that flying tin-can and as far away from it as possible. Then take whatever cover you can find.'

'What?'

'Do it!'

'What do you suspect? What proof...?'

'No proof except Intel from an ongoing search, plus there's a full moon tonight and my agitated entrails are insisting that you're Icarus.'

'No – Jamal is.'

'I've just spoken with him and he's at work in the basement of MI6 which gets my vote as the safest place in London. Humour me. On the off-chance that I'm right get the hell out of the sky and back on terra firma ASAP!'

He heard Philippe instruct the pilot to land immediately and his reply that he couldn't as an unscheduled stopover wasn't part of his flight plan. That was followed by Maigret's angry response along the lines of "to hell with it, land now – and since when do helicopter pilots need to lodge bloody flight plans?" To which the pilot stammered something about it being protocol because the Minister was on board.

By then Clive was incandescent with rage and shaking with fear.

'Tell the bastard to land now!' He screamed down the line. 'And if he won't, overpower him and land the bloody thing yourself! Or do you want an explosion in the middle of Paris?'

Whether the pilot understood English, or whether he reacted to the terrified tone in Clive's vocal tantrum, or even both, remains unknown. Sufficient to say that he swiftly decided to comply and landed safely on a recreation field near a picturesque country church. This was indeed fortunate since neither Maigret nor Saint-Valéry had ever sat behind the controls of any kind of flying-machine: Heaven alone knows what calamity might have ensued if a pair of inept amateurs had attempted to land in the midst of an emergency. They took what they could carry then jumped from the helicopter and ran as fast as possible towards the church.

The sprightly old priest, on his knees in front of the altar and the handful of the faithful seated in the pews, were startled when four breathless strangers burst into their sanctuary. Father Lascelles wisely decided to end the service right then with the triune blessing, followed by a generous glass of wine for everyone.

Then they prepared themselves for the explosion, which Maigret had warned was imminent. Except that it wasn't. They waited, and waited, until after thirty minutes, Christophe chose to terminate the charade.

In a concise statement he declared that he had no doubt the entire episode had been caused by a misjudgement on the part of the British Police, compounded by a serious over-reaction. That it was well-intentioned was not disputed, but the rationale had clearly been flawed. Then he thanked them for their patience and hospitality, concluding with the information that they would shortly be resuming their flight to Paris. As he finished speaking, Maigret's phone rang again.

'Are you safe?'

'Yes, for the third time Clive, we're absolutely fine! And it seems we always were. However Christophe's severely displeased and insists that the next time we meet I should...'

At that exact moment there was a tremendous explosion which shook the church's stained-glass windows and shattered most of the front-facing ones. Shards of metal and other helicopter debris went flying in all directions destroying anything in its path for what seemed like time without end. This was followed by an acrid smell which assaulted their sinuses and triggered sustained coughing. Eventually the hideous noise subsided and the fire took over, steadily reducing what was left of the wreckage to smouldering metal.

'What was that you were saying, mate?' The voice

on the other end said when the noise had somewhat abated.

'Er, um… Eternal gratitude Clive, er… we're forever in your debt.' Maigret mumbled, stunned by what they had witnessed happening in the sky above Paris instead of in an empty field. 'And so is the Republic. We were planning to land on the helipad on top of 36 Quai des Orfèvres.'

'That's your HQ. I've been there and it's in a busy, lively area.'

'Always is. The loss of life on the ground… And the injuries…'

'Don't torture yourself with what might have happened, my friend. It didn't; that's all you need to remember. By the way, why do you sound like you're being strangled?'

'Because I'm being strangled! When the helicopter exploded Meg threw her arms around my neck; now I'm almost bent double as well as being throttled.'

'Tell her to let go.'

'I will – but not yet. I'm rather enjoying the experience despite the discomfort. Now she's muttering something about it being grounds for divorce if I ever suggest we travel by helicopter again.'

'In that case, how do you intend to get to Paris?'

'Christophe's requesting a replacement copter from our Strasbourg garrison. If it were my decision I'd go home in the back of a cattle truck if it meant we arrived sooner. I'm desperate to sleep in our own bed, in our own home again. Hold on a moment…'

'It's me, Clive. I've just informed Philippe that the grounds for divorce stipulation will not come into force until *after* the flight in the helicopter from Strasbourg.'

When the helicopter finally arrived it was almost dark. Not to be deterred, Father Lascelles had arranged for the floodlights to be switched on at the football ground and the flight landed safely. Then he and his flock accompanied the visitors to the departure site where he blessed both them and the helicopter generously with holy water to ensure a safe landing in Paris. He also blessed Christophe for his assurance, on behalf of his department, that all damage both to the church and the playing field would be covered from the legislative contingency fund; as well as an ex gratia payment for any inconvenience caused by having a helicopter explode on his front doorstep.

A few minutes into the flight Philippe whispered to Christophe that he owed a number of people a debt of gratitude for his deliverance. When Christophe nodded, he produced a list he had already written in chronological order.

- The elderly Belgian farmer, name unknown, who rescued him from the compost heap;
- Dr Lucas Defoe, the country doctor who literally saved his life;
- The hamlet's police sergeant who remembered the Europol alert and identified Maigret despite his vastly-changed appearance;

- The consultants and staff at the Saint Luke Clinic;
- And above all, Chief Inspector Clive Scott who had saved them, and many others, from certain death.

'The farmer's name is Jakub Maes,' Christophe said. 'And the sergeant's Armand Willems. I agree with those names except for the personnel at the clinic; they submitted their accounts *tout de suite* and were paid promptly – and handsomely. None of the others, including Dr Defoe and his hospital staff asked for payment and actually *declined* it when offered. That makes them the real heroes in my opinion.'

'But we'll make a donation to them, won't we? And provide some new equipment to the hospital?'

'Ahead of you on that score; both are already under discussion. However, there's an omission from your list: Jamal Ahmadi. He risked his life when he escaped from the farmhouse to find help. And he supplied reliable coordinates to where he thought you were being held.'

'And yet the dear *grand-père* farmer found me! I trust we're talking about the Légion d'Honneur for outstanding service to our country, Christophe.'

'Of course. What else?'

'*Bon, bon.* So for the grand-père farmer – Chevalier? And Dr Defoe, Commandeur…?'

'Leave the ranks for me to determine. As you know there are limits on the numbers for some of the higher echelons…'

'Yes, but not for foreign recipients; they're supernumerary. You could recommend Clive for any high honour you chose.'

'Yes, that's true. I promise you won't be disappointed with the award I recommend for him or any of the others. Now, my friend, what about you? What recognition do you desire?'

'Oh dear God – no! I've been flying too high in the limelight already. And if Clive is right and the insurgents believed I was Icarus because of what we prevented in Berlin: followed by the promotions with overblown fanfare, then my best option is to clip my wings and stay in the background for evermore. After I'm dead you can do as you please.'

'Do we really need to collect the furry one from *maman* tonight?' Philippe asked as they touched down on HQ's helipad.

'Of course not, darling. Why don't you speak to her from the car so she knows you're finally home? Then we could join her for breakfast tomorrow and Moggs can come home with us afterwards.'

'I *was* planning to sleep late tomorrow.'

'Then so you will; tell her we'll come for brunch.'

Philippe's physical recovery was surprisingly speedy, but the spiritual and emotional healing took far longer than either of them had anticipated on that night when he finally set foot inside their home again. There were the recurring nightmares from which he woke screaming and shaking, and sometimes the demeaning night-sweats too, which sapped his energy and left him ashamed and depressed. He jumped if a car backfired in the street outside their apartment or when they were enjoying a coffee at their favourite rendezvous. Nevertheless he was unwilling to seek professional help, apart from one occasion when Meg insisted they see someone together. That visit had proved unhelpful in the extreme, which meant the subject was never raised again.

Three times during that challenging period Christophe Saint-Valéry offered him a prestigious position within his department, and three times it was declined: instead Philippe spoke wistfully of de-camping to Provence to grow flowers for the perfume industry.

CONCLUSION

As Clive was finally preparing to leave Willows Glen he received another phone call from Inspector Moreton who was still engaged in the search of the Clapham home of Ursula Speirs and Hamilton-Burgess.

'You really do need to be here, Chief. Masses of stuff in German, and the same with a couple of the computers.'

'First thing tomorrow morning I'll be there, Matt. In the meantime bring some of the most important-looking German documents back to the Yard with you and I'll give them a quick look at home tonight.'

'I'll tell you what, Chief – there are some highflying names on what appears to be a membership list I found stashed away in the secret compartment of a desk.'

'Give me some for instances.'

'Well, I'm not much for politics as you know, but so far I've recognised seven current members of the House of Commons, and four old codgers from the House of Lords.'

'What shade of politics are these quislings?'

'Three Conservative, three Labour, one LibDems – maybe, not sure what side he's on, and I don't know the alliances of the seat-warmers in the Lords either.'

'Holey-moley! This stuff's going to cause a hell of a ruckus.'

'We've only managed to look at a fraction of what's here; there's far more to uncover. We're going to be here for a long time to come.'

Inspector Moreton was right; it would take many weeks to collect and catalogue the evidence against Ursula Speirs, Blake Hamilton-Burgess and their associates. And close to two years for the case to come to Court. During that time two of the Conservative members of the House of Commons allegedly committed suicide, while another disappeared: it was widely assumed that he had followed that well-trodden path to Argentina.

The three Labour politicians escaped to Russia but were denied entry, refused asylum, and returned to the UK post-haste in a good-will gesture by the Russian President. The LibDems politician, anticipating arrest, escaped to the Philippines for extensive cosmetic surgery and is now pursuing a career as a Mariah Carey impersonator.

Inspector Moreton was also correct in his contention that all those involved – particularly Speirs and Hamilton-Burgess – were probably bonkers. Indeed they were, but perhaps not in the conventional understanding of that word. They believed that the long-dead Nazi leader had been channelling messages and instructions to them via Robert de Montfort's cryptic crosswords.

Delusional they might have been, with an overwhelming confidence in their own superiority amounting to full-blown megalomania, yet not so out of touch with reality for their defence lawyers to contemplate a plea of mental incompetence. Far from it; these two were highly-intelligent but fatally-flawed individuals. It was unfortunate that they had ever met; the world would have been far better-served had they not. Desperate for power and wealth, and absolutely convinced of their entitlement to both.

After dinner that night, despite his eventful day, Clive began to translate some of the German documents. His wife went off to her book club, returned hours later, made them both a hot drink, kissed him 'good night' then went to bed, but he continued to read. And the more he read, the more appalled he became, despite large chunks of it being the usual subversive rant and justification with which he was already familiar.

The West was fiscally corrupt and morally degenerate and grew steadily worse. Redemption was possible only by means of a blood-letting cataclysmic re-set. In the farthest extremes of radical Islam they had found their fervent fellow-travellers and a profane alliance had been born. Although Clive had not yet found it writ large in what he read, it seemed that the DDTRS – abbreviated to TRS (Dead riding fast) would supply the brain-power and the mind-altering, memory-erasing drugs similar to those they fed Robert de Montfort during his three day incarceration; while the Rad-Isms provided the brutal bloody muscle.

Europe was to be divided – as equally as possible – between TRS and the Rad-Ism faction who already had troops training in Afghanistan, Egypt and Syria with funds donated from an affluent European war-chest.

Austria, Belgium, Czech Republic, Germany, Holland, Poland, Slovakia, Switzerland, and so forth would be ruled by the right and could remain Christian if they chose. France, Spain, Portugal, Italy, Greece, Turkey et al would be Islamist countries following strict Sharia Law. The Scandinavian countries were also to follow Sharia law.

The division of the UK was considerably more complicated and was still in contention, although it had been agreed that Scotland would be Islamic, and so would the chapel-attending Welsh. All the Royal Estates like Windsor, Sandringham and Balmoral would be confiscated and the Royals sent into exile in the Southern Hemisphere. Ireland it seems was either too complicated or contentious to appeal to either TRS or the Rad-Isms, ditto Russia and her Caucasus: their fate had not yet been resolved. But then it was clearly a work in progress, as far as he could tell from the lunatic proposals.

As he read further he discovered what amounted to the Mission Statement of the Heracles Project.

More bloody Greek mythology, he muttered. *Why couldn't David Quinn, the Oxford Classics whiz-kid, have told me that Heracles was the original Greek name for the greatest of their heroes, whose Romanised name was Hercules?*

The fifth labour of Heracles was to clean the stables belonging to King Augeas which housed a thousand incredibly healthy – not to mention *immortal* – cattle which produced an enormous amount of manure every day. Moreover the stables had not been cleaned for thirty years and this labour was to be accomplished in a single day: a seemingly impossible task. But Heracles used brain-power to triumph: he diverted the course of two rivers to flush out the filth. And that's what this devil-inspired partnership would do too: they would flush away the West's degeneracy but with sluices overflowing with life-blood instead of fast-running rivers.

As Clive began to read the final page, his own blood ran cold. Someone within the TRS was not so completely deluded. Under the heading *'The Five Year Plan'* he read these chilling words:

Our Strategy is simply this: a sustained exercise in demoralisation as the road to victory.

However – nota bene – for advertising, marketing, recruitment and parliamentary selection, the name to be used at all times is 'New World Option.' *There is to be no mention of the parent company DDTRS or the abbreviation TRS, or the beloved Führer.*

Nützliche Werkzeuge und nützliche Narren: English translation, Useful Tools and useful Fools – all part of the softening-up process – are as follows:

- Our Islamist allies – many desirous of 'a meaningful martyrdom' (all sins forgiven)
- Control of the twenty-four hour broadcasting channels most already *compliant* – not a far stretch for them to become completely *complicit*

- Dedicated place-persons already working inside many of the management companies – need to increase numbers
- For those who are reluctant or resist, get them onside in the usual way: loads of cash and/or sex, drugs. Intimidation and Blackmail are useful tools
- Steady repetition of bad news: natural disasters, violent murders, deadly infections – *the mode becomes the message*
- Ten reasons for the timid sheep to be terrified before breakfast. Repeated traumatic images and issues: *saturation level demoralisation*
- Subtle, but constant use of words or phrases about what 'could' happen, or what 'might' or 'probably' will happen
- Frequent use of quasi-experts peddling their own agendas. Supposition is our friend: *Facts are our enemy!*

'God Almighty!' Clive cried aloud. 'Didn't I *say* this was happening? Didn't we all *know* that it was? The constant diet of bad news followed by even worse news? Didn't we know we were being set-up? And didn't we all feel totally powerless to do anything about it?'

Vindication at last – but not what I wanted. Not what any sane person would want. Never this bloody anti-Christ garbage. How the hell do we combat it? In the same way as we've always done, his sub-conscious replied. With courage, rational debate and freedom of speech.

The brilliant chemist, Ursula Speirs, was the Queen-pin of the TRS/NWO which was planning a serious challenge to the established Alternative for Deutschland at the next German Federal election. And Hamilton-Burgess was her besotted second-in-command. In a relatively short space of time, through his contacts in MI6, and dissenters in both the House of Commons and the Lords, he had tempted many to become followers. Their reward was to be their own fiefdoms when all ambitions were realised.

If I were a betting man my money would be on Heracles finishing the stable-cleaning job armed with nothing more than a bloody toothpick and a teaspoon, long before this rancid alliance made any headway with their plans, Clive thought as he fell wearily into bed.

First thing the next morning, as good as his promise, he joined the search at the Clapham house to discover the extent of the planned insurrection. He was sickened by the progress the plotters had already made, and the scale of their ambition. But the membership list that Inspector Moreton had found was what almost destroyed his faith in humanity. Internationally honoured and trusted organisations, revered philanthropists, captains of industry, clergymen, doctors, judges; all walks of life were represented in that record of those who had joined the seditious alliance.

'So all this was the New World Option attempting to gain the upper-hand, Chief?' Matt Moreton asked.

'There's no New World Option – or New World anything else,' Clive replied. 'Trace its roots, follow the money, and it's always just another version of the old totalitarianism of Stalin, Mussolini and Hitler, the Kim aberration in North Korea, and Mao Zedong – and his current successor in China, Xi Jinping – by a different name.'

'Another example of the Emperor's new clothes?'

'Yep. That poor old bugger never had any clothes at all and neither does this greedy collection of chancers. Now gather up the rest of the German documents and we'll head back to the Yard.'

'And our next move is…?

'I'll send out the membership list to all the democracies at risk via a restricted Europol alert; each country will need to decide what their approach should be. And here's another question: who will close down the training camps in the Middle East – the US or NATO, or who? While that keeps me out of mischief you need to liaise with the Crown Prosecution Service about what offences we can charge Speirs and Hamilton-Burgess and their assorted hobbledehoys with. Then I'm off to Downing Street to find out how quickly the UK and the other countries involved can legislate for the New World Option to become an internationally proscribed organisation.'

THE HONOURS

In April 2016 the following awards were made in the Paris HQ of the Légion d'Honneur, next to the Musée d'Orsay on the left bank of the Seine. This is the highest decoration in France, established in 1802 by Napoleon Bonaparte himself, to recognise distinguished service to France. The award of such a decoration is decided by the President of the French Republic subject to a very strict examination, and is divided into five degrees; Chevalier, Officier, Commandeur, Grand Officier, and Grand Croix:

To Jakub Maes, Belgian National, Chevalier (Knight)

To Sergeant Armand Willems, Belgian National, Officier (Officer)

To Dr Lucas Defoe, Belgian National, Grand Officier (Grand Officer)

To Jamal Ahmadi, British National, (under his witness protection name which cannot be disclosed), Commandeur (Commander)

To Chief Inspector Clive Scott, British National, Grand Croix (Grand Cross)

SUBSEQUENTLY...

In the summer of 2016, Fleur de Montfort and David Quinn were married in Fingest Church, Buckinghamshire; the same beautiful little Norman church in which Meg and Philippe had been married. Quinn, having decided that he no longer wanted to be a Bush-Baptist or a Bush-anything-else, had been confirmed in the same church two weeks earlier. And to everyone's delight Robert de Montfort's health was so greatly improved that he walked his daughter down the aisle.

Clive Scott, newly-promoted to Superintendent Scott and his sociable wife Katie were special guests.

As they walked towards the cars that were waiting to take them to the Reception in Oxford, Philippe asked Clive a question that had troubled him for months.

'Err... about your father's time in Berlin with the BAOR after the end of the war...'

'Yes, what about it, mate?'

'Err... I wondered if he... perhaps...'

'Brought some souvenirs home with him?'

'Yes. Did he?'

'Certainly. But nothing like a German Luger, if that's what concerns you. My father was an army doctor. As far as I'm aware he didn't even know what a Luger looked like, much less owned one. What he brought back was a set of antique beer steins.'

'Good.'

'I didn't kill that bastard who… I would have, given half a chance, but someone beat me to it.'

'But to do it in cold blood, Clive? I don't think so.'

'Then you're considerably more certain about that than I am.'

One morning, a few weeks after their return to Paris following the wedding, Meg had a distinct feeling that Philippe was up to something. She was right.

'I have an appointment to view some real estate later this morning,' he said as they were finishing their leisurely breakfast at their favourite café on the Boulevard Saint Germain.

'Are we moving?'

'No, not us,' he laughed, 'but some of *nos autres Amis* might be, if I can persuade them.'

'Our other friends? Who exactly?'

'Make a guess.'

'Err… well… Give me a clue.'

'People to whom I am indebted perhaps…'

'Oh! Louis, who found your wedding ring…?'

'Go on, you're in the right territory, Miss Marple.'

'Madeleine? You'll never get her to live in a house again – you know that already.'

'Ah yes. But what about a pretty little cottage in the 11th with Louis Allard and his kind and capable widowed sister?'

'You've seen it already – haven't you?'

'Yes, and so have they. It was love at first sight. They're confident it will be the same for the Duchess too, now she's growing older and the winters are more severe.'

'Let's go; I can't wait to see it. We'll buy it for them won't we? It will be our gift and they will have no rent to find?'

'Certainly. I have no desire to be anyone's landlord at this time of my life.'

'I don't care what anyone says, Monsieur; you're a decent human-being. At least I think you are.'

'That's good enough for me,' he said, tucking her arm through his as they left the café.

They strolled along the Boulevard in the warm sunshine, not speaking, just content to be together.

'Look at the sky,' she said after a while. 'See how blue it is? There's not a cloud in sight. A long time ago I heard a story about a woman whose grandmother was born in India. Every morning granny would go outside to look up at the sky. If there was enough blue in it to make an elephant's coat, she knew the day would be fine.'

'A charming story.'

'So how many elephants' coats do you think could be made from the sky above us right now?'

He thought for a moment.

'How many elephants make a herd? Ten? Twenty?'

She shrugged.

'Let's split the difference. Assuming there are fifteen elephants in an average herd, I'd estimate that the sky above us could supply er… *generously-cut coats* for about… forty thousand herds of normally-sized elephants.'

'Is that what General de Gaulle would have said?'

'Yes. But he would probably have been quoting Napoleon at the time.'

'He should have stuck to cheese,' she said, stopping in the street to kiss him.